Praise for
Corinne Holt Sawyer's
previous mysteries!

MURDER IN GRAY AND WHITE

"The flavor of this crisp, amusing novel is more British than Californian, the characters delightfully Dickensian."
—*Publishers Weekly*

"Sawyer has written this novel with wit and a sharp eye for whimsical detail. . . . The energetic and humorous plot has enough twists and redherrings to make it puzzling and fun."
—*Tallahassee Democrat*

THE J. ALFRED PRUFROCK MURDERS

"What's most enjoyable about this murder mystery is the characterizations of its elderly protagonists, formidable women in their 70s who haven't surrendered their roles as mistresses of all they survey."
—*St. Louis Post-Dispatch*

"The murder is definitely of the cold-blooded variety, but the efforts of the Miss Marple-like foursome will warm your heart and make you laugh."
—*San Antonio Sunday Express News*

Also by Corinne Holt Sawyer
Published by Fawcett Books:

MURDER IN GRAY AND WHITE
THE J. ALFRED PRUFROCK MURDERS

MURDER BY OWL LIGHT

Corinne Holt Sawyer

FAWCETT CREST • NEW YORK

A Fawcett Crest Book
Published by Ballantine Books
Copyright © 1992 by Corinne Holt Sawyer

Library of Congress Catalog Card Number: 92-53076

ISBN 0-449-22171-7

This edition published by arrangement with Donald I. Fine, Inc.

Printed in Canada

First Ballantine Books Edition: April 1994

10 9 8 7 6 5 4

For Wayne Stroup—
who labors heroically to improve my bridge and my
driving—and to keep me from walking into walls.

And of course for my sister Madeline Holt Campillo.

Introduction

BOUGAINVILLEA IS deceptive—at once glamorous and disappointing. For looks, it is unquestionably the Elizabeth Taylor of vines—gloriously beautiful, sinfully vivid, demanding of attention, the unquestioned star in any garden where it chooses to flourish.

And yet the delicate, richly colored flowers have no scent. In its mature years bougainvillea's lush growth can become a kind of careless abandon—a blowsy droopiness. Without proper nurturing, it can become embarrassingly, vulgarly overdone—a caricature of itself as it was.

This is the way it was with the cerise-flowering bougainvillea that grew in the garden of Camden-sur-Mer, the one-time luxury hotel now reincarnated as the finest retirement apartment complex south of Los Angeles. Sea mist gave the vine the humidity it loved and the moderate temperatures of the "golden crescent"—that stretch of Pacific coastline just to the north of San Diego—kept its colors vivid. But just as the hotel had once been neglected, so the garden had run down, and the vine had simply grown wild.

Like an old woman nobody loves, whose stockings sag, whose hair comes loose from its pins and strays in wisps about her face, and whose slip is always showing, the bougainvillea straggled along, each year in greater and greater disarray. It kept growing, but it had lost its sense of direction. Long streamers would reach down into the patio beneath, and it would pelt with flowers and leaves, helter-skelter, anyone sitting in its shade. On the hottest summer days, the uncontrolled growth obstructed the sea breeze from the occupants of the patio area. One of the residents

initiated a petition to the manager to have the vine chopped
down as a hazard and an eyesore. Of course, as with most
of the residents' petitions, this one was filed away and forgotten.

Then a gardener was hired to work at Camden. Rollo
Bagwell was a short, cross-eyed man, slightly retarded, but
patient and perpetually good-natured. He had a difficult
time reading the instructions on the back of the seed pack-
ets, but he had a magical touch with growing things and a
passion for his work. Since he had almost nothing else in
his life, the garden obsessed him, and he toiled gladly with
his plants from dawn until dark.

From the moment he started work at Camden, Rollo
loved the bougainvillea. Not a day went by that he didn't
spend at least a few minutes with the vine. He cut and
shaped and thinned, he fed and aerated and watered . . . and
finally, he could stand back to admire the most beautiful
flowering vine in the whole of Southern California.

On the evening of Tuesday, July 16, its cerise blossoms
were at their best, glowing nearly fluorescent in the golden
pink twilight that streamed directly onto the patio from the
seaward side of the hotel's grounds. The residents had finished their evening meals and had gone either to their
rooms to watch television or across the street to Camden's
own Tuesday night bingo game. Rollo was alone in his garden.

In the fading light, he had trimmed dead stalks from the
giant pots of clivea that stood on either side of the two
steps leading to the patio. He worked carefully, trying not
to nick the leaves as he cleared away the extra growth, because he was using the large shears normally reserved for
trimming grass at the edge of the walk—strong, spring steel
with long points, not really designed for pruning—and they
made him clumsy. The clivea had finished blooming, but
the leaf was still attractive, provided the flower stalks were
removed. Rollo stacked the clippings neatly in a pile and
laid down his shears. Then he stepped up onto the patio,
throwing his head back and gazing upward for one more
look at his beloved bougainvillea.

It took his breath away with its powerful beauty. Rollo

thought to himself that even if he had all the fine words in the world, he could never find a way to tell anyone how lovely the vine was, how special. He had never been in love with a real, live woman—but he thought perhaps he knew what love was, as he looked at the passionate rose red of the flowers, at the graceful arch of leaf and blossom, at the patterns of golden light and cool gray shadow on the patio floor.

Then very softly, from the garden behind him, he heard a tiny whisper of sound. A breath? Something *ssurrussuring* through the grass? But when he turned and looked, he saw nothing. He hesitated, waiting, but he heard nothing more—only the leaves scratching against each other, the woody vine scratching against its redwood supports, as the evening breeze picked up from the west.

He sighed in contentment and edged forward to sit down on one corner of a redwood chaise, something he would never have done if anyone had been around to see him. Rollo was a humble man—he knew his place—and it was in the garden, not up on the patio. But tonight, all by himself, when there was no one around to see, he could let himself imagine that this whole place was his—the building, the patio, the furniture, the grounds . . .

He smiled to himself. "The first thing I'd do, I'd move a bed out here and sleep right here with my vine. Yes, sir, right here." He looked up at the curtain of blossoms and leaves above him. "My vine," he said with satisfaction. "You are mine. They forgot you. They let you grow wild. But I took care of you—and now you belong to me . . ."

He frowned. There was a new branch growing at an angle that should be trimmed back. It was getting dark, but he thought there might be enough light . . . He sat up and half-turned to rise. He meant to go and get the shears. But the shears had come to him. The powerful points struck once into soft neck tissue . . . again into the chest . . . were pulled out and struck the neck again . . . and again . . . and again . . . Rollo had been dead for some minutes when the killer flung the shears away and moved off silently, down the garden path.

Night tiptoed into the garden, advancing in the shadow

of the building, pushing silently and powerfully against the last golden streaks in the western sky until, defeated, they withdrew into the purple fortress of the horizon. Victorious night advanced across the sky and raised its lantern, a sliver of silvery moon. Rollo lay on the chaise, unmoving forever and now forever unmoved, while over his head, the Elizabeth Taylor vine drooped in mourning and wept cerise blossoms over its fallen friend.

Chapter 1

Rollo Bagwell's body lay undiscovered for some time in the shadows that covered the patio that Tuesday night. But murder at Camden-sur-Mer was nevertheless the topic of conversation some miles away in the office of the San Diego County Police.

Sergeant Hal Benson was waiting, more than a little uncomfortably, for Lieutenant Martinez to get off the phone so Benson could claim time to discuss his latest case. He sat awkwardly in a wooden office chair (probably a Torquemada original) while Martinez jotted words into a small spiral-bound notebook. Benson shifted his weight impatiently until Martinez at last closed the notebook and put the receiver down.

"Now, Sergeant?" Martinez recognized him.

"Listen, if you're not in too much of a hurry—not going out for dinner or something? I need a short conference. Need you to fill me in. Tell me something about that Camden place and the people there. Save me a little time."

Lieutenant Martinez smiled. "Okay, Benson. No problem—glad if I can help. Let me get a refill first." Martinez got up from behind his desk and went to the coffee maker perched on the top of the bookcase across the room, poured his outsized Styrofoam cup full, then doctored it with sugar and some ersatz cream. "Heaven help me, I hate the powdered stuff, but it's better than drinking my coffee black."

"Why don't you keep milk?"

"Where? It would sour by this time of the evening anyhow. And if I put it in the little fridge out there—the one

5

the men use for their lunches—it wouldn't last the day. Even the San Diego County Police, admirable as they are in all other respects, aren't to be trusted when it comes to real cream in the office refrigerator. I'll make do. This will kill my appetite till supper." He carried the brimming cup back to his desk, set it on a scratch pad so the drips wouldn't fall onto the wooden desk top, and then made himself comfortable in his chair. "Okay, Sergeant. I'm set. Fill me in," he said. "You're up there at Camden for what—?"

Sergeant Hal Benson settled into his own chair and put a foot up on the rung on each side. The pose was like that of a schoolboy facing the principal after a spitballing episode. But Benson looked more like a middle-aged grocery store clerk than a schoolboy, or than a policeman for that matter: rimless glasses, neatly combed straight dark hair thinning on top, pale skin. His colleagues called him "Mr. Whipple" behind his back.

Now he sighed. "Okay. It's a stabbing. You heard about it, I know. Last week—a week ago this evening, in fact. A little guy named Enrique Ortelano who services drink machines for a living. I mean, he brings the soft drinks around and refills the bins and empties the coin containers and if anything goes wrong in between times, he's supposed to come out and make the machines work right again. There are a couple of 'em in this retirement center. That's what he was doing there.

"He got the first one. I mean, he'd restocked the machine and taken the coins out. He had several cases on a handtruck, and he'd pushed them along as far as a little patio behind the main lobby when somebody got him from behind with a knife. Dropped him in his tracks. One of the nurses found him lying there late that night as she came around with medication for some of the residents.

"So I've been up there at the center every day . . . asking questions, poking around . . ." He sighed and moved his glasses off his nose so he could rub the place on the bridge where the nosepieces rested. "I don't know . . . I don't know . . ." He eased the glasses back in place and sighed again—and just stared silently at the wall, his eyes slightly unfocused.

"Well, so what's the problem?"

"The problem is, I'm getting nowhere. I'm learning nothing. I can't find any motive—nothing in his life—and there doesn't seem to be any real connection at all between Ortelano and the place where he was killed—this retirement place. And those old people—they're making me kind of— kind of nervous. I can't explain. Anyhow, I thought you might save me some time and trouble . . ."

Martinez smiled. He was as handsome as Benson was plain, the living image of Gilbert Roland in his younger days: black curling hair, a pencil-thin black moustache, olive skin, strong jaw and white teeth that showed when he gave his devastating smile, snapping black eyes that too often gave away his emotions—a slim, well-muscled, broad-shouldered body that he moved with the unconscious grace of a trained dancer. It was small wonder that when he had been called to the retirement center at Camden-sur-Mer in a professional capacity, Martinez had, in a word, *wow*-ed the elderly ladies who made up two-thirds of Camden's population.

Camden-sur-Mer, named for the town in which it stood and for its situation overlooking the sea, had been a luxury hotel in the days of silent films and open roadsters, a favorite watering hole of Hollywood notables. But the fickleness of fashion and the San Diego Freeway—which detoured traffic away from the little town of Camden—undermined the hotel's popularity, and after World War II it struggled briefly and gave up. In time, a very clever group of investors bought it and restored it—adapting the main building specifically to the needs of the elderly. Perhaps the stockholders had meant their project as a tax write-off, but instead, with excellent management, it had prospered.

In the first place, the area's climate was the finest in the United States, without the smog that besets Los Angeles, and never varying in temperature far from the sixty to seventy-five degree range. The old hotel's location in a quiet little town was ideal for the elderly, for they could walk to the drugstore and the dress shop and the post office

without fear of being mashed by speeding traffic or mugged
by fast-moving teenagers. There were doctors and dentists
and lawyers available in town, at least sufficient for the residents' needs, and after a few years, the center built its own
health facility across the street from the main building—a
tiny hospital with a superior nursing staff and a resident
physician to care for residents when they became physically
or mentally incapable of caring for themselves.

Planning for the needs of the elderly had been excellent
from the first. The renovators put railings along the hallways, added seats in showers and baths, enlarged closets
and built extra storage shelves into each room—the elderly
cannot bear to part with all their mementos of the past.
What had been the hotel bar became a chapel or a movie
theatre, depending on which day of the week you visited;
the back wall served both as projection screen and altar. On
Friday night you could see Nelson Eddy and Jeanette
MacDonald in *Naughty Marietta*. On Sunday, you could listen to the Reverend Mr. Peabody—one of Camden's pastoral rota—pleading for your salvation, and be amused by the
fact that his face was bobbing about at the approximate location where, two nights before, you had been gazing at
Miss MacDonald's décolletage.

The former gift shop became a nurses' office. The ser-
vants' quarters, where the maids and valets of wealthy hotel
patrons had stayed, became a wing devoted to wheelchair-
bound residents. The nursery where hotels guests' children
were kept out of mischief became storage for residents'
luggage. The bellboys' station became the Pink Ladies'
lounge.

Residents took meals together in a common dining room,
and Camden employed a gourmet cook—a Mrs. Schmitt,
whose inventiveness and skill were legendary up and down
the coast—so that the food at the center was one of its most
potent selling points. A barber and a hairdresser set up shop
in a former janitors' closet; a podiatrist visited the center
twice a week and worked in what had been a newsstand;
and the center, while disposing of the extensive gym equip-
ment on which hotel visitors had worked-out to stay in

shape, had retained a whirlpool spa in which several residents at a time could soothe the pains of arthritis.

So while residents coming in from their own homes often felt crowded in their one- and two-room apartments, at Camden they exchanged space for convenience—and for security. Everything they might want could be arranged for them under one roof. In fact, the longer they stayed, the less likely they were to take vacations involving travel, to visit attractions that the tourists flocked to in Southern California, or even to take meals at restaurants in town "for variety's sake."

Now Martinez—recalling his own experiences with Camden and its residents—smiled at Benson. "I hope I can be of some use. But, of course, I don't know your case or anything about it."

"Well, that's it. There isn't any case. Not yet. There may never be! I said it before—I can't see any connection at all between Ortelano and those old people in the center ..."

"Have you interviewed them yet?"

Benson frowned. "Oh, sure. Whaddya think? Sure! But they weren't very useful interviews. I guess people get a little strange when they get older. Some of them talked around the point, never answered my questions at all— some of them acted like they were mad at me for interrupting them—like I was responsible for spoiling their day—like maybe I stabbed their soft-drink delivery man ..."

"Come on, Sergeant," Martinez said. "Everybody's like that. Nobody likes the police—until they need us. These people aren't that different ..."

Benson shook his head. "I know." He took his glasses off and wiped them clean with a limp handkerchief. "I'm not doing a very good job of explaining ... I think all I'm trying to say is that nothing I learned from them was any use at all. And I decided maybe the location was incidental. You know—that Ortelano was killed for some reason that had to do with him and had nothing to do with the old people, see? But I figure I better find out for sure ..."

"Well, what about the obvious? You said he'd just emptied the coin box in one of the vending machines."

"The money wasn't touched. Not that a sack full of coins is easy to handle. It's pretty heavy, and it clanks. But that wouldn't have stopped someone from toting the bag away, if that was the point of the murder. Anyhow, it wasn't—because the money was on the floor of the patio right beside him. Believe me, the first thing I thought of was the money. I thought—maybe some junkie down from the city, trying to get money to score . . . but unless Ortelano was maybe carrying a wad we don't know about, or something . . . Well, that wasn't very likely. Because even his wallet was intact! No, he wasn't killed for money. Anyway, not what he was carrying on him."

"You mentioned drugs. Could your man have been a dealer himself?"

"We thought of that. If he was, he was so discreet nobody knew about it. I mean *nobody*. We asked all our contacts. And the lab didn't find any traces of drugs around his clothes, in his truck, at his house . . ."

"What about his home and his family?"

"Divorced. He lived alone in a small frame house. And before you ask, we looked the place over from top to bottom. Naturally. Not even an unpaid bill. He was tidy, he paid his creditors . . . a model citizen." Benson looked glummer than ever. "Except, of course, that somebody speared him like a marshmallow at a weenie roast!"

"How about the ex-wife? Anything there?"

Benson shook his head. "She took the kids to her parents in Mexico City. Still there, according to the Mexico City police. Respectable family—her father's a teacher; she's clerking in a bank; kids are getting good grades in school—it just doesn't look like her family is involved."

Martinez raised a hand in apology. "I'm sorry, Benson. I'm not being very helpful, asking questions when I'm supposed to be answering them."

Sergeant Benson shrugged. "I understand. Occupational hazard, I guess. I should have said from the first we already looked at everything we could . . . we've had six full days, seven if you count Sunday."

Martinez smiled. "Detectives work on Sundays."

"Yeah, but other people don't. We had a hard time finding anybody around to question, you know? But anyhow, after a week, there just don't seem to be any likely possibilities in his work, his home life, his friends, his family. Well, so now I'm thinking again about the place where he was killed. I didn't find a connection, but maybe there is something—I mean, like maybe he rubbed somebody there the wrong way or something, you know? Or maybe he got onto something illegal going on around that retirement place and somebody tried to keep him quiet. And then I thought maybe—do you suppose one of those old ducks is maybe crazy enough to skewer him with that carving knife?"

Martinez nodded. "You've certainly thought through a list of possibilities. So why ask me? Surely you can find out more on the spot than I can tell you from a distance."

"Not quite true. It's what I said—you've been there at the retirement place on business before. I'm starting cold. And besides, I told you, it bothers me. The place—the people—it never seemed to bother you and that aide of yours, Swanson. Me it bothers. A lot. I don't know—seeing all those old people coming together in one place to die—it reminds me of the old elephants' burial ground in the Tarzan movies."

Martinez shook his head. "Oh, no. You're wrong. They didn't come there to die. They could do that anywhere! They come there to be comfortable and to be safe *before* they die! They're not vulnerable to thieves and con men like old folks living alone can be—they don't have to worry about getting sick in the night and not being able to get help—they're not likely to leave the stove on and burn the house down—somebody's there to watch out for them and they don't have stoves anyhow. At least, the ones in the main building don't."

"Oh, that's another thing . . . what's the story on those little houses out behind the main building? They call them 'the cottages.' "

"The retirement center filled up quickly after it opened, and that was one way of expanding. The 'cottages' are bungalows with maybe four or five little apartments in each one. They're slightly larger and more expensive than the rooms in the main building, and they do have kitchenettes."

"Costs a lot to live at Camden, doesn't it?" Benson asked curiously. "I mean, I know they feed 'em—give 'em linens and maid service—have a van that takes 'em on errands, keep an office staff and a desk clerk, have somebody plan activities . . ."

"Well, they can't watch TV all the time, when they're not eating," Martinez said, a bit defensively. "Yes, I guess it costs them. If Ortelano had been killed for that sack of quarters, it wouldn't have been by one of them. I'd say they're all 'comfortable.' Some more than others, of course."

"You like them, don't you?" Benson said curiously.

"Yes, I like them. I liked them from the first. But then, old people don't bother me. It may be a cultural thing. I come from a people who genuinely respect their elders."

"Oh, I don't mind old people—one at a time. It's just—in herds like that . . . I mean—for gawdsake, they even look alike! I can't tell one from the other!"

Martinez snorted. "I shouldn't laugh . . . that's exactly the way I felt at first. All that gray hair, all those glasses, all those bent shoulders and wrinkles . . . it took days before I could sort them out. I didn't realize how much we rely on hair to cue us in when we recognize people. The only ones who looked different to me at first were the bald-headed men . . ."

"And that's another thing," Benson protested. "Most of them are women! What happened to the men?"

"We die off, sergeant," Martinez said. "Men aren't a very hardy group. Women are. Amazingly tough! One seventy-plus-year-old there, for instance . . . I caught her climbing through a window six feet off the ground one time. It wasn't easy for her, but she managed, and none the worse for wear. Listen, you'll learn to sort them out, believe me. And you'll find them a very helpful, cooperative group, too, if you handle them right."

Benson looked skeptical. "Well, I asked if anybody knew anything about the murder, would they come and talk to me—and was I surprised! Nearly the whole bunch volunteered! As it turned out, there wasn't a one of 'em knew a damn thing. But they all wanted to come. You weren't going to leave them out! It reminded me of grade school— like a bunch of kids raising their hands to volunteer to recite, when they don't even know the answer . . ."

"Didn't you ever do that as a kid, Benson?" Martinez asked curiously.

"Oh, sure," Benson said, and had the grace to look embarrassed. "I thought everybody did. But I grew out of it. And these people . . ." He shook his head. "I don't know what they thought they could gain from coming forward except the pleasure of using up my time for no reason."

"Think about it, Benson," Martinez said. "You were the high point of their day—maybe their week! Ordinarily, they do pretty much the same things all the time, day in and day out. Oh, they like what they do, but variety is precious. That dead body on the premises is the most exciting thing to happen since Christmas, I'll bet . . ."

"Well, one *bi-i-ig* old girl did compare me to the Fourth of July fireworks show on the Oceanside pier. She was something else! She had a laugh that rattled the windows!"

"I bet I know which 'big old girl' that was. Did she wear a bright-colored, loose-fitting kind of robe thing . . . floor length . . . and did she have a rope of real pearls that were probably worth several thousand dollars that she handled as though they were wooden beads strung on grocer's twine?"

"Sure thing. You got her to the life. Mrs. Caledonia Wingate. I couldn't forget her name," Benson said.

"Widow of Admiral Herman Wingate, and the absolute queen bee of the hive, up there," Martinez filled in. "She's lived there ever since old Herman went to his reward— must be twenty years or so now. She's got the courage of a lion, she's smart as can be—hasn't lost any of her brains, that one—and she's got a heart of pure mush. It really isn't any wonder all the others up there defer to her and love her. If she told 'em to go out and dig up the street, you'd see half the residents hacking away with pick and shovel within the hour . . ."

"She had a little bit of a woman with her . . . a cube-shaped little pepper pot with a tongue that would slice roast beef! A Mrs. Benbow . . ."

Martinez laughed. "I hope that woman doesn't decide to operate on you, Benson. You're useful to the department, and if looks could kill, hers would bury you six feet under! Where she turns that icy glance, no grass grows ever! Mrs. Angela Benbow is an admiral's widow too, by the way, and I understand she used to be the absolute terror of Camden. The other residents seem to have got used to her . . . but they still won't cross her if they can help it. She's got no time for stupidity, she lets you know it, and she thinks and moves *fast*. She's the one I said climbed through a window."

"You know, the two of them," Benson said, "had the gall to offer to 'help me in my endeavors'? They even said you'd vouch for them."

"Oh, boy! My fault, Benson," Martinez said. "If I'd known you were going up there, I could have warned you. Those two old girls not only still have all their wits about them, they're keen observers. And whether because they're bored and gossip comes naturally, or because they mix in everything that's going on, or because people tell them things, they know absolutely everything. And they have been helpful. Extremely. You see, they have strong intuition and a lot of luck—pure, unadulterated, dumb luck! And that's what they seem to need to be able to come up with solutions to problems—and at exactly the same minute I do, with all my research and my experience. Sometimes even before I do . . ."

"Do you mean they really have helped you on investigations? That's what they told me, and I flat didn't believe them."

"Well, in a manner of speaking. I learned to use what they offered and to give them assignments—tasks that kept them out of my way. And out of harm's way, if you see what I mean? I called them 'part of my team' and kept them bringing me information, and in so doing I kept them out of mischief—and that kept them from getting their feelings hurt. That last was very important to me, by the way. I really like those two . . ."

"So they thought I'd make them the same deal?" Benson asked.

"You could do worse," Martinez soothed. "If you want to know how to take the residents—who to trust, who talks nonsense, who is forgetful, who might be slipping a cog— you could do worse than ask those two. But don't patronize them. That's one thing they're quick to catch on to—and to resent."

Benson shook his head. "I'd rather not get into that whole thing at all. It sounds like—like a nuisance, I guess, is what I'm trying to say."

"Suit yourself," Martinez said. "The point is, if you really think one of the staff or one of the residents might be involved, you'd better consult an expert . . . and they're experts, those two."

"I thought that was what I was doing right now," Benson protested. "Consulting an expert. You."

"Well, yes, but I don't know exactly what to tell you— where to start. I don't mind answering questions, of course . . ."

Benson shrugged. "And I don't even know what to ask. That damn murder seems totally out of context, totally unrelated. Not just to the guy's home and his work—but to the retirement center. Unless maybe it's a cuckoo— somebody riding along with one foot out of the stirrups. Someone who's about three bricks shy of a full load."

Martinez stood up and moved to the coffeepot again. "Sure you don't want one? Good, then I'll take the last cup out of this pot and unplug it for the evening. I tell you what. I think if I were you, I'd call in those two—Mrs. Wingate and Mrs. Benbow—and ask them if they think one of the residents might be disturbed enough to stab the soft-drink man. A lot of them do start getting forgetful, you may have noticed. Sometimes, it gets so bad they lose their way and can't find the dining room—eventually those people end up in a bed across the street, of course."

"Yeah," Benson said. "There's one old girl now who sits in the lobby all day long looking at the desk, because she can't remember when to come to eat and she's scared she'll miss a meal. She just waits there in the lobby all day. I'd say she had a screw loose! But I don't even have to ask anyone about her. She's obviously harmless."

Martinez nodded. "That's what I was starting to say about all of those folks—they are very unlikely to do anybody any harm at all, unless they irritate people to death by repeating questions. I bet that old girl by the desk asks 'What time is it?' every ten minutes."

Benson grinned, and suddenly he looked ten years younger. "She sure did. Every *five* minutes! If we're looking for a loon, she'd qualify."

"Actually, what happens to some old people—first, it's that they can't remember and they get cross about what's happening to them. Grumpy—like children at nap time. But not homicidal. Then they gradually get so they can't reason—can't work out simple things—how to add a line of figures, how to put things in alphabetical order, how to use a can opener—but when they get to that point, they don't seem able to hate, either. And after a while—they just get very pleasant. Very cheerful. They don't care about anything, much."

"But are all of the old ones like that when they get funny in the head? Isn't there any other kind of craziness running around there?"

"Now that," Martinez said, "I wouldn't know. And that, I suppose, is one of the things you'd better ask. Listen, do you want me to come up there and do some poking around? Is that what you're hinting at?"

Benson got to his feet. "Huh-uh. Captain Smith assigned me to this case and I'll do the work. I just wanted to get a better feel for that place. To know how to take Mutt and Jeff, for instance." He blew out a gusty sigh. "You know, they got to me the other day, talking to each other across my head as though I wasn't there—and about things I never heard of!"

"Like?"

"Like—oh, they introduced themselves to me as 'the trylon and the perisphere.' That's what the big one said. Ever heard of that? And when the little one says something about the modern age, the big one laughs and says 'And to think it used to be a big deal to go out on Sunday to watch the Ford Tri-Motor come in.' What the hell is a Ford Tri-Motor? I'm telling you, it makes me uncomfortable when I don't even know what they're talking about! I mean, as they were leaving, I sneezed, and the big one said something like it wouldn't do for Warner Oland to have a cold—and the little one said I might catch a cold if I hadn't taken my cod liver oil . . . I mean, they could have been talking Greek!"

Martinez laughed out loud. "You don't play Trivial Pursuit, do you?"

"Naw."

"The New York World's Fair in the late thirties—just before World War II—had the 'trylon' and 'perisphere' as its symbols . . . a tall triangular tower and a short round spherical building. They were just kidding about the difference in their heights. And the Ford Tri-Motor was the most modern plane around in the thirties. It had a big center motor mounted on the nose, and a smaller motor on each wing. And, what else was it? Oh, sure—you said they called you 'Warner Oland.' Don't you watch the late-late show? He was the first actor to play Charlie Chan . . . they were just saying you were acting like a detective."

"How about cod liver oil?"

"Now there you have me. I mean, I know what the words mean, but I never heard of anyone 'taking' it. Maybe you should ask them. Anyway—no secret code—just women talking about things you're too young to remember."

Benson shook his head. "Made me feel like a kid."

"To them you are. It doesn't hurt anything, does it?"

"Well, maybe you're right. I'll see. I'll be getting back there sometime tomorrow."

Benson underestimated the time interval.

Chapter 2

"Under the I—19!"

"Give me some of your corn kernels, Angela," Caledonia Wingate whispered across the table. "I've run out and I still don't have bingo."

"Well, just don't take too many—I need more myself," Angela Benbow said crossly. ("You'd think," Caledonia remarked to Emma Grant after one bingo game, "the way Angela acts, that she plays for corn kernels, instead of for prizes!")

Now the two were gossiping in hushed tones across the rough wood of the bingo table while the game progressed.

"I know what you mean, Cal," Angela was acknowledging softly, "it just doesn't seem as though the police are getting anywhere. It's been a full week tonight since that Mr. Ortelano was killed—right there on our patio—and what have they found out? Absolutely nothing!"

"Be fair, girl." Caledonia's rumble was more audible than her small friend's whisper, but she too was trying to keep it down. "This Sergeant Benson isn't our friend Martinez, after all. And he doesn't seem to me to have examined the possibilities very thoroughly . . ."

"UNDER THE O—72!"

"Bingo! I got bingo!" Dora Lee Jackson shouted. "Oh, sister, look—I got bingo!"

"Oh, rats!" Angela said, testily dumping her corn kernels off the card to start another round with a clean slate. "If Dora Lee doesn't fix this game, how is it that she wins right away, first thing every bingo night? She or her twin

18

Donna Dee. One of them always gets the first bingo. It's just not fair."

"You're right, of course." Caledonia scraped her corn into a neat pile to the right of her card, ready to begin again. "The rest of us don't stand a chance with them."

This was not strictly the truth, for the bingo games at the retirement center were arranged so that sooner or later, during each evening, everyone present won some little prize. It didn't soothe the real gamblers in the group, of which there were one or two, but it made most of the residents happy. Everyone went away with a tiny tube of hand lotion, a box of note paper, a four-pack of White Cloud toilet paper (so superior to the brand furnished by the Camden management!), or a Kennedy half-dollar, of which someone on the staff seemed to have saved up an endless supply to use for prizes in the games. Typewritten rules were posted saying that nobody could win twice in one night; once you won a prize, you were supposed to drop out of the game. Of course some people played on, just for the feeling of participating; the Jackson twins always did, although they usually won early, as Angela said.

"Maybe," said Caledonia, "we ought to ban the Jacksons from bingo entirely!" As she spoke, she swept the trailing sleeve of her lime green satin caftan back off the table and, in doing so, dislodged half of the corn kernels belonging to Tootsie Armstrong, seated nearest to her down the table.

"Oh, Caledonia," Tootsie protested, but rather faintly. Caledonia was not only a great favorite with everyone in the retirement center—so that whatever Caledonia did was generally thought to be right—but she was so big that people seldom contradicted her. Tootsie behaved as though, if Caledonia had knocked the corn to the floor, it must have been for a good reason, and she bent to pick up the kernels with great humility, as if apologizing for spoiling Caledonia's plans to grow a few rows of Seneca Chief on the carpet.

"I told you not to wear that—that robe to things where we're in close quarters," Angela hissed across the table. "This always happens."

Caledonia's laugh made the satin ripple in the light from

the chandeliers overhead. "I really don't have a choice, Angela. You know caftans are all I own."

Just a bit under six feet tall and quite a bit over 250 pounds—she would never say how much over and perhaps she truly did not know, for she had stopped looking at her scales some years ago—Caledonia had found twenty years before a caftan that suited her perfectly. It was concealing; it was versatile, for she could wear it for evening or every day; and it was above all comfortable, with no seams and bands to cut into her ample flesh. Indeed, stretched out, it was large enough to serve as a dust cover for a TV satellite dish.

"A wise people, the Arabs," Caledonia had told herself, and immediately hired a very expensive dressmaker to duplicate that first garment in a selection of materials and a rainbow of colors. She habitually topped off each outfit with a variety of fine jewelry, another successful camouflage maneuver, since a cluster of rubies or a rope of exquisite pearls will tend to rivet the eye of the beholder on themselves.

Now she placidly tucked her sleeve around her elbow as she bent to help Tootsie pick up the dried kernels they used as markers. "Hard to pick up, but they remind me of . . . well, these are just like we used to use at the Iowa State Fair," Tootsie was saying with delight, bent over so that her head was hanging upside down as she picked up her corn.

"Ready, everybody?" The bingo caller was the center's activities director, the indefatigable Carolyn Roberts, who acted as though there were simply nothing more thrilling she could do on a Tuesday evening than put on a bingo game for the residents. "Miss Jackson," she trilled, "has won a lovely box of dusting powder! And now, somebody else will be lucky, because we're starting another round . . ." She shook a homemade patchwork bag and reached inside it for a marker. "What will it be—what will it be . . ."

Angela leaned forward again, once she was satisfied that Tootsie's attention was centered away from them and onto her own card. "I don't like this Benson, Cal," she hissed. "He's not like Lieutenant Martinez. Martinez understood that we could be of help and he . . . well, he respected our intelligence. This man acts . . ."

"Like most people act toward anyone with white hair," Caledonia nodded. "As though we hadn't the brains left to be of use to anyone anymore. I know—it drives me crazy too. Oh, he's all business and no charm, that Sergeant Benson. But we couldn't expect Martinez to come here every time we had trouble . . ."

"But he knows us now. He knows how to use the resources here . . ."

"What you mean," Caledonia said, holding up a hand the size of an octagonal highway stop-sign, ". . . what you mean is that Martinez listened to our ideas and flattered us into thinking we were useful to him."

Angela tightened her mouth and raised herself in her chair as tall as her four-feet-eleven would allow her to sit, head held high and chin thrust out—the position her late husband the admiral used to call "flying her storm signals."

"Martinez didn't just flatter us," she protested. "We were useful to him."

"UNDER THE G—43!" Carolyn chirped. "G-43, ladies and gentlemen . . ."

"Bingo!" a voice cried out.

"You can't have bingo, Mr. Grogan. This is the first number I called."

Grogan stared at his card. "Got something on every damn number on the damn first row on this damn card!" he croaked hoarsely. He bent over and peered closer at it until he seemed about to pitch, face forward, onto the table.

Carolyn hurried to him. "Mr. Grogan," she said despairingly, peering at his card, "you left the corn on from the last game again. You do that every week! Now listen to me. Take if off. Take it all off."

"Last woman who said that to me was a blonde Swede on a TV commercial for shaving cream," Grogan said, leering blearily up at her.

Angela shook her head. "He's drunk again," she hissed across the table to Caledonia.

"Mr. Grogan," Carolyn was saying firmly, "just take the kernels off the card, will you please, so we can get on with the game? All but G-43, of course. Here, let me do it . . ."

She brushed an impatient hand across the card and then replaced the single kernel.

"Listen to me, Angela," Caledonia growled, as they waited for the game to resume. "This police sergeant doesn't want our help and we'd be fools to try to get involved. You didn't see poor Henry Ortelano and I did. I was walking through the garden when the men came to carry him away. I didn't mean to look, but I did. You know—you just *do*. Well, he was stabbed in the back and there was a great big knife handle sticking out between his shoulders. I tell you the truth, it scared the liver out of me. If there's some lunatic running around loose doing that to people, we don't want to get mixed up in this in any way. Do you understand?"

Angela threw back her head in a fair imitation of Scarlett O'Hara defiantly vowing that she would never be hungry again. "Well, I'm not saying we should get mixed up in it. It's just—I'm sure we can help in the investigation. I know we can. But that young sergeant just isn't ... he just isn't ... interested in us. He's not what I expected from a policeman at all. He's not an interesting person himself, he doesn't seem to have a sense of humor, he's not as ... as ..."

Caledonia grinned. "As handsome and as attractive as the charming lieutenant. That's what you're getting at, isn't it? And don't you argue back. I see your mind working behind your eyes. Well, things will work themselves out. For now, just play bingo, girl. We'll argue later."

"*UNDER THE O—91.* Got that, everybody? O-91." Carolyn's voice rang strong through the hall, and the game wound on.

The last winner was called just after 9:00 P.M.—late enough, as Tootsie Armstrong remarked, for half of the players to be yawning. The population of Camden was divided exactly in two between those who were early risers and began to droop long before the late-night news came on (like Tootsie and Angela) and those who liked to sleep late in the morning and often suffered through insomniac evenings spent in the company of Johnny Weismuller, Bela Lugosi, the Bowery Boys, or Maria Montez. The night owls included Caledonia, who never rose before 9:00 A.M. if she could help it, and who regarded dawn as suitable only for roosters, milkmen, and lunatics.

Bingo was played each week in the large hall attached to the health facility across the street from the main building. It was a room suitable for all manner of activities—meetings of civic clubs and PTAs, exercise and craft classes, dances—and of course bingo. Tonight, because of the unsolved death of the soft-drink man, the residents had been urged to walk to and from the activities room in pairs and in groups. Tootsie, Angela, and Caledonia made their way back across the street arm in arm until they reached the main building, where by tacit consent they let go of each other. It felt somehow much safer, once one was inside the perimeter of one's home territory.

Tootsie Armstrong had an apartment on the second-floor north wing; Angela's apartment was on the first-floor south wing; and Caledonia had a splendid double-sized apartment in the first bungalow beyond the end of the main building. Caledonia had rented two adjoining apartments and paid to have the separating wall knocked out, costly renovation that attested to her wealth, as did the exquisite antiques with which she furnished her rooms. Admiral Herman Wingate had come from a wealthy family and had been careful with his investments throughout his distinguished military career; his widow was more than a little shrewd with hers, and her net worth only increased with time.

Now Caledonia sailed through the darkened lobby of the main building, waving goodnight to Angela, who peeled off just after they entered, climbed the four stairs into her residence hallway, and disappeared through her apartment door—the first on the hall.

"Evening, Jimmy," Caledonia called to the freckle-faced young man acting as night clerk behind the main desk, tending the phones, conversing with lonely residents who called during the night, coping with emergencies (Mrs. Dalrymple had lost her teeth again, and he'd had to call a nurse to go up and help her find the misplaced upper plate), and studying for his exams at Camelot State College.

"Mrs. Wingate . . . Mrs. Armstrong . . ." Jimmy acknowledged them with a wave and went back to a heavy chemistry text, adjusting his glasses with a sigh.

"See you in the morning, Caledonia," Tootsie twittered vaguely, and stepped into the creaky old elevator which would save her walking up the stairs to the second floor.

"I wouldn't take that thing at night," Caledonia warned. "It's getting crankier and crankier—it stalled with the Emersons the other day and it took twenty minutes for the repair men to come and get it moving again. At night, heaven knows when they'd arrive. Maybe you better walk . . ."

"Oh, dear. Perhaps you're right." Tootsie looked alarmed and started to move forward to vacate the elevator, when the door slid shut with surprising vigor and the groaning commenced that indicated the wheels and pulleys were hoisting the cab and Tootsie Armstrong to the approximate level of her hallway (it had been years since the elevator cab had stopped at the exact level of the second floor).

"Don't worry, Tootsie, you'll be all right," Caledonia boomed toward the closed door. She really didn't know whether Tootsie could hear her or not through the massive oak door; they built elevators to *last*, in the 1920s! But at least, Caledonia's contented smile seemed to say, she had tried to be comforting. She turned and swirled her way across the lobby toward the garden door.

Just as Caledonia came out through the sliding glass door that led from the lobby to the patio, she caught the impression of a shadowed shape in the corner of her field of vision. But when she looked directly at the far end of the patio, she couldn't pick out from the darkness what she had seen.

"I've always hated stories," she told Angela on the phone later, "where the heroine in the dark house hears a noise at night, and does she call the police? No! She puts on her bathrobe and goes down to investigate. And you know what happens. The fiend *gets her!*"

"Cal! Get to the point! I'm sitting on my bed in my pajamas, my bare feet are on the floor, and I'm cold!"

"Well," Caledonia suggested practically, "*sit* on 'em. Your feet, I mean. Let me tell my story my own way. Now,

I meant to say that the first and only time in my life I had something happen to me like the heroine in the dark house, what did I do? I put on my bathrobe and went to investigate, too . . . just figuratively, of course. There I was, on my way home from bingo, cutting across the patio toward the garden, and I thought I saw something in the dark. So—did I stop to think it might be dangerous? Did I go back and get young Jimmy Taylor to investigate for me? Did I even think to pick up a brick I could hit the fiend with? Of course not. I just strolled over. And there he was!"

"The fiend?" Angela asked.

"No! The body! Another body. This time it's Rollo!"

"Rollo? Who's Rollo?" Angela asked groggily.

"Rollo Bagwell. Our gardener. Dead as a mackerel. Lying on the redwood chaise. Been dead for a couple of hours, they say. Stabbed—exactly like Mr. Ortelano! Only in the front."

To anyone who knew Caledonia, it would have been less than surprising that after she conquered her initial dismay and her nausea, she marched in to the main desk and told a wide-eyed Jimmy Taylor to call the police to come and investigate a second murder. It took her two repetitions before he closed his jaw sufficiently to put on his operator's headset and start to follow directions.

Satisfied that her orders were being carried out, Caledonia went back outside to mount guard on the body, a gigantic, lime green sentinel, palely visible in the moonlight that came and went behind thin clouds. She did not think once to be afraid for herself, and so she never bothered to turn on the patio lights, mounted overhead on the building's side. If the truth were known, she half dozed in the soft air of the July night, only waking when she heard a siren approach the front of the building some twelve minutes later.

To her intense disappointment, the policeman who arrived to take charge of keeping the curious away, asking questions, and sending for the laboratory crew—after verifying that there really was a crime, and that it was not some old lady's nightmare—was not their favorite Martinez, but again Sergeant Hal Benson, brisk and businesslike, not especially friendly toward the residents, and even to the most sympathetic eyes a very plain young man.

"Not that looks make a difference, really," Caledonia complained to Angela, as she made her complete report the following day. "But he looks less like my idea of a detective and more like—I don't know—like a storekeeper or something. Furthermore, tactful is not a word I'd apply to him either. He practically threw me out of there."

Actually, what Detective Sergeant Benson had said was, "Thank you, ma'am. That will be all for now. We'll be in touch," as he and his men took over the patio area, where the outdoor lights had been turned on to full brilliance. Of course, thanks to the pinch-penny budget of Olaf Torgeson, Camden's royally disliked but highly efficient administrator, "full brilliance" was sufficiently well lighted for the police to complete only the most cursory of searches and the removal of the body. Everything else would have to wait till the full light of the next day.

Dismissed from the scene, Caledonia sailed down the garden path to her apartment, where she could keep an eye on at least a corner of their activities through her view window while she phoned Angela.

"Are you awake?" she demanded when she heard Angela's voice on the line. Without waiting for the obvious response, she continued, "Well, do I have news! Angela, there's been another murder!" and she launched into the story of her discovery of the second body. But when she reached her punch line, ". . . exactly like Mr. Ortelano!" all she heard on the other end of the line was a magnificent yawn. "Come on, Angela," she begged. "A second body! Another murder! Isn't that incredible?"

"Please, Cal, I'll think better tomorrow. Right now all I see in my mind's eye, when you talk about a body lying on the chaise, is me lying in my bed, with my feet warm under the covers, and my eyes closed. Asleep. Please—talk to me tomorrow. 'Night." And she hung up on an exasperated and wide-awake Caledonia.

The next morning, of course, the situation was reversed. The women met at breakfast, a sure sign that Caledonia regarded the day as special, since the last time she had voluntarily risen to come to an early breakfast—without someone's urging—had been the morning after the attack on Pearl Harbor, and no Navy family had slept at all the night before anyway. On this July day, Caledonia was wearing a bright red-white-and-blue poplin caftan that snapped out from her body in the fresh morning breeze like a flag from an unusually stout flagpole. The colors exactly matched those in her weary eyes, as she tacked uncertainly toward the dining room to join Angela over coffee.

Three cups later, fortified with several freshly baked cinnamon buns and a great deal of melted butter, Caledonia was sufficiently alert to repeat her whole story. By the point at which she described the body and the blood and her wait in the moonlight, her own brain was functioning at reasonable speed, and Angela was flatteringly attentive.

"Maybe this time," Angela breathed reverently as Caledonia finished her recital, "we'll get to see our handsome lieutenant. Oh, Cal, wouldn't that be a pleasure."

"Oh, that's another thing. I'd have told you last night, but you were in no shape to understand a word I said. The same fellow showed up in charge of things—that Sergeant Benson."

"Surely not! Not again!" Angela's little face was a study in petulance. "Cal, can't they see he doesn't know how to deal with us? And he's not getting anywhere . . . I can't believe they'll leave Sergeant Benson on the case now. Come on." Angela pushed her chair back from the table, flung her napkin onto her plate, and started toward the garden doors. "Come on, come on . . . let's at least go and see!"

Caledonia heaved her bulk upward to join her smaller, spryer friend, and together the two admirals' widows strolled out the garden doors of the dining room. Once outside, they were on the far end of the patio from the area where the redwood furniture, the bougainvillea vine, and several policemen were presently situated. But they could see, past the busy men who came and went, that a great, brownish stain was being hosed off the plastic cushions of a chaise, and Angela—gulping mightily—seized Caledonia's hand and fairly pulled her away from the area, out into the fresh air of the garden.

"Come on, let's walk up and down out here. We can watch what's going on from a little distance ..."

"That's him, all right," Caledonia said. "I won't point, but look at the man in the suit standing by the big flowerpot with all those orangey things in it ..."

"Oh, dear. How disappointing ... He really is back." Angela glared grumpily across at Sergeant Benson, who would not have been flattered to hear her comment, "You know, he doesn't even look very bright!"

"Oh, I agree—positively stolid. Dull. Martinez is not just a handsome devil. He looks more ... I don't know ... more competent."

"It's odd the way you always just assume good-looking people are smart," Angela nodded.

"That's the truth," Caledonia agreed. "And yet the stupidest female I ever talked to was a gorgeous model ... I could have stared at that face for hours and envied her for months, if I hadn't asked her a question. One of my husband's staff had this incredibly lovely creature on his arm at a reception. Herman couldn't take his eyes off her, but when we went over to speak to them ... Well, to begin with, she was chewing gum"—Angela groaned sympathetically. Caledonia went on—"and she had a voice like fingernails on glass. But as if that wasn't bad enough, the woman was dumb as a rock! I mean, we were at a Navy reception, for gawdsake, and I asked her if she enjoyed participating in naval affairs ... and she said absolutely not! That quite the contrary, she never did modeling that involved showing her bare midriff!"

"Cal, you're kidding!"

"Absolutely, on my honor ... look there!" Caledonia broke off to point. Two of the policemen searching the garden had leaned into a bed of miniature agapanthus ... one holding the other while he bent down and reached across, trying not to leave his own footprints in the soft soil, moving aside the stiff stems of the Lilies of the Nile to bring up—held gingerly in a handkerchief—a pair of garden shears.

Even from several yards away—as near as they had dared to go—Caledonia and Angela could see the rusty color of crusted blood. Angela drew her breath in. "The murder weapon," she hissed. "Oh, Cal, a pair of shears! What was it the first time? Didn't you say a knife?" As she spoke, they had been craning their necks and edging slowly forward.

"Move along, if you would, ladies," one of the policemen said, pleasantly enough, stepping forward so that he blocked their line of vision. "Sergeant Benson will be talking to all of you residents today or tomorrow sometime. In the meantime, if you'd kindly move along . . ."

Caledonia Wingate drew herself up so that she seemed to tower over him. She made an imposing figure in her red-white-and-blue draperies, and to stand against her would have felt a bit like standing up to the Statue of Liberty.

"This is our garden, officer," she said. "We live here. We need to walk for our health, and this is where we do that. Here. In our garden. Are you implying that we would tamper with the evidence or otherwise impede your search?"

"Well, no, of course not," the policeman said. He swallowed nervously. He was very young and looking younger every minute as he backed, an inch at a time, up the walk toward the patio. "It isn't that you'd be in the way, ladies. Believe me. It's just—" Inspiration struck. "Well, suppose there were footprints? We need to see them and measure them before anybody else steps on them, see? Believe me, Sergeant Benson will explain things when he talks to you. Much better than I'm doing, for sure."

Caledonia grinned. "I doubt if there are footprints here on the sidewalk, young man." Her good humor restored, and her moral superiority established, she gave ground gracefully. "But of course we have no wish to be in the way. Come along, Angela. Let's walk down to my place . . ." She gestured across the garden in the direction of her cottage and led the way with stately, unhurried steps.

Once inside, she let go of her dignity and laughed. "Oh, that poor young man."

"You really did intimidate him, Cal," Angela said. "And for no good reason I can see."

"Well, it never hurts to let the hired help know they're

just that. Sometimes they seem to think they run the show . . ."

"Cal! Behave. And tell me all about last night."

"There isn't much more than I've already told you. Of course, last night you weren't awake enough to take it in." She shuddered. "The only thing I haven't really talked about was how Rollo looked. He was a mess. I hardly recognized him. But that walrus moustache of his—there's only one like it."

Angela shuddered. "I'm glad you saw him and not me. You know I can't stand to look at blood . . ."

"I can stand everybody's but my own," Caledonia said cheerfully. "I wasn't surprised that they found those garden shears. It had to be some weapon like that. I mean, he was badly cut up . . . on the face, but most on his upper body and in his neck . . . Someone just hacked and hacked . . ."

"Why would anyone kill Rollo, of all people? That simple, sweet little man. For that matter, why kill Henry Ortelano?"

"I've been thinking about that," Caledonia said. "We don't know anything about Ortelano—the police will have to find out about him. But Rollo? Well, everybody here knows all there is to know about him. He's not married, he lives alone—doesn't even have a pet. He's so simpleminded I can't imagine him getting involved with a woman or anything, so I'd certainly rule out a jealous husband. He lived a pretty ordinary life. He told me once that for fun, he mostly watched TV."

"Do you think someone killed him by mistake? That they thought he was someone else?"

"Now how on earth would they think that?" Caledonia snorted. "None of the men here has hair as dark as his . . . they're mostly bald or gray. And his moustache would warn them they had the wrong person anyhow—there can't be two moustaches like that around. I mean, there certainly aren't among our residents and staff, are there? Well, of course, Mr. Ortelano had a moustache . . ."

"You don't suppose," Angela said, "the killer was looking for Rollo all along and just killed the soft-drink man by accident? I mean, he did kill him at night—and he stabbed him from the back. Suppose"—she narrowed her eyes, visualizing the scene—"suppose he stabbed a man with a moustache—thinking he was killing Rollo. But later, when he realized he'd killed the wrong man, he came back, and this time he got the right man!" She looked hopeful.

"Too complicated. Besides, they didn't really look much alike, did they? Different size, different age, and even the moustaches were different."

"Well, how about if Rollo wandered into the garden when a thief came through on the way to rob some of the residents? And Rollo threatened to give the alarm."

"But how would he know he was looking at a thief?" Caledonia said. "Thieves look very ordinary on the outside . . . they don't wear labels, you know."

"Don't be so silly," Angela said haughtily. "I know that. But—well, suppose the thief was coming out of one of the garden apartments with a sack full of loot? Even Rollo would know the man was a thief, then."

Caledonia shook her head. "Rollo was such a trusting soul, if he saw me carrying out the crown jewels of England and I told him I was just taking them home for cleaning, he'd run to get me a bottle of Windex!"

"But it would be hard," Angela insisted, "to think of an innocent explanation for wandering around our garden at night with a paper sack that had silver candelabra sticking out of it!"

"Who do you know living here who has silver candelabra?" Caledonia jeered. "A thief might find plenty of jewelry, all right, but we gave up the big, bulky stuff when we moved in. I don't know of anyone that kept even so much as a calling-card tray. Nobody would hang onto candelabra! And anyway, suppose Rollo did find a thief who killed him in a panic. Are you saying the thief was also here last week, and Henry Ortelano stumbled across him, too? Or . . ."

Angela put her little nose up. "Well, it was just an example, after all! You think of something, then."

"Well," Caledonia said, "we once knew of somebody who killed to stop a blackmailer . . ."

"Yes, but that wouldn't be Rollo's case," Angela protested. "He was a very sweet-natured person. He wouldn't have anything he could be blackmailed about. And as for his being a blackmailer himself? Well, he was far too dense to be able to make something like blackmail work . . . even if he could think it up! That takes a certain amount of cunning."

"I agree," Caledonia nodded. "Well, what about Henry, our soft-drink man?"

"We don't really know anything about Mr. Ortelano, do we? So I think we should concentrate our efforts on Rollo—although there doesn't seem to be anything . . . Well, I mean, it couldn't be things like spies and that. Rollo couldn't keep a secret if he had one—he chattered all the time, to anyone who'd listen. It couldn't have anything to do with money. He didn't have any. And if he had, he couldn't have kept it to himself—he'd be trying to share it. So that's out . . . And if it was someone else's money, he wouldn't try to horn in on it . . . he was far too shy for that!"

"Uh-*huh*. Well, that means there was *no* reason we can think of anyone would want to kill him. Right?" Caledonia said, and sighed hugely. "We'll just have to wait till we talk to this new policeman, Sergeant Benson, to see what's going on."

Their turn to talk to Benson came that afternoon. But what resulted was not enlightenment as to motive—or anything else.

Chapter 3

Benson, like Martinez before him, had set up shop at the retirement center in the second-floor room that was called "the sewing room," although it served multiple functions. A uniformed policeman sat taking notes at one corner of the big table that was used by the residents and employees for everything from cutting patterns to holding staff meetings over a bag lunch. The uniformed man, a youngster with embarrassing freckles on his nose, a rookie named Charlie Jeffers serving his first year on the force, kept his head down and his mouth shut, and neither Angela nor Caledonia could gather much impression of him other than that he was there. At least, not at first.

Benson was another matter. He bore out exactly their first impressions of him from their previous contact. He was briskly businesslike, almost unfriendly. Nothing about him inspired either their confidence or their confidences.

"Ladies ..." He gestured toward a pair of chairs and smiled, the smile stopping at the top of his upper lip, not extending into his eyes, which were cool and shrewd behind his rimless glasses. "I bring you greetings from a friend of yours ... Lieutenant Martinez said I should be sure to tell you that he will certainly stop by to visit you soon; he apologizes for having let it go so long."

"Ohhhh," Angela breathed, beaming. "How is that young man? Such a *nice* boy ..."

There was a small noise from the throat of Charlie Jeffers in his corner, the only uncalled-for sound he made through the whole interview. Anyone listening closely might have thought the sound was an imperfectly smothered gust of laughter, quickly controlled!

Benson nodded and sat down opposite them, across the table. He ignored Jeffers' response and kept his own face rigidly straight. "He's doing very well. I'll tell him you asked after him. But he did warn me about you two, so I thought I'd see you together, at the same time, and set things straight."

Caledonia looked at Angela and back at him, her large eyes innocent. "Warned you?" There was the suggestion of a grin starting to tug at the corners of her mouth.

"What do you mean," Angela said with indignation, "you want to set things straight?"

"About our investigation and your part in it."

"Oh! Our part?" Angela said hopefully.

"Well, perhaps I put that rather badly," Benson said hastily. "Let me rephrase. To be completely accurate, you have no part at all in this matter. But Martinez said you were very good observers and I'd find out a lot about this establishment from talking with you—about the other tenants and the staff, for instance. Of course, until last night, I couldn't see any reason to suppose that your knowledge was going to be of help in this case."

"Why not?" Caledonia challenged. "Why wouldn't our special knowledge be just as useful to you as it has been to . . .?"

Benson held up his hand. "I was about to say—we couldn't see that the first murder was really connected to this place and to the residents here, unless of course you know of someone given to homicidal rages. Like maybe one of the residents who isn't traveling with both oars completely in the water. Somebody"—he tapped his temple meaningfully—"whose wiring isn't wrapped all that tight. Someone who's leaning far enough off his hinges to stab this fellow . . . uh . . ." He looked toward the note-taking policeman and snapped his fingers. "This fellow . . ."

"Rollo Bagwell," the note-taker supplied.

"Bagwell? No—I meant the first guy . . ." He snapped his fingers again and Jeffers responded, "Ortelano. Enrique Ortelano," without looking up.

"Yeah. That's the one. Of course the killing of the gardener changes things."

"How so, Sergeant?" Angela asked innocently.

"Well, policemen don't like coincidence. Not coincidence like that, anyhow. Somehow those two deaths have to be linked." He leaned back in his wooden straight chair, tipping it so that the front feet came off the floor and the back rested against the edge of the table behind him. He clasped his hands over his shirtfront, and he looked, Angela thought with distaste, like a fat man twice his age.

"Now," Benson was saying, "as I see it, the case is likely to go in one of three directions: one way, it's Bagwell they meant to kill and Ortelano was mistaken for him."

"We thought of that, too," Caledonia nodded, "except they're not very much alike, really."

Benson frowned and went on. "Second, the two men are connected in some way we haven't come across yet and were both killed for the same reason."

"Like they both knew where a buried treasure was, and someone was trying to find the map . . ." Angela said excitedly. "I saw this movie on television last Saturday morning. Of course it took place in South America, but it could be something like that . . ."

Benson ignored her. "Third, of course, it might be Ortelano they meant to kill all along, and Bagwell just saw something he wasn't supposed to see—so they came back and got rid of him later, before he could tell someone what he'd seen."

"That's a possibility! I hadn't got to that one!" Angela said.

"I beg your pardon?"

"I was trying to think earlier of all the reasons someone might kill Rollo, and we threw them all out. I mean— spying secrets, blackmail, drugs, an affair with someone's wife, a fight with someone. Well, Rollo couldn't keep a secret, he wasn't a cruel person like a blackmailer, he wouldn't be involved in drugs or in a love affair, he avoided arguments . . . I'd gone down the whole list and almost nothing fit. But I just hadn't got around to that one yet—that he saw something or somebody he wasn't supposed to."

Benson's eyes were slightly glazed and he gave his head a shake, as though to clear it. Then he went on, "What I'm getting around to is this. I take it that you know the staff very well here?"

"We know some of them as well as family," Caledonia said. "The new ones—like the beginning nurses and the handymen—they come and go all the time and we never do learn much about them. But some have been here since the place was converted . . ."

"Well. All right. Would you like to fill me in on what you knew about Rollo Bagwell then?' Benson asked. The women hesitated. "How about you?" He pointed to Caledonia.

"Well, Rollo was around here every day but he was—you know—a little simple. You couldn't have a conversation with him—unless it was about petunias or something."

"We don't have any petunias in our garden, Caledonia," Angela corrected.

"Well, peonies then."

"Or peonies either!"

"The point is, Sergeant," Caledonia turned toward him, making sure that Angela got the back of her head, "all he seemed to know about, and certainly all he cared about, was flowers. The only way I can imagine him getting in a fight would be if he saw someone trying to cut some of his precious blossoms to make a bouquet. He'd pitch a fit about that!"

"He didn't like for people to cut the flowers, you see," Angela put in. "He thought of them as his, not ours, and he thought flowers looked best growing in the garden, not cut and standing in a vase . . ."

"So do I," rumbled Caledonia. "He'd get no argument from me."

"Besides," Angela went on, "cutting flowers is against the rules. And Rollo, being so simple, always kept the rules—to the letter! I remember one time he scolded Sadie Mandelbaum for feeding the pigeons, after Torgeson told us we mustn't do it. It didn't really matter to Rollo, except it was a rule. He kept shouting that she mustn't break the rules! And she's too deaf to understand what he was saying, so she kept on crumbling the bread and scattering the crumbs—and Rollo was coming along behind her with a broom, sweeping them up and shouting at her! Everybody heard the fuss before it was over."

"Why is it against the rules to cut flowers?" Benson wondered.

Caledonia laughed. "Oh, come on, Sergeant. There are more than two hundred of us living here. Suppose even half the residents decided to cut just one fresh flower to go on the breakfast table every other morning? In a week the garden would be stripped of all its bloom. The best thing is just to say that nobody can cut flowers. Except staff, of course—for the dining table when there's a special guest."

"Well, then," Benson said. "I take it you're saying that if he'd found one of the residents cutting his flowers, Rollo would have scolded the man—or the woman. I wonder—would someone take the scolding badly and fight back, maybe with the first weapon that came to hand, like the garden shears they were using to cut flowers?"

"Don't be silly," Caledonia snapped. "Sergeant Benson, those were Rollo's own shears. At least, I assume they were. He carried an old basket everywhere he went—with a pair of leather gloves and some twine and a trowel and a can of bug spray—and a pair of long-pointed shears—so he'd have his hand tools and things right with him when he needed them. Sort of like a businessman carries his brief-case everywhere. And Rollo didn't lend his tools out. He was very fussy about it."

"So Rollo probably had his shears with him," Angela said eagerly. "And the murderer could just have reached out and grabbed the shears from Rollo's basket . . ."

"I agree. That's probably how the killer got his weapon," Benson put in hastily, as though he were trying to seize control of the conversation once more. "We did find a basket on the patio with some implements. No shears. They were . . . well, they were somewhere else."

"In Rollo, you mean," Angela said brightly. "Don't be shy about saying the obvious. Blood and gore don't bother us in the least." Off in the corner, Charlie Jeffers ducked his head lower than ever over his notes.

"You know, my own theory is that Rollo couldn't have been killed for scolding someone who cut his flowers," Angela went on, as Charlie Jeffers' hand came up in such a way that it shielded his mouth from view, though the corners of his eyes were crinkled in an expression either of sharp pain or enormous amusement. "I mean, it's a quaint idea, Sergeant, but people don't cut flowers at night. At least—well, I seem to remember my mother saying they should be cut first thing in the morning, anyway."

"I wouldn't know about that," Benson said. "I'm not a gardener myself at all." He passed a hand over his brow, and his expression was dazed. Things seemed to be moving past him and the conversation moving of its own accord— without him.

"At any rate," Angela put in, "it's not very light out in our garden at night. Nobody could see to pick flowers in the twilight, could they?"

"Well, what about a thief?" Caledonia said. "Angela and I didn't really like that idea, but still . . . you know, like supposing Rollo saw an intruder, and maybe it was a thief and when Rollo challenged him, the thief got scared and killed him. But we decided that wasn't really a good theory. If Rollo had seen a stranger, he'd just have assumed they were here on legitimate business and left them alone." Then she snapped her fingers! "But—I just thought of this— suppose it was kids up from the beach! They come into the garden sometimes—we see their sandy footprints on the walk in the morning. If some kid came up here in a bathing suit—Rollo would have realized right away he didn't belong. Once, Sergeant, they went through and stole all the flowerpots."

"Stole the flowerpots?" Benson was a little bewildered. "What for?"

"Well, they were full, of course," Caledonia said. "I understand a beautiful, full-grown plant can fetch several dollars on the market . . . I don't keep plants around my own apartment, but some of the others do. And I wish you could have heard the complaining up and down the walk . . . Plants were stolen right off the porches of the cottages."

"Even Mr. Grogan! He had a giant old burro-tail cactus in a hanging basket," Angela said. "And there was Mary Moffet's fuchsia plant . . ."

"What they didn't steal they broke. Just out of meanness," Caledonia continued. "Picked 'em up and threw 'em or just dropped 'em."

Angela nodded. "Mrs. Toliver had a strawberry jar with a little begonia growing in every pocket . . . it was smashed all to pieces."

"Of course the noise got everybody up out of bed, too," Caledonia said. "I woke up myself. The boys were just running away, carrying off their prizes, by the time I got out onto the porch. It takes a while for us to get up and moving, at our age . . . get our bathrobes, fetch canes or walkers . . . We just saw the youngsters running off. Not much out of their teens, if that. Laughing . . . having a wonderful time. Of course we couldn't do anything about it. Poor little Mary Moffet cried for a week over that fuchsia. She'd worked so hard . . ."

"Okay-okay-okay," Benson said, determined to take charge once more. "The violence involved in breaking a flowerpot is a lot different from stabbing someone. I don't really think it was teenage vandals. But it's always a possibility," Benson said, his eyes narrowed speculatively, "that Rollo saw some stranger . . . someone who didn't belong . . . here the week before—on the Tuesday night when Ortelano was knocked off. And that Rollo was killed to keep him from identifying that stranger."

"Then why was Henry Ortelano murdered?" Caledonia asked. "If Rollo Bagwell was killed because he was a witness to something that had to do with Henry Ortelano's killing, then to identify the killer, you need to know why Ortelano died. Right?"

"I'm afraid that's right. And so far that's a complete dead end, Mrs. . . . Mrs. . . . ." He snapped his fingers at the note-taking policeman.

"Mrs. Benbow," Jeffers said, not even looking up.

"No, I'm Mrs. Wingate," Caledonia rumbled. "She is Mrs. Benbow."

"That's what I meant," Benson said. "I meant the big one," he said crossly to Jeffers. " 'Scuse me, ma'am."

"No offense taken," Caledonia said easily. "You'd have to be blind not to notice my size, and that's the truth. Well, why on earth was our soft-drink man murdered? It always gets back to that."

"And I get back to our dead end. Unless you can maybe think of one of the residents who's walking along with one foot off the pavement—you know, somebody who's about two eggs short of a dozen, and half of those are cracked."

"Crazy? That's what you mean?" Angela asked.

"Well . . . yes. Someone whose roof leaks just enough to make him decide to kill somebody. Somebody who's really unplugged from a couple of his sockets."

"Well, we've certainly got more than our share of eccentrics . . . it comes with getting a lot of old folks together under one roof. Not that I think any of them killed Henry Ortelano and Rollo Bagwell. The Jackson twins, for instance—they really are eccentric—they wear nothing but pink and dress like they were still back in the 1930s at a sock hop. But they wouldn't stab anybody."

"Mr. Grogan," Caledonia said, "is drunk three-quarters of the time and thoroughly disagreeable during the rare moments he's sober . . . but the man wouldn't kill a sand flea."

"Tootsie Armstrong doesn't think very clearly," Angela put in. "Her mind is as woolly as her hair. And Mary Moffet is innocent to the point of lunacy—she thinks the best of everybody, and you know in this day and age that is neither practical nor intelligent."

"There's Trinita Stainsbury," Caledonia suggested. "She keeps changing the color of her hair. It was rose pink last week . . . periwinkle blue the week before. Now that is crazy, to me!"

"And Mrs. Gardner . . . Lena Gardner . . . who sits and snuffles into her handkerchief all day . . . she's new here, or relatively new," Angela explained, "and sometimes new residents have a terrible time getting adjusted. She's one who didn't want to come in ... but it apparently wasn't safe for her to live alone any more."

"And Hazel Hanson," Caledonia reminded her. "Hazel," she explained to Benson, "talks to the sea gulls. She goes down to the beach every morning ..."

"Well, could any of them turn violent? You know—go off the diving board headfirst into shallow water and end up killing someone? Because that is about all I can think of." He shook his head. "Desperation thinking, I admit. Of course, that doesn't fit with the theory that the killer was sane enough to see Bagwell as a danger and knock him off to save being identified ... lunatics don't work in straight lines like that. None I ever met." He sighed.

"Of course," Angela said shrewdly, "a lunatic just might kill two people for the same twisted reason. I mean, like suppose he didn't care for moustaches. Do you see what I mean? That's a reason that doesn't make sense to us—but it would account for both men being killed by the same person."

Benson looked at them in dismay, and then suddenly swiveled around to look at the uniformed policeman. The man had his head down, but Benson frowned ... was that a smile on Jeffers' face?

"Well," he went on, assuming a businesslike manner, "do you have anything at all you can think of that might be relevant? Anything unusual that's happened recently around here that might somehow be related?"

The two women shook their heads regretfully. "But we'd be glad to look around for you, Sergeant," Angela said hopefully.

"Thank you, but that won't be necessary," Benson said, rising and moving to open the door to the hall. "Or, let me put it another way. That is not just unnecessary, it's highly undesirable. I told you that I heard about you two second-hand, and Martinez may have put up with your puttering around, but I definitely don't want you interfering. It's very dangerous for you and lord knows what you might do to evidence—meaning well, but blundering ... I hope you're going to leave this whole business to us. We know what we're doing ... and if we hit a snag and need you, we know where to find you." He gestured the way out to both of them. "Ladies . . ."

"Well! Well! *Well*!" Angela was speechless with annoyance, which she managed to express all the same, once they got clear of the room and out of Sergeant Benson's earshot. *"WELL!!!"*

"It isn't well at all, Angela. If we're looking for excitement, we're in for a disappointment. I think we just got the clearest kind of a signal not to try to get involved. Agreed?" Caledonia asked.

"Well, sort of, but I can't understand why. If Lieutenant Martinez told him about us—"

"Uh-huh . . . Obviously he did, and that's why the sergeant is making such a point of easing us out. I mean, we have poked our noses in where they weren't wanted in the past, haven't we?"

"But we were a big help!" Angela protested. "Lieutenant Martinez said he couldn't manage without us. Maybe this young fellow will find out the same thing. I tell you what, Cal. Let's ask around a little and see if we can turn up anything interesting. If we could—well, that would prove our point to Sergeant Benson. What do you say?"

Caledonia grinned at the same time she shook her head. "I say absolutely not! You know perfectly well I'm every bit as curious as you are. It isn't often we get something so . . . so bizarre around here . . . and yes, I'm dying to know more about it. But it's no deal. Sorry."

"Caledonia! Why?"

"Because somehow this scares me. Really scares me. There's something about death by stabbing . . ." She shivered hugely.

Angela tossed her head with disdain. "It's just that you saw the body for yourself, Cal. That's all. The other times you had people telling you about it, secondhand. You never saw for yourself . . . Now, I did. I once saw a woman who'd been beaten to death—and Rollo can't have been any more gruesome than that. But that didn't stop me! Oh, dear—I wish Lieutenant Martinez was here. This Sergeant Benson is nice enough, I suppose, but—"

"—but he isn't Martinez. At least we can agree on that!"

"Well, yes. And every time we have a murder, we've had Martinez here—they just seem to go together!"

Caledonia burst out laughing. "Did you listen to what you just said, girl? 'Every time we have a murder' sounds like it's something we do every week, like bingo. As though it was something we enjoyed!"

Of course, despite Caledonia's protest, it was. Up to a point.

It was less enjoyable for Benson, who had bruised his foot badly, kicking a chair after the women left. He turned to Jeffers. "Don't you ever tell Martinez about this," he warned. "Never! He warned me those two old women were clever as hell ... but I thought I could handle them easy. And they turned me inside out—got me talking more about the case than they did. I answered their questions—they didn't answer mine! *Damn!*" He kicked the chair again. "Just don't you tell anybody, and especially not Martinez! Clear?"

"Yessir," Jeffers said solemnly. But the smile was still lurking, just behind his eyes, as Benson, his face thunderous, called in for an interview the next resident on their list ... an interview that proved as useless as all the others, that whole long day.

Chapter 4

"WE MAY be getting a sprinkle of rain later," Mr. Brighton predicted to the group that gathered outside the dining room just before lunch. He leaned heavily on his cane and sighed as he adjusted an arthritis-crippled hip to take less of his weight. "Joint's giving me a fit today. I've been thinking that she's having such a hard time adjusting, perhaps we ought to make a special effort with her."

The change of subject wasn't difficult for his little group to follow. "She" and "her" did not refer to his hip, but to Camden's newest resident, the quiet, depressed-looking woman named Lena Gardner who had moved in six days before, and who seemed to be finding the transition difficult. Each day, while they waited for the recorded sound of the Westminster chimes to signal that the dining room was opening, Camden's residents gathered in the lobby. This week, there were two topics of conversation across the room: the murders and the newest resident. Mrs. Gardner sat dispiritedly gazing at her hands folded around a lace handkerchief in her lap, seldom glancing up to meet the eyes of other residents, never volunteering a comment, though politely answering when she was spoken to.

"She's really taken the move very hard," Angela Benbow agreed. "I don't remember anybody who moped that long about it."

"Well, we all hate change," little Mary Moffet said tentatively. The only woman in Camden who was smaller in stature than Angela, she was diffident with almost everyone. "It's a bad time of life to be leaving everything that's

familiar and trying to start all over again with new surroundings, new friends . . ."

Today, the Jackson twins stood beside Mrs. Gardner's
chair attempting to make conversation with her. The twins,
tubby women so unremittingly cheerful and optimistic that
they were often offensive and always tiresome, were
dressed as usual in their favorite color, pink. This time it
was a pair of identical pink-and-white-striped seersucker
skirts, cinched in at the waist with belts woven of pink-and-
blue fibers, and topped with little pink linen blouses that
were, seemingly, two sizes too small. Each of the twins,
Dora Lee and Donna Dee, had fastened a pink taffeta bow
at a coy angle in her iron-gray pageboy.

"I swear, that's enough to kill my appetite, and I don't
imagine it's helping Mrs. Gardner much," Angela Benbow
declared. "Thank heaven they're the width of the lobby
away from me. Up close to all that rosy glow I might just
have had to say something about it—something I'd probably have regretted. Don't those two know better than to
wear belts pulled so tight?" She ran her hand over her own
loosely belted and almost nonexistent waistline. "They look
like two sacks of red-skinned potatoes tied in the middle!"

Across the lobby, the twins labored valiantly but without
success to get some flicker of positive response from Mrs.
Gardner. From time to time she sighed and seemed to agree
with what they were saying, but her subdued murmurs
would have discouraged less-determined women. The Jackson twins, however, merely strained harder, their gestures
growing more animated, their faces set rigidly into smiles.
"They look," Caledonia Wingate whispered, "as though
rigor mortis has set in, and their grins are in place unto the
grave!"

Mr. Brighton's little group, formed up in a splash of sunshine that streamed through the glass sliding doors to the
garden, would all have denied most vigorously that they
were gossiping; they would have stoutly defended themselves as merely showing friendly interest. Mr. Brighton,
himself a kindly and cheerful man despite being in almost
constant pain, was merely indulging in one of the favorite
sports among Camden residents, guessing—or trying to

guess—the personality, age, marital status, interests, wealth, and short-comings of every newcomer to the retirement apartments. It was an exercise Mr. Brighton called "Weighing 'Em In," and one of which he and his fellow residents never tired.

These few minutes before the big double doors to the residents' common dining room swung open were the best times to share a little news and a few opinions. One could join any of the several groups that formed throughout the lobby or drift from group to group, gleaning the best offerings of each. Besides Brighton, the group by the garden door included Caledonia, Angela, Emma Grant—tall and gaunt, with a prominent hearing aid—and Mary Moffet, a cherubic little innocent who thought the whole world to be as well-meaning as she. "I swear," Caledonia had once remarked of Mary, "she's like all three of those 'Hear No Evil' monkeys rolled into one!"

"I remember when I came in," Emma Grant was saying now. "I had a hard time, too, so I know how Mrs. Gardner must feel. I felt terribly lost and lonely for weeks."

"That was because you couldn't hear a blessed thing, Emma," Angela Benbow said tartly. "You didn't get your hearing aid till last year, and you were deaf as a post up till then. You got so paranoid you were hard to deal with. You always imagined we were talking about you, because every time you came up to us when we were in conversation, we seemed to you to lower our voices so you wouldn't hear. Anyway, that's what you thought. Because you couldn't hear. And then you'd get mad at us. Really dumb!"

"Oh, Angela," little Mary Moffet squeaked. "That's not kind! Emma didn't know she was so deaf, after all . . ."

Emma nodded. "It does sort of come on you gradually, you know. It's not like—like one day you can hear everything, the next you're deaf. It's more like—one day you start thinking how the commercials are the only things they make loud enough on TV—and you notice how soft the news reporters talk." The others all laughed and nodded with appreciation. There wasn't one whose hearing was up to standard.

"Then you notice," Emma went on, "how commercials

made with music are terribly hard to understand. You can't pick out the voices when there's mood music in the background—the sounds kind of mush together. And they use so much music!" She laughed ruefully. "I never knew what product they were advertising, because they always have music along with the announcer. I used to have to wait to see the picture or the name of the product at the end!"

"And even then, you might not know it. I mean, the picture doesn't always tell you," Mary Moffet said. "All those cars, for instance! They all look alike to me. My grandson can tell them apart—but I'll never know how he does. And their names! I mean, what company makes the horses and what company makes the wildcats? And all those initials . . . XKE—GTE—GTO—I don't know what they're talking about most of the time when I can hear them!"

"They don't really care whether *we* watch the ads for cars or not," Caledonia Wingate said, smoothing the folds of her lemon brocade caftan. The cloth shimmered in the sunlight and seemed to cast light of its own. "Of course, I used to know quite a lot about cars. But these modern ones look alike to me, and even if we can tell one car from another, we're not about to buy one. And those advertisers know it. So why worry whether we can understand the words in their ads or not?"

Mr. Brighton nodded. "Our driving days are over, alas. Except for you, of course, Mrs. Grant." He gave a small bow in the direction of Emma; one of only twenty or so residents who still drove for themselves, she kept a car parked in the lot across the street.

"Well, to be fair about that, we don't want to go much of anywhere. I mean, everything we want is right here for us . . ." Caledonia gestured around the expanse of the lobby, cool and heavily shadowed except where light streamed through the doorways. It was much the same as when the old building had been a hotel.

The furniture was elegant, and—as in many old hotel lobbies—built for titans, but titans who didn't care one way or the other about creature comforts. Scattered around the lobby there were gigantic, high-backed, stiff-cushioned velvet chairs with legs so long and seats set so far off the ground that half the residents could not touch the floor if they perched on one. There were sofas upholstered in expensive brocades, ten feet long and so deep that if one of the residents tried to lean against the back, he found himself lying down flat instead. At several places through the room there were heavily carved cocktail tables of blackened oak, large enough to hold a Greco-Roman wrestling exhibition. Expanses of cream stucco wall were disguised by massive tapestries depicting gallant medieval knights and their ladies fair. The floors were of solid marble—slippery for canes and walkers, so now hidden at intervals by imitation Turkish carpets. And on one side of the lobby there was a copper-hooded fireplace with a monstrous wrought-iron spit on which one could have roasted a Percheron—whole—assuming one ever wished to do so.

But the residents gloried in their antiquated monster of a lobby and basked in its elegance. Two years ago, in a burst of generosity inspired by an unusually profitable quarter, Olaf Torgeson—known to the residents whom he served as administrator as "The Toad" or "The Wart Hog"—had offered to modernize the lobby for them—to make it, as he put it in his memo:

> . . . a tribute to our good taste. My dear wife, who as you know is a decorator herself, has suggested we consider going "art deco," and I agree that the notion is amusing. I shall be happy to entertain any alternate suggestions.

The suggestions Mr. Torgeson received caused his blood pressure to rise another notch and gave him a severe headache. If one were to summarize the gist of the notes, using only polite terms, one might quote the song: "Don't change a hair for me, not if you care for me." Of course, the terms were not really that polite. Torgeson never mentioned redecoration again.

The truth was, Camden was home to its residents—at least, as soon as they became accustomed to it. The transition was often difficult, as Emma Grant had remarked, but one was swapping independent living for safety and convenience, and most of the residents considered it a fair trade-off.

"You're right, of course," Angela Benbow said now, as the group basked in their sunny lobby corner. "Advertisers aren't selling cars to such as us. For that matter they aren't selling us kitchen-tile cleaner or barbecue sauce or detergent or soft drinks either! We are definitely not the Pepsi generation!"

Mr. Brighton shook his head dolefully. "I haven't seen an ad for my favorite soft drink for years. You'd think they'd quit making root beer, for all anybody advertises it."

"Ooooooh," Mary Moffet breathed blissfully. "Remember Black Cows? Rich vanilla ice cream floated in foamy root beer?"

"I remember once in Laramie, Wyoming, in the early thirties," Mr. Brighton said. "We had come in on the train from Omaha. Hot? I mean, there was no air conditioning on the trains then, of course, not even in the sleepers. My folks and I went into town, and I saw a sign on a drugstore advertising 'Creamy Root Beer.' Well, that's what they called it everywhere—you know, the root beer with the big collar of foam—creamy. So the folks gave me a dime—and believe me, that was a big investment, back then. And I ordered me a creamy root beer.

"Well, sir, you'll never believe—when the root beer came, they'd actually dumped a half-cup of pure cream into the stuff! It was in a glass mug, and you could see the cream swirling through the brown root beer ... I nearly gagged!"

"But that might be good," Caledonia said, "kind of like when the ice cream from the Black Cow melted and mixed in."

Brighton laughed. "I didn't think so at the time. Kids aren't much for experimenting, you know. I went out of there almost in tears ... and I didn't even try my nice drink. I bet you never ran into root beer with cream in it anywhere else, either. That had to be a Wyoming special!"

At that point, the silvery sound of the Westminster chimes rang through the lobby and the double doors leading to the dining room were swung open by Dolores, the headwaitress. The waiting residents surged forward, and the individual groups ceased to exist as all heads turned in a single direction, all bodies moved forward as one, and two hundred souls generated a single thought: LUNCH.

When Caledonia and Angela arrived at their assigned table—separately, because Angela moved quickly, while Caledonia allowed herself to be carried along by the human tide around her—they found it already occupied. Cora Ransom, a still slim and still pretty woman who dressed in high heels, tidy little suits, silk blouses that tied at the neck—who wore modest but becoming makeup—and who could easily be taken for an active business woman—an administrator, perhaps, or an expensive executive secretary (they dress identically)—Cora Ransom was already seated at one of the two chairs.

"Oh, dear," Angela muttered. "Not again."

"Be nice to her, now," Caledonia whispered.

Angela glared at her large companion. "Cora, my dear," she said pleasantly, "your table is over there—by the front window."

Cora looked up in mild confusion. "I'm already by the window," she protested, without conviction.

"Yes, Cora," Caledonia put in, "but the wrong window. This is the garden window. You're over there—across the room—by the front window."

"Oh, of course. How silly of me." Cora sighed. "I was thinking of something else when I came in . . . and I just saw—you know—leaves and sunshine—and I sat down." She pushed her chair back and shrugged in apology. "I'm afraid I already ate one of the rolls," she said, pointing to the crumbs on the bread plate.

"We'll just have Chita bring us another," said Angela, beckoning to the little dark-haired waitress bustling through their section with a huge tray of soup cups balanced precariously above her head.

Cora Ransom made her way between the tables toward her own, smiling and exchanging greetings with the other diners as she went, her momentary embarrassment forgotten.

"It's amazing. You couldn't tell by looking at her that

anything is wrong. And tomorrow, she won't even remember she did that," Angela sighed.

"Tomorrow! Hah! She won't remember three minutes from now," Caledonia said. "Ah, well . . . Chita, Mrs. Ransom ate one of our rolls . . . when you get time?"

Conchita Cassidy, one of the prettiest and most popular of their waitresses, deftly slid a small cup of French onion soup, loaded with grated cheese and croutons, before each of them. "Don't you worry, ladies. I get you more rolls. You gonna like the soup today . . . one of Mrs. Schmitt's best, I think. But be careful. It's *hot!*" Chita's accent came and went with the moment. Sometimes she talked more like her Mexican mother, whose Latin good looks she had inherited, sometimes like her Irish-American father from whom she took her bubbling good cheer and optimism. "Rolls coming up when I finish with the soup," she said, as she slid away to the next table. "I promise!"

"How's Chita's romance with that young detective coming along? You know who I mean—that tall, skinny kid who came around with Martinez all the time," Caledonia asked. "What's the latest word on that?"

"She saw him three times last week, but he hasn't called yet this week," Angela said.

"Migawd, how you find out all the details like that I'll never know!" Caledonia laughed aloud, the gust of her amusement setting a series of miniature tidal waves moving across the surface of the onion soup, engulfing croutons and swamping islands of floating cheese. "I would have been happy with a general report."

"Well," Angela said defensively, "I hear things, you know. And let me tell you, people are mighty concerned. I mean, it's Thursday today, isn't it, and last week by this time they'd had two dates. People are thinking maybe they had a quarrel . . ."

"Shorty Swanson isn't easy to get riled up," Caledonia said. "But I bet Chita's a little wildcat if she's mad. But what would she get mad about? She takes everything here in her stride—nothing ever seems to upset her. Remember the time Emma Grant had her hearing aid in for repair, didn't hear the kitchen doors open behind her, and backed right into Chita, coming out with a loaded dessert tray?"

Angela laughed at the memory. "There was lemon pie everywhere, that day! What a waste—Mrs. Schmitt's lemon pie is a work of art!"

"So is this soup! Lord, lord, but we're lucky, here at Camden. I could drink a gallon of this stuff, of course, and all they let me have is this little taste . . . but oh, that one little taste! I think the day I found this place, the good shepherd had me under the protection of his rod and staff for sure!" Caledonia sighed. "Better pass me one of the rolls. Chita will be bringing more, but I need one now."

Angela moved the plate within Caledonia's compass and nodded across the room to where Cora Ransom was sitting with the new woman, Lena Gardner. "Look at them . . . one of them is so down-in-the-mouth she couldn't work up a smile for Christmas . . . the other one is getting so she wouldn't even recognize when Christmas comes! Now there are two women who really need this place!"

"Cora for sure," Caledonia agreed, buttering her roll carefully. "But I'm not certain Lena Gardner would agree with you. She didn't want to come here . . . and I don't think she feels much better about it now, after nearly a week! She's a little absent-minded, but she's not as bad off as Cora, and she really hates this place, I'm thinking."

"But that absent-mindedness is why her nephew brought her here, remember," Angela said.

Like every other resident at Camden who could find a way to do so, Caledonia and Angela had managed to manufacture excuses to be in or to go through the lobby while Mrs. Gardner moved in. That was the game they all played. They would pretend to admire the flower arrangements the chapel's Altar Committee had moved, after the Sunday service, to grace the lobby's many tables. They would stop by the main desk to talk to Clara, the cheerful, red-headed day clerk, while she put up the residents' mail into little numbered pigeonholes. They would make an issue of reading Torgeson's interminable memos posted on the bulletin board outside the office door—and any of these errands could use up fifteen or twenty minutes, during which time they could get a look at the newcomer.

A few minutes were usually all the experienced residents needed in which to gauge the newcomer's furniture (Mrs. Gardner's was Grand Rapids Chippendale); her clothing (Mrs. Gardner wore a black rayon dress, long-sleeved and with a small white collar—a dress designed for Whistler's grandmother); her luggage (Mrs. Gardner's was nylon-sided, of a repellent shade of dull garnet strapped in dusty black webbing—probably, Emma Grant suggested with un-characteristic cattiness, bought with Green Stamps because nobody would pay cash for something with that color scheme!); and even the relatives who came to assist in the move (Mrs. Gardner's move seemed to be accomplished by a group of young people—apparently friends of the tall, thin, palely handsome young man with dark hair and a bright smile, who stopped to talk with Mrs. Gardner every few minutes and who called her "Aunt Lena.")

The young people chattered noisily as they unloaded the U-Haul and carried in small tables, lamps, chairs, pictures, stacks of bedding up to the second-floor south, where Mrs. Gardner's apartment was situated at the end of one hall-way. They spent their bright energies on each other, how-ever, and ignored Mrs. Gardner completely. She sat quietly, as though she were in shock, her hands folded to-gether in her lap, her lips pressed tight, her eyes solemn and—it looked to the curious residents—slightly moist.

Mr. Brighton had a room on the south hall, first floor. He was limping slowly out toward the lobby and had just come to the four little steps that led from the residence hall down into the main room when a girl in jeans and an oversized shirt that hung almost to her knees bustled through with a lamp in one arm, the shade perched on her head like a hat, and a huge family photograph in a gilt frame dangling from the other hand. She simply didn't see Mr. Brighton, and though it was a minor bump, as collisions go, it was dev-astating to Mr. Brighton. He gasped aloud in pain and dropped his cane . . . then clutched wildly at the stair rail to get his balance, since he was unable to move his legs freely to compensate.

It was the nephew who leapt forward to lend a hand. "Here, let me help you, old-timer," he said, totally unconscious of having given offense. He put a strong arm around Brighton's shoulders and eased him into a chair near the steps. "Here—your cane . . ." he said, handing Mr. Brighton his stick. "Okay now?" he added breezily. Then, without waiting for an answer, he walked over to his aunt, seated not ten feet from Mr. Brighton. Thus it was that Brighton was a witness to the conversation between the two.

"Why are you doing this to me?" Lena Gardner was saying mournfully. "I loved my little house. I don't want to be in this big, dark place. I want my little garden. They won't let me have my cat . . . what's going to happen to my Morris-Two?"

"Aunt Lena, you know we've found a nice home with Mrs. Walters for Morris-Two. He was over there half the time anyhow, because she always left food out for him; he never knew which was really his home, your place or the Walters'."

"Oh, Robbie, he loved me," she insisted. "He'll miss me."

"Yes, I'm sure he will," the nephew insisted. "But, Aunt Lena, what were we to do? You know you couldn't stay in that house all by yourself any more. You're far too frail . . . And you're getting forgetful. How about the time I came over for lunch and found you'd gone shopping and the gas stove was still hissing gas—but there was no fire going? How about the time you left the iron on and it burned right through the board and onto the floor?"

"All right. I know about those," she said, with a tiny show of spirit. "But nothing ever happened. I mean, you found the gas going—Mrs. Walters found the iron . . . she used to check on me every day."

"Well, you know she's going to take a job at K-Mart. She'll be much too busy, Aunt Lena."

The old lady looked at the floor, her mouth set in unyielding lines. "Robbie, I could have taken care of myself! I'm not senile yet!" she insisted.

"Of course not, Aunt Lena," he soothed. "But you do forget things."

"No, I don't."

"What about your checkbook? You were going to write me a check for my tuition and you couldn't find the checkbook . . . remember?"

"Everybody misplaces things," she protested.

"Then there was Aunt Hattie's brooch," he reminded her.

"Yes, I lost that somewhere. I felt really terrible about it. Such a lovely piece—little pearls all around that picture done in black enamel on gold—so unusual. And besides, it was my sister's . . ."

"Aunt Lena, you're always forgetting things . . . losing things. You know I worry about you. And here they can help you . . ."

Her woebegone face sagged even further and she shook her head. "I don't want to be taken care of. I want my own little house . . . I want my own friends . . . I want my dear old Morris-Two . . ."

He sighed and shook his head. But though he stood beside her another few moments, smiling hopefully down at her, she would not look up at him. She touched her eyes with her handkerchief and stared fixedly at the carpet. So eventually he moved on to carry another box of papers and books from the U-Haul truck, through the lobby, up the stairs, and presumably into her apartment.

Mr. Brighton's legs had stopped throbbing and he roused himself to go over to her.

"Tom Brighton, ma'am," he said with a tiny bow—all his hip joints would accommodate. "One of the longtime residents here. I'd kiss your hand, but I can't bend over far enough to get hold of it with mine . . . I'll wait till you're standing up—or until a warm, sunny day. My arthritis is the very devil before the morning fog burns off . . ."

Mrs. Gardner nodded sadly. "I know just what you mean, Mr. Brighton. I can predict rain more accurately than a TV weatherman, these days, myself. And I used to love to go for walks . . ."

"Well, perhaps on a sunny day, you'll join me for a walk around our building. We residents who try to keep up our exercise have almost worn a path. There are morning walkers and afternoon walkers—I'm an afternoon type myself. Hope you are . . ."

She smiled a tiny smile. "Oh, yes. Now that I have no household duties and no pets to feed, I can afford to sleep late. So I suppose I'll start a new set of habits. It's nice to meet you, Mr. Brighton."

He bowed. "Look forward to seeing you again, as the days go on," he said, and moved off to join others of the prelunch crowd, standing in their little discussion circles.

But settling in had apparently proved difficult for Mrs. Gardner, just as Brighton predicted to his friends that it might be. The residents speculated to each other in a mild way why the new lady seemed to be having such trouble, and how long a cure might take. Everyone had an explanation, a guess, an opinion.

"It's taking in everything new at once," Tootsie Armstrong said sympathetically. "She'll get it sorted out. It takes time."

"I'm not sure she can get it sorted out," Mary Moffet said. "She may just be going slowly downhill, you know. Like that woman in the second cottage—the one who moved in one week, got lost the second week, ran away the third week, and took to her bed to stay at the end of the month, remember?"

"I hope the poor lady isn't getting Alzheimer's," Angela said.

"Oh, a little absentmindedness is no sign the whole structure is crumbling," Caledonia shrugged. "We all forget things. There's probably not a thing wrong with her but the shock of the move. Give her time. She'll perk up."

But now, as they looked across the dining room, they agreed that Mrs. Gardner didn't seem much happier near the end of her first week of residence than she had on her very first day.

"You know," Caledonia said thoughtfully, "I think we'd better give that lady a little get-acquainted party. Help her feel a little more at home. She's not going to make it unless somebody does something to help."

"It didn't improve matters for them to assign her to a table with Cora. You can't get a sensible conversation from

Cora anymore," Angela said. "That wasn't a good idea. I don't think they give enough thought when they assign new people—I must mention that at the next Residents' Council meeting."

"Well, it was better than putting her with Grogan. He's got one of the few other tables with an open place. He's always in a raging bad humor, when he's sober, though he's cheerful enough when he's drunk. No, she's better off with Cora. At least Cora's happy all the time." She glanced across the room. "I think we'll have to give her a get-acquainted party soon. Immediately. In fact, I'll ask her right after lunch—when Cora's gone, of course. I don't want to hurt Cora's feelings, but I'm not having her come and get lost on the way from my living room to the bathroom. Pass the butter again, will you, please? I'll just take this last roll—there'll be another for you when Chita brings a refill."

"Cal, do you realize," Angela said, handing the butter plate across, "that we've spent the whole lunch hour and we haven't mentioned our murders once?"

"You're right. That's remarkable. Because that's the biggest news that's hit this place for months . . ."

Angela sighed. "I just feel so out of things, where that's concerned . . . I used to feel part of everything. But I feel as though I've been shoved aside—made a spectator . . ."

Caledonia leaned across the table and patted her hand. "There, there . . . there's plenty else to keep you busy. And you're better off. Remember what I said—this business smells of danger, to me . . . I'm happier that you're involving yourself in doing a good deed with me."

"Arm, Mrs. Wingate," Chita trilled, "move your arm, please," as she reached to take Caledonia's soup cup and replace it with a plate of chicken Marengo, a spear of steamed broccoli lying beside it, and half a small baked pear on the side. "You'll love the chicken . . . Mrs. Schmitt says she left out the garlic on purpose, but the sauce is superspecial anyhow. Here you go, Mrs. Benbow."

"Oh, Chita," Angela said slyly, as the girl whisked away the second empty soup cup. "What ever happened to that nice young man . . . Detective Swanson?"

"Oh, he's fine, Mrs. Benbow. Was the last time I saw him. Doing fine," Chita said, taking the empty breadbasket and substituting a full one. "Are you going to need more butter?"

"This'll do," Caledonia rumbled. "I shouldn't have the bread, either, but I can make my conscience clear by going easier on the butter, thanks."

"I will tell Swans-sohn you asked about him, Mrs. Benbow. When I see him." And Chita was gone.

"You've got nerve," Caledonia marveled as she put a fork into the chicken. "I'd never have had the gall to ask her about her love life ... oooooh, you've got to try that chicken, girl! What a triumph. Mmmmmmmmmm ..." Her eyes closed in sheer bliss.

"We didn't find out much from Chita, did we?" Angela grumbled. "I might as well not have asked. Oh, you're right! This is incredibly good!" And for a few moments both women, like everyone else in the dining room, concentrated on chicken Marengo and baked pear. The hum of conversation was at half-volume, and heads were bowed over the meal as though in adoration of the gods of Mount Tappan. Even a person with a failing memory, dim eyesight, and a hearing aid can appreciate a work of art from the kitchen. Gossip, good deeds, and murder sat on the shelf and waited.

Chapter 5

CALEDONIA DECIDED on Monday afternoon as the best time for her party in honor of Mrs. Gardner, and through the intervening days, she and Angela amused themselves with a guest list of noble proportions.

"Please remember that my apartment isn't quite as big as the lobby," Caledonia said, as Angela added yet another name.

"No need to be sarcastic, Cal. You want this to be a lively get-together, don't you? Well, the more people talking and laughing, the merrier. And of course we do want her to get to know the nice people. Speaking of which, why on earth did you add Trinita Stainsbury to the list? That woman gives me a royal pain . . . I was trying to think of a word to describe her. 'Pretentious' springs to mind!"

Caledonia shrugged. "She had me over for a coffee two weeks ago. I owe her. It doesn't pay to let your obligations mount up—pretty soon you'd have to rent the L.A. Coliseum to give the party! Besides, she'd have her feelings hurt if I left her out."

"Well, so would the Jackson twins, and you didn't put them on the list."

"Oh, yes, I did. I asked them last night."

"Cal! Not the Jackson twins?"

Caledonia nodded. "I know, I know . . . but they're bright and cheerful . . ."

". . . to the point of idiocy! Nothing makes them discouraged or downhearted or . . . I bet they had forgiving smiles on their faces during the last earthquake!"

"It wasn't much. Just a little quiver, really. Not enough to get excited about," Caledonia protested.

"Yes, but nothing to be pleased over, either . . . 'If you can't say something kind, Dora, don't say anything at all, as Mama used to say to us back in Anniston,' " she whined, in wicked imitation of the twins' Alabama drawl. "I bet they would even find something kind to say about Rollo's murder!"

"Speaking of which . . ." Caledonia pointed to her view window that faced a bank of rose bushes, just across her porch, then the expanse of the garden.

"Yes. I noticed. The police seem to have gone. Or at least there's no activity in the garden and Benson and his friend aren't in the second-floor sewing room any more. I'd say they've given up on us, wouldn't you?"

Caledonia sighed. "If it were Martinez here, we'd have heard what was going on, wouldn't we? Boy, that Benson! You talk about someone who gives you a pain! Well, it probably doesn't matter, because he may be gone from here for good, now. I agree with you—they've given up completely." She sighed. "Anyway, there's a bright side to it; at least they won't be poking around out there spoiling the view while we're having the party, will they? Now—how about the Emersons?"

"Good," Angela agreed. "I like him. And she's all right, of course. A little colorless, though."

"Angela, you think anybody's 'colorless' who doesn't go-go-go-go-go every blessed minute! Just because you've got the energy of a forty-year-old—try to remember, there are a few of us who feel our age as well as look it!"

Angela, who had never thought of herself as middle-aged, let alone old, grimaced. "But she just sits around and knits all the time! He plays shuffleboard, he plays bingo, he goes to the Library Committee meetings, he helps put up the trestle tables on the lawn for our barbecue parties . . . If he just wouldn't tell those interminable fishing stories! But anyhow, even with the stories, at least he's alive and interested in things. She stays in that room most of the time and makes things for her great-grandchildren!"

"She's nice enough," Caledonia said mildly.

"Oh, I grant you . . ."

"Well, then," Caledonia scribbled in EMERSON with her pencil, followed by a 2, "Well, then, the Emersons are in." She lifted up the list. "Look at this thing. I think I've got everybody here but Grogan! I might as well have asked him, I guess—except he wouldn't be sober! Let's see . . . I've got twenty-five guests. And counting us, that makes twenty-seven. Wow! I better go ask Mrs. Schmitt what she can produce for tea for twenty-seven on Monday . . ."

Approached in her kitchen while she poured a rich onion gravy over pork chops, ready to put into the oven to bake for Saturday night's dinner, Mrs. Schmitt cheerfully suggested a molded shrimp-salmon mousse, cucumber sandwiches, others made with walnuts and sliced white grapes in cream cheese, and tiny, thimble-size cherry cupcakes. "No problem, Mrs. Wingate. Glad to have the extra money, always. You want one of the waitresses to serve?"

"Good idea," Caledonia agreed. "How about Chita Cassidy?"

"Okay," Mrs. Schmitt said. "I'll talk to her. If not her, well, one of the kids we use in the kitchen has a father who's sick and can't work. She wouldn't be as good as Chita, of course, but she'd be glad for an afternoon's extra pay."

"Fine. Suits me. You'll bring the things down to the apartment after lunch Monday? Say about two or two-thirty? I'll nap awhile after lunch, and then I'll be ready to help get things set up."

Mrs. Schmitt nodded and it was agreed.

Caledonia cut across the dining room, out the garden door, and was skirting the edge of the patio (funny how nobody seemed to want to sit out there anymore, even on the warm July afternoons) when she heard her name warbled by a pair of soprano voices.

"Caledonia . . . Yoo-hoo—Caledonia . . ."

It was the Jackson twins, wearing matching tent dresses of dazzling rose-pink polyester crepe, rippling out about their stout frames, and matching rose-colored nylon stockings, making them look like soft-sculpture pyramids set up on pink stilts. They came tripping along from the lobby, waving and calling . . .

"I'm so glad we caught up with you," Dora Lee said. Or was it Donna Dee? Caledonia could not tell one from the other until the speaker identified herself.

"We were on our way to see you, weren't we, Dora Lee?" (Ah-*hah*! Now she knew—the one with the rimless glasses was Donna Dee, the one with the plastic rims was Dora Lee. *Today*, at least. Caledonia suspected that they changed glasses, from time to time, to confuse matters.)

"We certainly were, sister. About your party Monday, Caledonia . . ."

"Yes?"

"We can't come."

"We're desolate! Truly! But our grandniece is coming in for a visit from Birmingham . . ."

"Of course, our apartment is much too crowded with the two of us in one room for us to have her living there. She'll have to stay at a motel, if there's no empty apartment in this place."

"Oh, have they started renting the empty apartments to our guests again?" Caledonia asked. "Torgeson said that was too much trouble, and he stopped it for a while."

"Well," Dora Lee said, "we asked, and he said that if one was vacant when she arrived, our Sue Nancy could have it for two weeks. That's all I know."

"It'd be a lot cheaper than a motel, that's certain," Donna Dee said. "And Sue Nancy isn't what you'd call wealthy."

"Of course, on the other hand," Dora Lee said unhappily, "there's that ol' murderer running around loose still."

"I don't feel safe, and I'm not sure Sue Nancy should be exposed to that kind of thing . . ."

"What kind of thing do you mean?" Caledonia said curiously.

"I just meant," Donna Dee said unhappily, "well, you know—murder and killing and policemen everywhere—that's not the atmosphere for a well-brought-up young lady. Sue Nancy's mother would have a pea-pure fit, if she thought we exposed Sue Nancy to—you know—worldly things of that sort."

"On the other hand," Dora Lee twittered, "I simply hate the idea of a child like Sue Nancy staying in a hotel all by herself! That doesn't seem right, either."

"How old is this little girl?" Caledonia asked.

"Well, now," Dora Lee said, figuring on her fingers. "She was born the same year Cousin Emil's house burned. And that was the year before the county fair was closed down for having a lewd show—remember that, sister?"

"I surely do," Donna Dee replied. "Everybody in Anniston was talking about it. 'Course I don't have the faintest idea what kind of show that would be, but I remember Daddy said it was lewd. I remember his using that very word. That was the same year as the hurricane that tore up the sea front at Mobile—all those nice old places . . . you remember, sister, that must be . . ." She did some finger calculations.

"She's twenty-two last March," Dora Lee said triumphantly. "Right, sister?"

"Absolutely."

Caledonia sighed. "I'd have thought she was old enough to know a little bit about the real world already," she suggested.

"But she isn't married!" Donna Dee gasped.

"You can't have young girls like that seeing just any ol' thing!" Dora Lee said.

"Think of the influence on their lives!" Donna Dee added.

Caledonia grinned. "Sounds to me a little like not letting pregnant women see squashed tomatoes for fear the baby will have a red birthmark!"

Dora Lee furrowed her brow. "I never heard of that one," she said. "Is that something like why you don't let pregnant women see automobile accidents? I've heard of that."

"Exactly," Caledonia said. "But about your grandniece . . . what's her name again?"

"Sue Nancy Butler."

"Well, why not bring Sue Nancy along to the party? I mean, if you think she won't be bored stiff with a lot of old people. She'll probably want to go to San Diego a couple of days while she's here, maybe see Sea World and the

Wild Animal Park and the zoo . . . she may decide to skip the party entirely."

"Oh, I hope she wouldn't be that rude!" Dora Lee said, shocked. "Of course she'll come!"

"Besides, she can't go to all those places alone, now, can she?" Donna Dee added. "She'll want to wait till we can go with her. Not really chaperones, you know . . . more like companions."

"Sure," Caledonia said, registering grave doubt with a monosyllable. "Well, anyway, if Sue Nancy isn't busy and if she doesn't think she'd be bored, just bring her along. One more won't matter."

But, of course, it wasn't just one more. The next morning after church the guest of honor, Mrs. Gardner, stopped Caledonia on the way in to lunch. Granted Mrs. Gardner didn't know she was the honoree; Caledonia and Angela had both decided it was better to be more casual, to act as though she were just another of the guests. All the same, the party was for her benefit, and all the other guests had been told that. But to Caledonia's dismay, Mrs. Gardner had sought her out to tell her, "I can't come to your little get-together tomorrow."

"Oh, dear!" Caledonia was genuinely dismayed. "Oh, that would be a terrible shame. What's the problem?"

"Well, you know my nephew Robbie? The young man who helped me move in? The son of my youngest sister. She's dead now. All my family is—except for Robbie. He's a wonderful boy—a genius, I'm told! Of course, we get along like friends, instead of aunt and nephew. But he's been so busy over at the college he hasn't had time to come by to see me here since the day I moved in. Well, he's finally got time off from his computers and he's told me he wants to spend Monday afternoon with me."

Caledonia sighed and shifted toward her sternum the rope of pearls, which had been hanging slightly askew around her neck. "Dear Mrs. Gardner, why not bring Robbie with you? I'm sure he'll be bored to tears with us— we're no match for genius, certainly—but we'd like to meet him, of course, and it will be a chance for you to get acquainted with a few of your fellow residents as well—

people you haven't met yet, I mean. Tell him it won't take much of his time. We don't have parties that drag out and drag out, you know . . . we're far too old to stand around balancing teacups for very many minutes." She smiled her broadest, warmest smile. "Please?"

"Well," Mrs. Gardner said unhappily, "if you're really sure . . . I don't know that we'll stay very long. But yes, I'll surely tell Robbie, and I feel certain he'll agree."

Caledonia shook her head at the retreating back of her guest of honor—the one who nearly got away. It had been a near thing, keeping the fish on the line. A near thing—and of course the party would have been pointless without her.

"Oh, I'd have gone ahead with the party anyway," she told Angela. "But what a waste of preparations. I can buy a cheese ball from the deli counter at the Big Bear Market and lay out some chips, if it's just us." Angela smiled, thinking of the elaborate crystal and elegant silver with which Caledonia had always entertained—and of Caledonia's preference for gourmet delicacies, whether for herself or for guests.

Monday morning Lola, the chubby maid, cleaned with special care, moving the furniture and dusting the mopboards, swiping overheard with her broom, as well as underfoot . . . "You don't want cobwebs in the corners, Mrs. Wingate. Your guests would think I don't take care of my people right."

Just after two o'clock, Caledonia arose from her nap, bathed, and dressed herself in a jade-and-silver caftan, upon which she fixed at the point of the V-neck a handful of midnight-blue sapphires dancing in a swirling platinum clip.

At two-twenty, Mrs. Schmitt and two kitchen helpers showed up with trays of food. Caledonia directed them to the table set in one end of the extra-large living area she had achieved by combining two apartments into one. She had already laid out an array of serving dishes, which they filled, bringing the surplus to the kitchen, ready to be served when supplies on the table began to run out.

At two-forty-five Angela arrived, chic in a raw-silk suit

of ivory with an old-rose blouse trimmed in creamy lace. At her throat she had fastened a small antique pin she'd bought from her favorite jeweler downtown—pearls and gold, nestled down into and just visible among the frills of a jabot that spilled ecru lace out of the jacket front. Angela had looked with satisfaction at her image in the mirror and thought smugly that this was how the maker of the little brooch had meant it to be displayed when he fashioned it nearly a century before.

At two-fifty-five Chita Cassidy arrived, wearing a stiff white apron over a neatly pressed maid's uniform. "I'll stay in the kitchen till I'm needed," she said cheerfully, closing the folding doors of the kitchenette area behind her.

Promptly at three the doorbell rang. "Okay," Caledonia said, rising and smoothing the folds of her caftan as she glided to the door, "up and at 'em, Angela . . . here we go." She swung the door wide. "Lieutenant!" she gasped. "Lieutenant Martinez!"

"Delightful to see you, Mrs. Wingate!" It was indeed their friend, the handsome police officer. It was really amazing, Caledonia thought, how vivid the man was—how his presence seemed to make things look somehow brighter—more intense. She beamed a welcome at him like a great lighthouse illuminating a trim clipper ship tacking near its shoreline.

"Ah, Mrs. Benbow is here as well. How fortunate. I stopped at your apartment on the way into the center, Mrs. Benbow, but no one answered my knock and I thought I'd missed you!"

Over his shoulder Caledonia could see, coming down the walk from the lobby, Mr. Brighton, limping gamely on his cane, his hip obviously giving him trouble today. Up the walk came Mary Moffet, tiptoeing diffidently, as though her footsteps might disturb someone—still fifty yards away.

"Come in," Caledonia boomed. "You're just in time."

"Oh, we're so glad to see you," Angela sighed. "You have no idea! Not just because we don't like that other policeman, mind you . . ."

"You don't like Sergeant Benson? I'm sorry to hear that.

He's a nice enough person. What seems to be the problem?"

"Too businesslike, for one thing," Angela said. "It's hard to explain—oh, we've got so much to tell you ..."

"But not right now," Caledonia amended. "You will stay, Lieutenant? Till the party's over, I mean?"

"I see I've come at a bad time." Martinez had entered the room far enough to see the festive table. Through the crack in the folding doors of the kitchenette, he caught a glimpse of a black-and-white uniform. "You're giving a party. Oh, my dear lady, I am so sorry. My fault—I should have phoned ahead and asked if you were busy ..."

"No, please don't leave." Caledonia caught his arm to stop him from edging toward the door. "We both want to see you, to ask you questions in your professional capacity ..."

"And we want to visit with you as a friend, of course," Angela put in. "Can't you stay?"

"I'll tell you what, ladies," Martinez said. "I will come back in two or three hours when your get-together is over and done with. You see, I've met a number of these people in the line of duty. I interviewed many of them when I came here to look into your—your other troubles," he said tactfully. "I'm afraid it would make them uncomfortable to have me here, trying to make small talk. People often have that reaction to policemen, I've noticed. And besides, suppose I should have to interview them again? Social encounters could set the wrong tone for me professionally. You understand?"

"Just so you understand *we* don't feel that way," Caledonia said. He nodded and she went on, "I bow to your better judgment, of course."

"I'm very disappointed, you know," Angela said, cocking her little head coquettishly to one side to peer up at him from the corners of her eyes. "You haven't been here for simply ages, and now you're leaving ..."

"Only for a couple of hours, believe me." With his usual gallantry, Martinez bowed over each lady's hand, and was going out the door as Mr. Brighton and Mary Moffet simultaneously arrived at the porch. "Mrs. Moffet—Mr.

Brighton—" He nodded pleasantly to both and swung off rapidly toward the main building.

"Official business?" Mr. Brighton asked shrewdly.

"Oh, what did that charming man want?" Mary Moffet said.

"Just a friendly call—but when he saw I was already entertaining, he said he'd come back another time. Do come in . . ." Caledonia said, swinging the screen door wide. And the party began.

Within fifteen minutes, there were thirty people jammed into Caledonia's rooms . . . twenty-five guests, Caledonia and Angela, the two visitors, and Chita Cassidy moving skillfully to and from the kitchen with refills for the plates and with fresh tea. (Caledonia had disposed neatly of Trinita Stainsbury by asking her to pour, and Trinita was glorying in the honor, her hair shining bronze with a new spray-on color she was trying over her natural silver-white.)

The party progressed smoothly enough through its first half-hour or so. At nearly three-thirty, Caledonia managed to ease herself away from Tootsie Armstrong and Emma Grant, who then quite naturally half-turned to begin a conversation with Hazel Hanson just as Hazel was disengaging herself from Janice Felton. Janice then was able to move another few feet along and position herself where she could pass a few words with Sadie Mandlebaum and one of the only two husband and wife couples in the room, George and Adele Trimble. And so the groups formed and re-formed around the room.

Freed for a moment from her guests, Caledonia sought out Angela. Making sure they weren't overheard, she bent down to bring her mouth close to her ear. "Did you see the Jacksons' grandniece? Over there . . . by the door." She gestured cautiously—it wouldn't do to point—to a very blonde young woman standing beside one of the twins.

Angela nodded. "It always looks to me," she said, "as though these girls had reached into the bathtub to turn the water on, hit the button that turns on the shower by mistake, and only had time to dry off—not to set their hair!"

Caledonia uttered a series of sharp, barking noises that might pass for coughing, to cover her involuntary snort of laughter. "That frizzy hair may be fashionable," she whispered, "but to me it looks like a bad permanent wave done by a beginning student at the El Cheapo Beauty School!"

"Tell me," Angela said, "is that really the Jacksons' innocent little Sue Nancy, who can't be exposed to real life? Heaven help 'real life' if she gets near it."

As though aware she was under inspection, Sue Nancy raised a languid hand to idly brush a stray hair from her cheek, and her ox-blood-red nails were fully an inch longer than her fingers. The cheek she stroked was liberally highlighted with blusher, and her eyes were rimmed above and below with smudgy blue and black lines, making her look at once fatigued and knowledgeable—an exhausted Cleopatra.

"What are those clothes supposed to be? She looks like she dressed in the dark," Caledonia said.

"Oh, that's the very latest," Angela assured her. "She's been desperately seeking Madonna, I think."

"Who? Seeking what?"

Sue Nancy's sleeveless blouse hung unbelted to her hips, and one shoulder was bare as though the garment were too loose—flashdance style. Her skirt—what there was of it—could have been applied to her by means of aerosol spray. She towered over her two grandaunts, thanks mainly to the four-inch heels of her slippers, and her legs were imperfectly covered in black fishnet stockings.

"Never mind," Angela said, "never mind. I'll explain later. Just take my word, it's high fashion for the younger generation that you're looking at—one form of it, anyway."

"I haven't seen stockings like that since the last performance of *Irma La Douce* at the little theatre," Caledonia marveled. "Where's she staying, by the way?"

Angela grinned. "In the empty room across the hall from the Jackson twins' place. Torgeson let them rent it for her. And do you think Sue Nancy was pleased to be living here with all of us? Look at that expression of sheer joy and rapture!" As they looked, Sue Nancy yawned visibly and sighed.

Caledonia smiled back down at Angela. "You know, before the party, I was thinking maybe our Sue Nancy would get together with the boy genius—Mrs. Gardner's nephew, Robbie. Two kids close to the same age—but they don't seem at all well matched."

She nodded across at the far side of the room, where Mrs. Gardner and her nephew, Robert Hammond, stood side by side, talking seriously to the Emersons. Robbie had glasses on today and looked a little as though he were missing his textbooks. He shifted his weight and sighed, from time to time, but he was listening to Mr. Emerson ("... another fishing story, I bet," Calendonia whispered) and even smiling and putting in a word from time to time.

"How do you think the party's going? I mean, other than Miz La Douce, over there, who is monumentally bored, of course," Caledonia whispered. "Does Mrs. Gardner seem any more cheerful?"

"I can't really tell," Angela whispered back. "I haven't had the chance to talk to her. I'll drift over that way in a minute. It wouldn't do to let the guest of honor leave without my talking to her, and I suppose people will start to go home just any time now." She checked her own watch. "Yes, it's nearly four ... I really had better get over there, Cal." And she began to make her way across the room— slow progress with a word here, a smile there.

Caledonia moved as well, first to the head of the serving table, where she had pressed Trinita into service by asking her to pour. "How's it going, Trinita? Have enough tea? You're doing *such* a fine job, my dear," she encouraged heartily. "Splendid! Splendid!" She moved briskly away before Trinita could respond with any details.

Across the room, Angela insinuated herself into the guest of honor's little group. As she approached, Mr. Emerson was saying, "... a fine big trout, best I'd ever caught," and his wife was checking her watch, her expression grim and her eyes glazed over. Charlotte Emerson had heard about this particular trout more than once. Angela's arrival was Mrs. Emerson's chance to put a hand firmly on her husband's arm and say, "Oh, dear, Howard, I do believe it's getting close to four. You know I have to get back to take my medicine before we go to dinner ... where has Caledonia got to? Come along, dear, and we'll say our goodbyes . . ." She began to ease away from Mrs. Gardner and her nephew, keeping a firm grip on her husband's arm so that he was towed behind her.

"Well," Angela said. "So you're the nephew. Do tell me . . . you're a student at the college here in Camden?"

"Yes, ma'am," he replied and smiled a lovely, boyish smile that Angela found enchanting. But he didn't go on to expand his answer. Not skilled in small talk, Angela noted to herself.

"What are you taking in college? I don't mean what courses—I mean what are you majoring in?" Angela prompted.

"Computer science," he said. "I'm going to be a programmer. I haven't accomplished anything yet of importance, but my aim is to devise a better computer language for astrophysicists to use. Right now, most of the data input is in one of three or four languages that . . ."

"Robbie, dear," his aunt broke in. "I'm sure Mrs. Benbow doesn't want to hear all those details. He gets quite carried away with enthusiasm for his work, you see," she apologized to Angela. "He doesn't realize that to the rest of us, it's a little too complicated."

"I'm afraid computers came along after my time in college," Angela said pleasantly. Robbie looked startled. "Well, it's true—there was a time when there were no computers, you know!" she said.

"Well, certainly," he said, a bit uneasily.

"Relax, young man. I do understand," Angela said. "I used to feel that way about telephones and airplanes . . ."

"I beg your pardon?"

"You know—that they'd always been around. But they were just invented during my parents' lifetime. Now you feel that way about computers—that they've always been there, and that we're pretty dim not to understand them as well as you do."

He looked earnest and very concerned. "Oh, I understand what you mean, Mrs. Benbow. And maybe you're right . . . sometimes it's hard for me to figure people out. Aunt Lena says it's because I have such a high I.Q. I can't relate to people. My roommate used to say it was because I know more about computers than about people—and I always expect people to behave like computers . . . logically. You know? To follow straight lines of reasoning and . . ."

Angela smiled pleasantly. "My dear young man, as soon as you start talking logic you lose me. I was an English lit. major in college, and I never studied logic, let alone computers. I wouldn't have studied them even if we'd had them to study," and she swung slightly away from him, trying to signal an end to their conversation. She really did not intend to spend the afternoon talking about his problems in figuring out how people thought! She maneuvered so that her back was slightly toward him as she turned toward their guest of honor.

"How about you, Mrs. Gardner? How are you getting along? Getting the feel of the place, are you? Those of us who've been here a long time and who love the place always hope that everyone who comes in will feel as we do about it."

Mrs. Gardner did not respond. "I know you were tired at first from the move," Angela rattled on, hoping to strike a spark, "but now that you know . . . Is something the matter, Mrs. Gardner?"

Lena Gardner was standing transfixed, her mouth slightly agape, staring as though paralyzed straight ahead at Angela's chin.

"Aunt Lena," Robbie said, "what is it? Is there something . . .?"

"Robbie, she's got my brooch!"

"What are you talking about, Aunt Lena?"

"Mrs. Benbow. She's—Mrs. Benbow, you've got my brooch on!" Lena Gardner raised her voice and her hand at the same time. She was pointing straight at Angela's throat where, peeping out of the foam of lace, the edges of the antique pin were just visible . . . one line of pearls along an edge—the sheen of gold, the tracery of black enamel . . .

Angela's hand flew protectively to her throat. "Oh, dear, no, Mrs. Gardner. You're mistaken. That's my pin. I bought it at a jeweler's here about two months ago . . ."

"It's mine!" The woman's voice rose higher, and conversation around the room began to die away. Heads turned.

Caledonia moved swiftly across the room toward them, her face concerned. "It's mine! Robbie, make her give me back my sister's brooch!"

"I assure you this is not yours, Mrs. Gardner," Angela said, quite at a loss as to what else she could say or do to calm the woman, who was getting quite pink in the face, tears beginning to course down her cheeks. "Here . . . have a handkerchief . . ."

Angela held out a little square of lace and Lena Gardner pushed it abruptly away. "I don't want your handkerchief. I want my brooch! Robbie . . ."

The young man put his arm gently around her shoulders. "Oh, God . . . Aunt Lena, *please* calm down. I'll get this all sorted out . . . I'm terribly sorry, Mrs. Benbow. She gets upset like this, and confused . . . it happens when she gets tired, you see. I'll take her to her room. I shouldn't have let her stay so long, standing up, meeting so many strangers . . . Aunt Lena, please come with me . . ." He tugged her forward, and she resisted.

"Robbie, you know how much that brooch means to me. Please, make her give it back. Mrs. Benbow, I don't know how you got it, but it's mine. It was my sister's. Hattie's. Please, won't anybody believe me? It's *mine*! The pearls . . . the enamel on gold . . . Hattie inherited it from Grandmother, and I've had it now for twenty years. Since Hattie died. It's just . . . I lost it a while back, you see, but here it is . . ."

Tears were streaming down her face as she reached out to the embarrassed guests as though pleading for help, moving among them, first to one then to another. "Honestly . . . Mrs. Wingate, that pin is my pin! Please . . . Miss Jackson, it's mine . . ."

Her nephew kept the arm around her shoulders, his face agonized as he moved with her, half guiding, half trailing as she made her way through the other guests. "I'll get her home to bed and come back later to explain all this," he said to them. "Come on, Aunt Lena. I promise I'll look into it and find out about it . . . just come on home now."

"Home? Can we go home, Robbie? To my own little home?"

"Oh, Aunt Lena, we've been all through that over and over . . . this is home now. I meant, we'll go home here—to your own apartment . . . come along . . ."

She turned as they reached the door. "It's a terrible thing not to have anything that's yours anymore. They won't let me have my own home . . . they took my cat away . . . he was such a nice tiger cat—such a gentle old boy . . . and I know he isn't happy without me. And my little brooch . . . now you've taken away my brooch . . . I don't know what's mine anymore and what is going to be taken away from me!"

Her nephew guided her out and the sound of her sobbing died away as he led her up the walk and into the main building. For a long moment nobody said a word, and then everybody started to talk at once.

"Well, I never . . . nobody in Anniston ever behaved . . ."

"I don't understand—whatever did she mean by saying Angela stole . . ."

"My Lord, Cal, did you hear all that . . ."

"Dear lady, how embarrassing for you . . . if I can be of service . . ."

"We really have to go, Howard . . . my predinner medication . . ."

"What's with all that, Auntie Dora? I never saw anything like . . ."

And then, in rapid succession, a series of hasty goodbyes. Nobody knew quite what to say, and it was all very awkward, but Trinita Stainsbury seemed to think she had found exactly the right words: "Well, Caledonia, I don't know when I've been to a more fascinating party. You certainly do know how to entertain your guests!"

The room was empty of strangers by four-thirty-five, leaving only Angela, Caledonia, and a concerned and protective Chita Cassidy. "Mrs. Benbow," Chita soothed, "don't you be upset. She's a crazy lady, that one. Crazy. Nobody thinks you stole her brooch. Believe me. Mrs. Wingate, I'll carry one tray of things up to the kitchen now and come back for the rest after I serve dinner. I'm really sorry I have to go, but I have to help set up now. Listen, Mrs. Wingate, I'm real sorry your nice party was spoiled like that." And she hurried away, swinging along as though the tray full of used cups and sandwich plates weighed absolutely nothing.

"Strong as a horse, that little girl," Caledonia mused. "Angela, are you all right? You better sit down here . . ." She helped her friend to the small rose-colored velvet chair Angela always chose because it was the only one in the room in which she could sit and have her feet touch the ground at the same time, all other furniture having been selected to match Caledonia's ample proportions.

"Phewwwwph!" Angela sat down and let out a gasp of air. "Cal, that was the . . . the oddest . . . the most upsetting . . ."

"I'll say it again, are you okay?"

"I guess so. If it had been anybody else I'd have been furious, of course. But that old lady really thought . . . Cal, she really thought I was wearing *her* pin. That I'd stolen it from her somehow. And she was simply crushed!"

"Well, is it stolen property?"

"Cal!"

"I don't mean did you steal it . . . I know you didn't. I mean, is it possible your dealer got hold of stolen property somehow? Could it be Mrs. Gardner's brooch?"

Angela thought about that. "Well, you know, that didn't occur to me. I'll have to ask him. We can go down to the shop and say . . . well, we can say . . . Cal, how do you ask a jeweler if he's dealing in stolen goods?"

"Well, we can't do that, of course . . . all you'd get would be rage, if you put it that way. He'd think you were calling him a crook. We'll be more tactful. Like, for instance, for starters you could tell him he may have been taken in by someone else . . . or you could say there's been some accident . . . we'll think of something. But, Angela—before we go down there—think. Is there anything shady about that dealer?"

"Absolutely not. I've bought odds and ends of pretty jewelry from him ever since I moved to Camden. He has the usual watches and stuff—all new—and then he has this one counter where he handles fine secondhand jewelry and antique pieces . . . some very good, some not very expensive,

but all usually very pretty. He's a regular jeweler is all ...
But I tell you what. Let's ask Martinez!"

"Good thinking," Caledonia said. "And now, Angela, I
think you deserve a little something to calm your nerves. I
know I do ... first the strain of putting on the party ...
then standing and talking for an hour or so ... and then
that sad, bizarre business with Mrs. Gardner ... I tell
you ..."

She heaved herself out of the love seat and moved over
to her little bar. "How about a nice sherry? I have a new
bottle of Dry Fly, if you like it ... or my usual amontillado.
Oh, I know—I remember that I got this last week just for
you ..." She reached into the back of the cabinet and
pulled out an unopened bottle of Bristol Cream sherry.

"Cal! How very thoughtful of you!" Angela was
touched. Caledonia was a terrible snob about liqueurs and
aperitifs and ordinarily would not tolerate a sweet sherry in
her home. But Angela doted on sweet sherry and for Caledonia to indulge that taste was a real act of friendship.

"Here you go, girl. Sip slowly now, Angela. You've been
upset, and that gets the blood to stirring, so this might go
to your head if you gulp. Sip—sip—atta girl ..."

And they sat for a few minutes, neither saying a word,
sipping their respective sherries in companionable and comfortable silence.

Chapter 6

Two visitors came to the apartment in the postparty, predinner hour while Caledonia and Angela sipped their sherry and talked.

First there was a subdued, apologetic, and sweaty-looking Robbie Hammond. He knocked timidly at the screen and entered at Caledonia's bidding, pulling out a handkerchief to mop his forehead.

"I've had a terrible time with Aunt Lena. Mrs. Wingate . . . Mrs. Benbow . . . I can't tell you how sorry I am. I owe you our apologies . . . both of you, of course. I can't believe she could do that . . . it was so embarrassing . . ."

"Don't think anything of it," Angela said with unaccustomed charity. Her heart went out to this scrawny, studious-looking boy, patting the perspiration off his damp forehead. "Did you have a hard time getting her to bed? You seem—so very upset."

He sighed. "I finally had to send for the doctor to give her a shot. The man came from your little hospital across the street . . . I don't remember his name . . ."

"Carter. Dr. Carter. We tease him about his liver pills," Caledonia said, "and that makes his name easy to remember." Robbie looked completely blank. Caledonia sighed— these kids—Then, conscious of his stiff lack of ease, his embarrassment over his apologies, she said, "Young man, it's all right. We understand. You needn't be so upset about . . . Look, can I get you a drink?"

He hesitated. "Well, I'm not sure . . ."

Caledonia got to her feet and went to the bar. "Will you join us in a sherry? Or would you prefer a little splash of something stronger? I have some Scotch, a little Canadian, some vodka . . ." Caledonia considered bourbon a drink suitable only for field hands, and not very discerning field hands at that, so she did not keep any in stock.

"Scotch would be good, thank you. But with a lot of water. No ice. Thanks." He turned to Angela while Caledonia worked. "I didn't get a good look at your brooch before, Mrs. Benbow. Sitting here, without all the commotion to distract me—well, I guess I can see Aunt Lena's problem. That is very much like Aunt Harriet's pin . . . Harriet was Aunt Lena's second-oldest sister, the one she calls Hattie. Both pins are square and made of gold—and decorated in that black paint—and they both have white beads down each side."

"Pearls! Real pearls," Angela said, in the tone of voice one reserves for a bumpkin who takes filet mignon to be round steak, or a Maserati to be a Ford Thunderbird . . . nothing wrong with the less expensive models, you understand, but the mistake shows a certain lack of sophistication. Then more kindly she added, "But you didn't see it up close, so you couldn't be expected to know that. This is a Victorian mourning brooch—that's why it has the black enamel decoration. Did your aunt's brooch have real pearls on it, as well?"

"I never really looked at it too closely, myself. I don't honestly know. She says so." He sighed deeply. "I didn't know what to do with her . . . she was so upset, she couldn't stop crying when I got her home. Oh, thank you, Mrs. Wingate." He accepted a tumbler of Scotch and water from Caledonia. "That tastes good. I think you're right—I needed something like this. I just didn't know how much."

"Well, you say she's all right now?" Caledonia said.

"Oh, gosh, no, far from it. The doctor gave her the shot and she cried herself to sleep. I didn't leave till I was sure she was asleep—several minutes . . . I was afraid she'd wake up again. Honestly, I don't know what to do about all of this. I'm afraid she'll just start in again tomorrow, unless . . ."

"Unless what?"

"Unless she forgets all about it. She might just as easily

do that! That's why she's here, of course. Confusion, forgetting, and the past and present getting all mixed up together . . . I didn't realize how bad it was until she got lost coming home from the grocery store one day, and the police had to call me. Got me right out of a class. She lived over in Escondido, you know, and she had my name and number in her wallet on one of those cards: 'In case of emergency call . . .'

"So I came and helped her get home and that's when I knew she couldn't live alone anymore. I put in an application for her to get space here. But of course there's a waiting list . . ."

"I didn't know that," Caledonia said. "We always seem to have an empty room—somebody dies, or goes into the hospital for permanent care, or moves out to some other place all the time . . . so I didn't know there was a waiting list for apartments."

"Oh, yes," he assured them, taking another sip of his drink. "We waited a couple of months before they called and said they had that second-floor apartment. Those were the longest months of my life, while we waited for a space to open up." He sipped again and looked back into his memory for a silent moment.

"What's the problem?" Angela said. "Stroke? Alzheimer's?"

"They say it's arteriosclerosis. But they all act about alike, don't they?" he said.

"Oh, no," Angela said. "There are vast differences . . ."

"Angela!" Caledonia interrupted. "I'm sure the young man isn't interested in clinical details of aging. Mr. Hammond, we hope there's some way we can help out. Especially with this—this crisis."

He shook his head. "There isn't anything anybody can do. She's been getting worse for some time, but it just never seemed so bad as this. I mean, when she was in her own house among familiar things, she could operate perfectly well—habit carried her through, I guess. She didn't have to think about where things were, for instance.

"Now she spends a lot of every day in total confusion, because she has to think about everything she does . . . and that's difficult for her. And the confusion depresses and frightens her, and the depression and the panic make the confusion worse ..." He sighed. "I don't know—maybe I did the wrong thing bringing her here ... I don't understand people. I really don't. Computers are easy to figure out. People ..."

"Now-now," Angela said firmly, reaching out to pat his hand. "Problems like hers are nothing you can deal with by yourself. They'd take up all your time and worry you to death ... and people like your aunt, who are physically healthy, may live for years and years. Why, think what it would be like caring for your aunt in her condition for twenty more years or so!"

He looked sad. "I guess you're right. It was getting awfully hard to study, with her demanding attention all the time. I mean, I couldn't turn my back for fear she'd wander off and get lost ..."

"And you have your whole life to think of, not just your school work," Caledonia reassured him. "If you had to move in with her, or she with you, that would blight your social life."

"Oh, I don't know about that," he said with a rueful smile. "I don't have all that much social life to blight! People didn't come to see me at the house very often after Aunt Lena started to get so odd. Once when I had some friends in, she flew off the handle at them—said they were trying to take over the house—that they had no manners— that they stole things ... All they did was help themselves to some stuff in the refrigerator and you'd have thought World War Three was starting!" He shook his head. "It was hard to make friends with no place to ask them over to, if you see what I mean. But a few of them still talk to me ... you saw some of them helping us move Aunt Lena in. But generally, I guess I'm just not the social type—I spend a lot of time with my studies ..."

"It's been hard on you, I'm sure. Well, you've found the one place where you can be certain your aunt's going to be well cared for, and where you don't have to worry. And she will settle in, given time. We'll help all we can," Caledonia said.

He got to his feet and returned his emptied glass to the bar top. "Thank you for the drink. I didn't mean to talk about my troubles. I only wanted to apologize for what happened and to explain."

"Oh, we understand. Don't worry about it," Caledonia said.

"By the way," Angela said, just as he got to the door, "there isn't any chance this is your aunt's brooch, is there? I mean, I bought it a couple of months ago from a dealer in town. He's perfectly honest himself, and I know he'd never buy stolen goods, but perhaps he bought it from someone who found it, rather than stole it, you see . . ."

Hammond shook his head. "I shouldn't think there was the slightest chance. You say you bought the brooch two months ago?"

Angela nodded.

"Well, Aunt Lena only lost her pin a couple of weeks before we came in here. At least, I don't know exactly when she lost it, but that's when she discovered it was missing. So—I couldn't swear—but anyway, I don't see how that could be hers. Anyhow, I wouldn't worry about it, if I were you. You bought it from a dealer, and it's yours now, isn't it?"

He swung out the door and smiled that lovely, boyish smile of his. "Thank you for being so understanding. And thanks for the drink."

"Is your aunt all right for the night? Does someone need to check on her?" Caledonia called after him.

"She should be perfectly okay, thanks. The nurses will check every half-hour or so." He shook his head. "Poor Aunt Lena. It doesn't seem fair she should have all the problems in the family, does it? Well, goodnight, and thanks again . . ." and the screen door swung shut behind him with a metallic *clap* against its aluminum frame.

"Nice boy," Caledonia said, turning back and coming to sit on the love seat next to Angela's chair. "I like it when a young person is concerned for one of us older people."

"She's his only living relative," Angela reminded her. "He ought to be concerned. I'd worry about him if he wasn't! Oh, dear, I think it's getting on for dinner time, and perhaps . . ."

And that was the moment at which their second visitor appeared at the screen door. Lieutenant Martinez had returned.

"Good evening, ladies," he said, standing in the center of the screen door so they could both see him clearly. "I didn't want to startle you . . . I wanted to be sure you knew exactly who it was. With the kind of trouble you've been having here at Camden . . ."

"Trouble?" Caledonia said.

"Yes. The murders."

"Oh. Those! You know, for a minute, I forgot completely. Very thoughtful of you, Lieutenant, to try to avoid frightening us. But we were halfway expecting you. It was in the back of my mind that you were coming."

"Not in the front of your mind, Mrs. Wingate?" he teased, as he stepped through the door. "I'm really disappointed."

"Well, after what happened here this afternoon . . . it was so strange . . ." and interrupting each other, correcting each other, and making a long story much longer, the two women bubbled over with the tale of their unusual afternoon.

Martinez was clearly intrigued. "You're right to call it 'strange.' That's not something I can recall happening to any one of my friends before," he said to Angela. "You have some explanation, perhaps?"

She shook her head. "None. Except that the woman's confused, and getting more so all the time. Of course, it did occur to us that the brooch might really be hers. I only bought it two months ago, or thereabouts. And even though I'm sure the jeweler's completely honest . . . well, of course, her nephew says she lost her pin only recently. But even so, it could still show up at my jeweler's . . . I mean, if she lost it, for instance. Why, almost anybody might have found it. They could have advertised for the owner—you know, like people hang signs in the drugstore windows for lost dogs? Of course, I always thought it wasn't very likely you'd see the one sign that pertained to you ... and she might have missed this sign, you see."

Martinez held up his hand. He was shaking his head in bewilderment. "Missing dogs? Signs in a drugstore window?" Martinez said. "I'm afraid I'm losing you ..."

"Maybe they don't do that so much in California ... maybe it's a custom that died out, except in small towns. But when my husband was stationed in the South, at Charleston, we lived in a small town—a suburb of Charleston, really—and everybody used the drugstore as a kind of free bulletin board. You brought in a three-by-five card with your message ... kittens that were lost, car keys that were found, furniture for sale, baby-sitting available, manuscripts typed reasonably ... and everybody in town checked the window at least once a week ..."

"It must have made the drugstore a very popular place," Martinez said. "You're right, we don't do that around here—at least, not that I know of."

"Doesn't either of you realize," Caledonia said despairingly, "you're way off the point? Angela, for Pete's sake—go on with your story about the brooch!"

"Oh, I'm sorry. Where was I?"

"You were saying," Martinez prompted, "at least I think you were saying, that Mrs. Gardner might have lost the brooch some time ago without even knowing it, and that it might have been picked up by someone who advertised— some way or other—for the owner. But when the owner didn't respond, likely because Mrs. Gardner just didn't see the notice, then ..."

"Oh! Yes! Well, then the finder would consider the pin belonged to him. And he'd feel perfectly free to sell it to a jeweler. I told Cal we ought to ask my jeweler tomorrow."

"Here in town?" Martinez asked.

"Yes. Mr. Singletary," Angela said.

"I know John Singletary," Martinez said. "We're old friends. Back when I was in uniform, I interrupted a robbery at his place once. He always said I saved his life, though it isn't true. But we stay in touch. Why not let me ask him about it? It's a touchy subject, but he wouldn't take it badly from me, just in the line of duty. Oh, and may I take the brooch with me?"

"Of course, Lieutenant." Angela unfastened the chain-and-pin assembly that acted as a guard. "Here you are."

Martinez wrapped the beautiful little pin carefully in a clean pocket handkerchief and slid it into a side pocket of his coat. "That's a real find, that pin. Unusual and I'd say worth a lot of money."

Angela looked faintly embarrassed. "Well, yes, I did pay quite a bit for it. But I thought it was worth it, too. Fine workmanship . . . Oh, I do so hope it isn't her pin. I'd hate to give it up . . . it goes perfectly with this blouse. But of course if it's hers . . ."

"Well, we'll cross that bridge when we come to it. Now, you said you had a lot of things to talk about with me?"

"Oh, my goodness," Caledonia said, frowning, "the murders went right out of my head, I was so busy with the story of the brooch. I haven't thought of them all afternoon, as a matter of fact. But it occurs to me to tell you that I think we could be of help to your Sergeant Benson. You know—in the same ways we've always helped you: by reporting things we hear and see, and by asking a few questions. But of course he made it plain that he isn't interested in our help!" She sounded outraged.

"Indeed he isn't," Angela joined in. "He was curt and almost cold . . ."

"Well, was he rude to you?"

"No, I wouldn't go that far," Angela amended. "Perhaps 'cold' isn't a fair word either. More . . . more . . ."

"Businesslike?" Martinez suggested.

"Yes. I'd say so," Angela agreed.

"Well, Mrs. Benbow, shouldn't he be all business?" Martinez asked.

"It's partly a matter of personal style, of course," Caledonia said. "No denying we like your style better than his."

Martinez bowed and looked faintly amused.

"But there are limits . . ." Angela said. "I mean, he practically threw us out of the interview after we offered to do some looking around—on his behalf, of course. Not for our own pleasure, you understand."

"Oh, of course not!" Martinez agreed hastily.

"Are you being sarcastic, young man?" Caledonia said suspiciously, and then she started to grin. "I guess you'd have a right to be. We've pretty obviously enjoyed it when we've had the chance to contribute to your investigations . . ."

"He practically showed us the door!" Angela was saying again. "He told us in so many words to keep out of his way!"

"Ladies, that's why I'm here," Martinez said. "The good sergeant came back to the office the other night considerably worried about you two. He had the distinct impression that you weren't listening to him when he warned you not to get involved in this investigation."

"Not true!" Angela protested. "We both heard every word, didn't we, Cal?"

"Ah, but did you pay attention? I mean, did you agree—in your hearts—that he was making a wise request? That getting involved was potentially very, very dangerous?"

Angela and Caledonia looked at each other. At last Caledonia said simply, "No."

"Ah-*hah*!" Martinez said, popping up to his feet and beginning to pace. "Forgive me if I lecture, but I thought as much. And so did Sergeant Benson. He wasn't cold-shouldering your offer of help because he didn't like you. He wanted you out of the way because he was concerned that you might get into a situation that had deadly potential. And he got the idea that you might be planning to ignore him and go off detecting on your own. Am I right?" He whirled on them, pointing a finger like an accusing district attorney.

"Mrs. Benbow, confess! You intended to ask a few questions, perhaps even to tiptoe down to the patio and wait in the dark to see if you could spot any suspicious activity. Mrs. Wingate," he fixed her with a stern eye, "you were going to go from one resident to another asking simply 'Did you do it?' and 'How do you feel about sharp blades—do they make you want to stick them into people?' just to see if anyone looked embarrassed or guilty!"

"Oh, come on, be serious, Lieutenant," Caledonia begged. "Of course we weren't. It's just that we think we know everyone here a good deal better than either you do or the sergeant does, and sometimes someone from the outside can be deceived by appearances. That's all."

"But he didn't want us!" Angela said.

"So you objected and decided to go off on your own?"

"No! At least . . ."

"At least what?"

"At least not yet," Angela finished meekly. "I tell you the truth, we hadn't decided what we were going to do."

"But you'd have done something, I'd bet my pension on it," Martinez said. "Well, if you haven't gone out advertising your interest in these matters yet, I'm still in time. And I want you to listen, and I want you to believe me, because I'm serious. Dead serious—no pun. We're very worried, the sergeant and I. Worried about you and about all the residents here. Because somebody killed two apparently harmless men for no good reason that we can find out. And that means maybe we're dealing with a person who's completely deranged. If that's so, we simply wouldn't know who to be suspicious of or who to protect. And we won't—not until we can work out a pattern—some of the killer's reasoning, however insane. And it's got us very, very concerned for all of you here. And particularly for you two."

"Why us, especially?" Caledonia said. "If this person kills for no reason at all, wouldn't everybody be equally at risk?"

"Maybe he just kills whoever is handy. And you two have a way of getting into everything—of making yourselves available—that makes me nervous to think about. And if you make yourself even slightly conspicuous, you might draw a madman's attention. This is a time to keep—as they say—a low profile."

"I'm done for, then," Caledonia shrugged. "No way I can do that."

"Now, Mrs. Wingate," Martinez reproved, "you know exactly what I mean. I mean don't draw attention to yourself and don't go anywhere around here alone and unprotected."

"We thought at one time that we'd worked out the pattern," Angela said diffidently. "We decided the only thing the pattern could be was moustaches!"

"Moustaches?" Martinez asked, a smile starting to twitch under the corner of his own slim black moustache.

"Well," she shrugged, "I know it doesn't make sense, but that seems to us to be the only thing those two men had in common! I mean, we were joking about it, because who would kill someone just for having a moustache? But I ask you, what else is there?"

"They had one other obvious thing in common neither of you has mentioned," Martinez said. "Two such sharp-eyed detectives as you should have noticed it. And of course it's what brought me here."

"I don't follow . . ." Angela furrowed her brow.

Caledonia shook her head. "No, me either. I really don't see it."

"And I thought you two were so clever! The other thing they have in common is Camden. They were both *here* when they were killed." Angela and Caledonia looked at him without a word.

"And that may mean one of two things," he went on. "It may mean there's something here, at this place—something we haven't found yet—that links the two victims together and perhaps links them to the killer; or it may mean that the killer is here at Camden-sur-Mer—one of the staff or one of the residents—someone you see every day . . ."

Caledonia suddenly shivered. "Oh, dear, I think it's getting chilly, with the sun going down. I'll put a shawl around my shoulders before I go up to supper."

"Of course," Martinez smiled. "And I should be going home myself."

"So soon?" Angela protested. "But we haven't had a chance to catch up on all the time between now and last time we saw you. We haven't talked about anything but the brooch and those murders . . ."

Caledonia grinned. "Any other time, those would be two wonderful topics of conversation. But we wanted to ask you all sorts of things . . ."

"I'm well and Shorty's well," Martinez said, smiling and

moving for the door, "and anything other than that will
have to wait awhile. I don't want to keep you two away
from supper. Besides, I told Shorty he could lurk around the
dining room while I came down here, so he could talk to
Chita. But she's working, of course, and that makes it tough
on any romantic conversation. You don't get many sweet-
nothings said while you're dealing out water glasses and
silverware to seventy-five tables . . ."

"So those two are still interested in each other," Angela
said. "We wondered, you know, because they've been seeing each other so regularly, and then last week . . ."

"Last week we were busy over in Rancho Santa Fe,"
Martinez said. "Someone broke into the linen storage at the
inn and stole all the damask tablecloths. The manager was
about to have a stroke. He can't buy replacements—not of
that quality—on short notice, and we couldn't get a lead of
any kind . . ."

"Anybody launch a new sailboat last week? Someone
who ran out of money before they bought the sails?" Caledonia suggested. "You might watch the next yacht races to
see if somebody hoists damask instead of canvas."

"That's about as sensible a suggestion as any that occurred to us so far. I might just do that. What's the date of
the next regatta? Look, ladies—dear friends . . ." He
stepped outside the door. "Now I am on my way, as I told
you, so that you won't be late for your elegant meal. I hear
it's beef burgundy tonight . . . and Shorty will be shattered
that we can't stay. You know that next to Chita he loves
these meals your Mrs. Schmitt prepares."

Martinez was on the porch and about to step into the garden, when he turned back, his face completely serious. "We
can joke all we like, but I'm very serious about one thing.
These murders ought to have you scared enough to lock
your doors, to walk everywhere in pairs, and to avoid giving anyone the impression you are prying into the matter
yourselves. Just for once, my dear friends—please, please
be sensible. Good night . . . I'll see you soon, I promise."

Caledonia waved goodnight and then turned back to
Angela. "Well, we certainly got told, didn't we? You know,

I think I will get that wrap. I know it's July, and the thermometer says seventy, but I still feel a chill, somehow."

"Your imagination is working overtime," Angela said with a toss of her head. "I certainly don't feel a chill—real or imaginary." But she shivered all the same.

Chapter 7

Dɪɴɴᴇʀ ᴛʜᴀᴛ night was a triumph and a disaster at the same time.

The triumph was the menu—Mrs. Schmitt's beef burgundy spread an aura of blissful contentment over even Mr. Grogan, whose sole complaint was that he wasn't allowed seconds. With the main dish Mrs. Schmitt served a tiny green salad with a vinaigrette dressing and a little scoop of baked escalloped apples—light, sharp flavors on the side to contrast with the rich mellowness of the main dish. Dessert was a little sherbet dish full of cranberry-raspberry fluff, so light the dishes almost floated to the table on their own. Even the fussiest eaters cleaned up every scrap, and as empty plates and dishes came back to the kitchen, Mrs. Schmitt's smile grew broader and broader. Nothing pleases a born cook so much as to see that there's not a forkful left on anyone's plate.

The disaster was the way everyone behaved to Angela. They all wanted to say something—but nobody knew quite what to say! Word had spread so that even people who were not at the party themselves had heard at least a little about the set-to with Mrs. Gardner, and as Angela and Caledonia entered, there was a massive hush that settled on the room, followed by a surge of renewed conversation ... "Don't just sit there with your mouth open staring at her ... pretend to be talking ... talk about the weather if you have to!"

One by one, various residents stopped by the table Angela and Caledonia shared, ostensibly to pass the time of day. In actual fact, those who had not heard the accusations for themselves were trying to find a tactful way to ask for details. Those who had been present were trying to find soothing words that didn't imply either anger at Mrs. Gardner or suspicion of Angela.

Only Donna Dee Jackson seemed to notice that the brooch was gone from Angela's blouse, when the twins and their niece stopped by the table on their way out of the dining room after the meal.

"You've lost it. Or have you lost it? Did you give it to Mrs. Gardner? Sister, look it's gone! Where is the pin, Angela?"

"Please, please," Caledonia shushed. "Angela gave it to the police to see if they could trace its original owner—find out if it really was stolen, Or lost. Or whatever."

"Very sensible," Dora Lee said. "I told Sue Nancy you were going to find just the right thing to do. Didn't I, Sue Nancy?"

"I thought it was so *awful*!" Sue Nancy said, running her blood-red nails through her tangled blonde curls and patting them, as though she had produced some semblance of order. "I was *so* embarrassed! I don't know how you kept so calm. I was all upset . . . I didn't know whether to laugh or cry! I thought it was the strangest thing I ever saw! I didn't know what I'd have done if I was in your place, I really don't. I told Aunt Dora and Aunt Donna, I don't want to run into that woman. I'd be afraid she might start in on me like she did on you, and I don't know how to handle things like that when they happen to me, I really don't."

The threesome moved on and Caledonia nearly burst out laughing. "My heavens! Can't that child think of anything but how she feels?"

"Did you count the '*I*'s' by any chance?" Angela grinned. "There were at least a dozen in that one statement."

"And she only said 'you' twice that I recall," Caledonia chuckled. "I'm telling you, that child thinks the way she dresses . . . as though there's nobody outside . . . as though she was moving through a world peopled entirely by wooden dummies, in which she was the only living creature. What's wrong with that kid?"

"Weren't you like that when you were her age?" Angela said. "I was. The world revolved around me ... I was going to be a big success ... I was going to live forever ..."

Caledonia nodded with understanding. "And then we grew up. What a disappointment the world is to the young on that morning they finally realize their own mortality!"

"Dear lady, how are you feeling now?" It was Mr. Brighton, kindly as ever, the strength of his concern showing in the fact that he had limped his way clear across the dining room to stop by their table, although he could have chosen a much shorter route to the exit.

"I'm much better, thank you. I was surprised and my feelings were hurt, but there's no permanent damage."

"Did you find out what was behind it all?" he asked, diffidently. "Forgive my curiosity, but ..."

"Her nephew came back later," Caledonia filled in. "She seems to be suffering worse mental problems than we thought when she first arrived. He says she's got a lot of confusion, though it comes and goes."

Brighton shook his head. "Oh dear! I thought she was completely sensible when I talked to her the day she arrived. I thought she was just suffering from depression and the shock of change. I'm sorry to hear that she's ... you know ... like that." He started limping toward the exit. "Glad things are well with you, my dear."

Of all those who had been Caledonia's guests earlier in the day, only Sadie Mandelbaum was still in the dark as to what had happened. Sadie was nearly completely deaf, with vestigial hearing in only one ear, and that had not been the ear turned toward the quarrel. Janice Felton, who lived in an apartment near Sadie's, had therefore tried to fill Sadie in as they walked home from Caledonia's in the afternoon. But it had been an exercise in futility.

"She said what?" Sadie shouted, her own voice far too loud, because she could not gauge its volume.

"She said," Janice enunciated with care, her mouth bent close to Sadie's good ear, "that Angela had stolen her brooch."

"Eaten a roach? In our food? Made in our kitchen? That's terrible!"

"No, Sadie. A pin. She thought Angela had her pin."

"Had to begin? Begin what? I don't understand."

"Let's go back. Sadie, do you recall the *pin* Angela was wearing on the lace *collar* of her *blouse*?" Janice panto-mimed as she talked and mouthed the words so Sadie could pick up the movement of her lips. Sadie had a little lipread-ing, as most of us do, and relied on it more than she real-ized, as most of us do.

"Blouse?"

"Yes, yes," Janice nodded vigorously. "And Mrs. Gardner ... you know, Mrs. *Gardner*?"

"Yes, Mrs. Gardner ..." Sadie was with her so far.

"Mrs. Gardner accused ..." Janice made pointing mo-tions with her finger ... "accused *Angela* of *stealing* the pin from *HER*!"

"What? Stealing the pin?" At last Sadie had the gist of things. "That's silly. Angela's a rich woman. She wouldn't steal. She can go and buy anything in this world she wants ..."

Janice sighed with satisfaction. "I know. I know. It's silly to even consider. But Mrs. Gardner was terribly mad ..."

"Yes, it is bad. Very bad." Janice didn't correct Sadie's mistake. Sadie was at least in the ball park, with what she understood, and Janice's voice was getting hoarse from shouting. Together, in a friendly silence, they had walked on to their own apartments to get ready for supper.

Now Sadie stopped by the table, and Angela braced her-self.

"Sorry to hear about the pin you stole," Sadie shouted. Heads turned, as some of the diners picked up on the word "stole."

"I didn't steal it," Angela said. "I bought it."

"Ought to what?"

"I say," Angela raised her voice, looking self-consciously around at the other diners, "I say I didn't steal it. I bought it!"

"Oh. Oh, of course you did. Only a crazy person would think you would steal something. Why did that woman say you did?"

"She lost hers a while ago." Sadie's brow furrowed, and

Angela repeated quickly, to stop the question, raising her voice again, "She *lost one like it*."

"Yes, I liked it," Sadie said. "I thought it was beautiful. A Victorian mourning brooch, wasn't it? I thought so," she said with satisfaction as Angela nodded. "Had one a little like it myself. Don't know what happened to that one. If I find it in my things, I'll haul it out to show you. I'll look for it tonight."

"Oh dear, Sadie—don't bother."

"Yes, Father gave it to me. It was his mother's. You'd enjoy seeing it."

"You really shouldn't, Sadie . . ." But Sadie was gone, happily on her way to spend an evening sorting through her dresser drawers, searching for her own mislaid brooch, leaving Angela and Caledonia shaking their heads.

"Why doesn't she get a hearing aid?" Angela sighed.

"Wouldn't do a bit of good. She's got a different problem from Emma Grant's. Sadie's one ear's gone completely and the other is going fast. She does use a phone amplifier for the one—when she remembers. But why go to the expense of a hearing aid that might help only a little, and for only a few months?" Caledonia said sensibly.

"Well," Angela said, "what I'd do, if I was Sadie, is learn sign language and teach the rest of us!"

"Too late for her to teach me," Caledonia grinned. "With my memory, it would go in one hand and out the other! Maybe a course in lipreading . . ."

"Well, she better do *some*thing. People are going to start avoiding her if they have to shout all the time. Oh, glory, here comes the Stainsbury!" Angela threw down her napkin and pushed her chair back. "One thing I don't have to stay put for is another conversation with her. You like her, you talk to her."

And Angela sailed out of the room, waving cheerfully to Trinita as she passed her, and muttering a "Got to run!" which successfully short-circuited Trinita's remarks and left her frustrated. Trinita recovered immediately, however, and changed direction to go and pass a few words with the Emersons instead.

The next day, after a light breakfast of fruit and a single

waffle with apple butter, Angela walked the perimeter of the garden, strolled down to the sea-cliff and watched the gulls wheeling and diving on hapless whitebait below, and generally killed time till she dared knock at Caledonia's door. Caledonia's late rising was not just a habit, it was very nearly a religion, and it wasn't often even her best friends dared to risk her wrath by interfering—by trying to get her up even ten minutes earlier than her usual hour.

At 9:00 A.M., as Caledonia opened her front door to go for a quick pot of coffee before the dining room closed at nine-thirty, she came almost face-to-face with Angela.

"Oh." Caledonia was given to monosyllables at what she considered the early hours of morning. "Hi."

"I was waiting for you," Angela said brightly as she danced along, trying to keep pace with Caledonia's purposeful strides. Nothing slowed Caledonia down on her progress toward caffeine, and anyone who wanted to see her on business had to do what Angela was doing—tag along; Caledonia would stop for no one, before her first cup.

"I've had a sort of idea . . ."

"Not yet. Wait."

"You can listen, Cal, even if you can't talk yet," Angela said. "And I have this idea about . . ."

"No. Wait!" Caledonia placed herself cautiously onto her chair, pulled herself up close to the table, righted the cup which lay upside down in her saucer, and when an auburn-haired girl brought a thermos-pot of coffee and asked about her order, Caledonia waved the girl away wordlessly and poured herself a cup. It required great caution, but she managed the job without spilling more than a few drops. Angela handed over the cream and sugar wordlessly, and while Caledonia doctored the mixture, Angela waited.

Finally the first cup was gone and Caledonia began the second. Angela waited.

At last, Caledonia spoke. "Who was that kid?" she said, waving a hand toward the kitchen doors.

Angela, experienced at interpreting Caledonia's morning ellipses, said, "One of the youngsters from the kitchen. I think her name is Ginnie. Or maybe that's Agnes. Or Sylvia. I don't know all those dishwashers and table-setters. Once in a while they help out here in the dining room, you know, when one of the waitresses is sick. It means a little extra money for them for that day."

"Haven't seen her before." Caledonia took another sip. "Okay . . . what?"

"Are you sure you're ready?" Angela said. Caledonia lifted the cup again, nodded, and sipped again. But her eyes were focused, as she gazed over the cup at her companion.

"All right, then," Angela said. "I think we ought to try to find out something about Rollo Bagwell."

The eyes that showed above the cup closed for a moment, then opened, and the brows above them were furrowed. The cup came down. "What on earth are you playing at, girl? Didn't you hear one word Martinez said to us last night?"

"Oh, that. Surely. Of course I did. But he says the same thing every time there's a case around here. He did last time, remember? 'Don't get involved, ladies. Promise me, now,' remember? Almost the same words as this time." She did a fair imitation of the silky accents, and stroked an imaginary moustache as she did so.

Caledonia leaned forward, bringing her face very close to Angela's. "Now listen to me. You won't listen to Martinez, so listen to me. Do not—and I repeat *not*—get yourself out on a limb. A murderer who slashes people up with knives and grass-trimmers is probably some kind of nut. He's not going to stop to ask whether you've found out anything important or you're just having a little fun! He's going to let fly with some sharp blade, and you'll find yourself a sudden and very surprised angel!"

"Oh, Cal, don't lecture. And don't be so grim. All I want to do is go to Rollo's apartment over on Catalpa Street— before you ask, I looked it up in the phone book—and we could check through his things a little. See if there's anything there that . . . you know . . . that rings a bell, that looks out of place, that could connect him with our soft-drink man, Henry Ortelano . . ."

Caledonia put a restraining hand on Angela's arm, so that she could no longer gesture with it. "Angela—stay! And listen. The police have already done that. Don't you believe they have?"

"Oh, of course. But we have always been able to recognize clues they haven't thought were important. Because we knew the people involved, you see."

"This time we don't."

"We did too know Rollo! I don't know what you mean!"

"Angela, we didn't. We knew what he looked like, we knew from saying 'Hello' in the garden that he was simpleminded, we knew his talent for growing flowers, and we knew he liked to watch TV and was an honest man. And that's *all*!"

"That's more than we know about a lot of people," Angela said defensively, "and more than the police knew. To begin with."

Caledonia shook her head. "This time you have no defense. You've talked me into an exploration with you before, using that argument, but this time it won't work. No. *Nein. Nyet.* Absolutely not!"

"I don't understand you, Cal," Angela said. "If there isn't anything important at Rollo's apartment, then the killer won't care whether we go there or not, and neither will the police. If there is something important, then somebody should certainly go and find it. And they will—eventually. Somebody will. So why not us? The murderer wouldn't take it out on us—that wouldn't make any sense. And it's a way to be of real use to Sergeant Benson, so he'll take us seriously and he'll really talk to us. It's a way to get involved in this matter without any danger! And if you can't see that, you need another cup of coffee. Quick!"

"I have my third cup," Caledonia said, lifting it in a toast. "And I have to admit, you finally got to me."

"I did?"

"Angela, you're either getting smarter in your old age, or something. But I am convinced. It's a reasonably safe thing to do and it could be a genuine service. Besides," Caledonia grinned, and showed her teeth in a smile that would have terrified a Doberman, "you're right about one thing— it's going to be interesting! So I say, let's do it!"

"This morning?" Angela said eagerly.

"No, I suggest we wait till this afternoon."

"But why?"

"Have you forgotten the handsome lieutenant took your brooch to the jeweler? I know Martinez—so do you! You should guess he'd be there at the jeweler's right away asking questions, and that if there's anything to tell us, he'll come right back here to see us. Barring another murder or emergency that calls him—like maybe somebody stealing the Rancho Inn's napkins to go along with those tablecloths—he'll visit your jeweler first thing this morning. If we're both gone at the same time, he's smart enough—he knows us well enough—to be suspicious. I say wait till afternoon."

"Now it's your turn to have a good idea," Angela conceded generously. "This afternoon it is." Then she had a sudden afterthought. "What if the lieutenant doesn't come this morning, though?"

"In that case, we ought to wait till tomorrow. One day isn't going to hurt at this point. If anything, it will make our trip all the less dangerous!"

"All right, Cal, you're on. I'll wait till Martinez has checked with us."

Of course, Angela didn't wait patiently. She turned on TV back at her apartment and fidgeted during "The Price Is Right," getting up and going to her wardrobe in the bedroom from time to time to select and lay out another piece of clothing suitable for housebreaking. A cotton skirt, a casual shirt of Oxford cloth, low-heeled soft-soled shoes. The TV had just started a spirited second round of "Jeopardy" when there was a knock on the door and Angela opened it to the smiling face of Lieutenant Martinez.

"Oh, Lieutenant, come in, come in . . . what have you found out?"

"I'm sorry to disappoint you, Mrs. Benbow, but not a great deal. Oh—here's the brooch."

"Thank you. That's really very kind." She took it and laid it on the little side table next to her chair.

"Your jeweler, John Singletary, says one of the prongs holding the pearls is weakened so it may come off," Martinez added. "He can fix it himself but he just didn't have time today. It might be smart to go down there tomorrow—at least before you wear the brooch—and leave it with him. I didn't want to leave it today, without checking with you."

"That's very kind," she told him, beaming as he smiled back indulgently. This was all working out, in Angela's view, to serve her purposes very nicely. "Now, Lieutenant, what about the source of the brooch?"

"Well, Singletary thinks it came in with a group of other pieces, all of them brought in by a local girl named Ruthie something—her mother's things, after her mother died, you see. He took them all, and he wrote a brief description of the items into a kind of logbook he keeps of such transactions."

"How very prudent!"

"Well, you're dealing in a highly marketable commodity, one that can be stolen and resold without too much trouble. An honest jeweler who deals in antiques or estate jewelry may buy stolen goods without meaning to. It pays for him to keep notes—and to make the information available to the police readily."

"I just didn't know they did that, that's all."

He nodded. "I don't suppose the general public does know. But we're fortunate that men like Singletary are so careful. Well, anyway . . . we'll ask this Ruthie some questions, if you want us to. But it all looks perfectly kosher, at least on the surface."

"Are you satisfied, Lieutenant?"

"Well, for now anyway. It sounds like it's just what the nephew said: your Mrs. Gardner is a very disturbed lady, and this brooch and hers may look something alike, but this pin isn't her pin. Unless you want me to look into things a bit further?"

"I really am grateful for your taking the time you already have. I don't want to impose on you more than I have. Besides, there doesn't seem any reason," Angela agreed. "Can you stay awhile this morning?"

"Oh, no, I'm sorry, but Shorty's waiting in the car. At least, I think he's in the car. I told him we didn't have time enough for him to slip in and see Chita on this trip—but he may have tried anyhow. There's no such thing as putting up a barrier to love—'Shorty laughs at locksmiths,' so to speak. But we really must be going along. We do have several things on our agenda for the day. Another time perhaps there'll be a half-hour or so to sit down and chat. I hope so."

"So do I, Lieutenant, but I understand." She saw him to the door. "And thanks again. I really will take the brooch to Singletary's today. Perhaps this very afternoon, as long as I'm going through downtown anyway."

And that was why Caledonia and Angela felt so virtuous when they stopped at Singletary's shop about one-thirty the same afternoon to leave off the brooch for mending. They had a legitimate errand that allowed them good reason to do what they had every intention of doing anyway.

Chapter 8

"**M**RS. BENBOW!" John Singletary sang out with delight. "Always a pleasure to see you!" Angela was not a cynic and she rather liked the man, but she knew that part of the warmth of his welcome could be attributed to his knowledge that to her the price tag was no significant barrier when she wanted to make a purchase. She had not been to the shop for some time, though she frequently stopped by when she was in town to spend a pleasant half-hour looking over his latest acquisitions. Her main interest was always in the older pieces he displayed in a special case, and he walked in that direction now.

"We have a string of fine baroque pearls that just came in. Can I tempt you?" he said. "And there's a nice dinner ring with eight small canary diamonds around a particularly good blue topaz, if that intrigues you."

"You know it does, John, but that's not why we're here," Angela said. "Oh, while I think of it, this is my special friend, also living up at Camden, Mrs. Wingate."

"But I've met Mrs. Wingate. Perhaps a dozen years ago, you came in to buy someone a Christmas gift. Do you remember?"

Caledonia laughed. "I remember. I'm just surprised you do!"

"Remembering customers is a special knack I've cultivated. Besides, Mrs. Wingate," he added mischievously, "you're a lady it would be hard to forget."

"You can say that again," Caledonia snorted. "But I'm not center stage today. It's Angela who needs your atten-

101

tion. I just came along for the ride. So to speak," she added with a slightly bitter note in her voice.

Before the two had set out from Camden after lunch, there had been the inevitable argument between them that surfaced every time they went anywhere outside the confines of the retirement center itself: how to reach their objective. Caledonia, who didn't really approve of walking, had wanted to call her limousine hire service. But Angela had balked. It would mean having the car wait for them while they were at the jeweler's, then letting the driver know their second and most important destination, Rollo's apartment. "I don't like having a witness," Angela said.

Caledonia then suggested they get Emma Grant to take them. "At least she won't ask embarrassing questions. She will hardly notice where she stops, and she can use the gasoline money." Whenever they asked Emma for a ride, they bought her a tankful of gasoline to repay her. Emma hardly ever bought her own gasoline anymore.

"Is she having a hard time with expenses?" Angela had asked.

"Well, not really, though she hasn't got anything like the money you and I have. I'm sure she's not reduced to selling off her possessions or anything."

"Then I say we walk."

"Walk!"

"Cal, it's only a few blocks. We don't have to share where we're going with anybody, if we just walk. And frankly, Emma Grant's driving makes me so nervous I can't eat for a week." Emma Grant was not a speedster. On the contrary, and there part of the trouble lay: on the superhighways, Emma refused to go faster than thirty-five miles an hour. She stuck to the extreme right-hand lane, it's true, but she created a hazard for other drivers, who speeded around her, blaring their horns and shaking their fists.

"I can't bear it with all those people yelling at us!" Angela said. "And it's even worse in town." In town, Emma was a menace of another sort, for if she didn't travel faster than thirty-five, neither did she travel slower. She maintained a steady speed, even when cornering—a maneuver that often took her in a wide, swooping arc that cut across into the lane of oncoming traffic.

"Last week," Angela said, "Emma was taking me to my dentist's office and we stopped at a light. There were a lot of cars coming the other way, straight at us on the same street, waiting across the way for the light too. But when the light turned green, Emma turned left right across the whole stream of oncoming traffic. Well, you should have heard the noise—brakes shrieking, men shouting, horns blaring . . ."

"My heavens," Caledonia said. "Was Emma upset?"

"Oh, she was," Angela assured her. "But not the way you think. Emma was angry because they were angry. She said to me, 'What's the matter with all of them? I had my turn indicator on!' I didn't say a word. I just prayed—a lot—till we got to the dentist.

"That woman drives like she's got a team and wagon— and like everybody else does too," Angela said. "She's going to kill herself one day, and everyone who's silly enough to be riding in the car at the same time. Cal, just this once, let's walk."

Reluctantly, Caledonia agreed.

Now they were at their first objective, the jewelry store just three blocks from home, and they were both breathing heavily from the unaccustomed exertion of the walk. "I'm afraid I'm not here to buy today," Angela panted as she followed Singletary across the shop.

"Then it must be your brooch," he said. "Lieutenant Martinez showed it to me this morning, and I need to keep it a couple of days if I'm to make all the pearls completely secure. Tiny prongs like these are so vulnerable . . . I hope you'll leave it with me."

"I brought it for you to look over," she said, handing it across the counter. "Did Lieutenant Martinez tell you the problem I've had with it?"

Singletary had fixed a loupe into his left eye, so that he was scowling ferociously as he worked away at the little brooch while he talked. "No, not really. Is there something besides this prong?"

"It's not the pin. It's where the pin came from. One of

our ladies up at Camden, Mrs. Gardner, seemed to think the brooch was hers. An old family piece. The lieutenant said he'd check your records to be sure. I mean, well, maybe she did lose it and someone found it and eventually they might have brought it here and you might have bought it without knowing . . ." Singletary was frowning, and Angela hurried on in an apologetic voice. "At least, that's what we thought. It needn't have anything dishonest connected with it, you see. Anyway, we know this can't be her pin, because her nephew says hers was lost a while back, but certainly after Lieutenant Martinez says you took this one into the store. Am I making sense?"

"I think," he said, still scowling through the loupe and working away on the side of the brooch with a pair of tweezers, "you know me better than to believe I'd get involved in receiving stolen property. Uh-oh—I was right . . . this prong is torn straight through." He held the brooch up, but Angela could see nothing.

"My eyes aren't good enough . . . I can scarcely see that those are pearls any more, they're so small. And I can barely make out that there are metal points holding them."

He waved the brooch. "I'll need more than a few minutes . . ."

"No problem. We're on our way . . . uh—shopping. We'll come back tomorrow or the next day," Angela said. "And when I do get back here, I might just look at that dinner ring of yours, if it hasn't been sold already. Remind me."

"Oh, I'll remind you," he said. "All right now. About where I got this brooch, the lieutenant did tell you where it came from, didn't he?"

"Yes, he said some girl you knew from town named Ruthie brought in her mother's jewelry?"

"Some pretty nice stuff it was, too. Ruthie doesn't have much money and neither did her mother, but the pieces she brought—well, people can surprise you. Oh, for instance there was this brooch of yours. Several highly unusual pieces like that . . . all very handsome. I went ahead and bought the whole bunch. A couple of the items I hadn't seen duplicated anywhere else. Let me see . . ." He went to the case where the antique pieces lay and unlocked the back. "Yes, here's one of hers ... a cross set with rectangular, faceted garnets, with a pearl at each point of the cross and in the center. Victorian, I think."

While the women examined the lovely little cross, he picked up a leather-bound book from behind the counter somewhere. "Here's the entry—I have it marked because I looked it up for Martinez this morning." He opened to a page on which he had briefly described six or seven items and entered a block price, $600. "That's what I paid," he said, "for the whole lot."

"That's her name at the top?" Angela pointed. "Virginia Ruth Robertson?"

"That's it. That's Ruthie. Her father ran the laundromat down on Smoke Tree Lane. He died about ten years ago, and Mrs. Robertson ran it for a while. I think they sold it before she passed away. Ever take anything down to that laundromat?"

"Not if I can help it!" Caledonia said.

"We wash everything we can in the laundry room up at our place. Well, it's free," Angela defended.

"Sure. I understand. I only meant, that's where you might have run into Mr. and Mrs. Robertson before. At the laundromat. Of course you might have seen Ruthie almost anywhere—she holds three jobs altogether, and—"

"Very interesting," Angela said, obviously bored. "But about the jewelry itself—is that all you can tell us?"

"I'm afraid so," Singletary said. "Well now, is there anything else I can do for you? The brooch will be ready by close of work today."

"If we have time on our way back from our errand today, we'll stop in. Otherwise we'll pick it up tomorrow," Angela said. "Thank you so much, Mr. Singletary. I am really grateful."

And the two ladies swung out of the shop to get on with their detective work.

Rollo's apartment was located in what had been a garage behind a house three blocks beyond the jewelry store. The street was easy enough to find; Catalpa Street ran across the width of the town and intersected every other major street which ran the length.

In the main part of Camden, the short streets running east and west were named for plants, the long, north-south streets for states. If you were on Michigan or Washington or Idaho, it didn't matter—sooner or later you'd find Catalpa Street—and Ivy Road—and Sage Brush Avenue—and Magnolia Gardens—and even Kudzu Lane, the latter being the private whimsy of a developer whose entire acreage on the southernmost edge of Camden was annexed to the city, street names and all. Residents had tried to change the street name, but there were always a few whose sense of humor was like the developer's and who refused to sign the petition.

Catalpa Street was the next after Golden Rod Circle and Caladium Avenue, as the ladies walked south on Nevada. Number 1306, the house in front of Rollo's apartment, was a small stucco bungalow with torn screens, a faded rainbow windsock hanging on the front porch next to some bamboo wind chimes and a macramé plant hanger, and torn window shades that filled the windows at uneven levels. The house looked derelict and exceedingly shabby. The yard around it was of beaten earth—no grass, no flowers.

Up the driveway—two strips of concrete separated by more hardpacked sandy soil—stood the garage, its big overhead door closed. Mindful of the possibility that some practical joker or some drunk might try to slide the door open and expose to passers-by the tenant of the garage apartment, an early landlord had nailed large wooden blocks to either side of the door and nailed the blocks in turn to the adjoining wall. There his interest had stopped—no one had ever painted the blocks, now weathered to silver gray.

As Angela and Caledonia got farther up the drive and the angle of their vision took in the side wall of the garage, they could see a small concrete stoop and a little overhang of eaves sheltering what they soon discovered was the only usable door to the apartment, a door on which wooden cutouts, painted blue and nailed in place, proclaimed "1306-B."

Nobody accosted them from the house as they walked

gingerly past. Indeed, they were both convinced that the house was untenanted, although as they moved down the drive beside it, walking toward the garage apartment, Angela thought she caught some movement out of the corner of her eye. She turned quickly, but the torn shade in the window just over her head hung still. "I guess I just imagined someone was there," she told Caledonia in a half-whisper.

"What's that?" Caledonia rumbled back, but she kept her voice low, too. "Somebody where?"

"Inside the house. In the window. Watching through the crack in the blind."

Caledonia halted her forward progress for a moment and burned the silent house from attic to ground with her intense glare. "I don't think there's been anybody there for months, let alone somebody there now, watching us. Come along."

The little apartment too was silent. There was no police seal on the door, and no padlock. When Caledonia pulled back the screen door and turned the knob, the door opened easily under her hand. So, there being no barrier to speak of, they went in.

"A cottage Goldilocks would have taken to right away," was how Caledonia described it later. Rollo's place was neat and tidy. The simple furniture was painted in bright primary colors; even the upholstery looked new and unused, its pretty chintz flowers vibrant and crisp. The cupboards with their stenciled Pennsylvania Dutch motifs were organized so that even the soup cans stood in drilled rows, the jam jars all the same distance from the front of the shelf, all the labels turned exactly forward.

"I suppose," Angela remarked, "that, especially if you don't have normal intelligence, you still need some activity to fill your time. Straightening things would have been a good activity for someone like Rollo."

"He must have spent years lining up the pantry shelves so perfectly," Caledonia marveled. "Look—he's even piled tea bags, one on the other, in a careful stack ... all the edges exactly even ... I don't believe this guy!"

"I'm surprised the police didn't mess things up a little looking through his possessions!"

"Maybe they did and old sobersides Benson made 'em put things back just as they found them," Caledonia said. "Oh, my glory!—look at this!"

She had pulled open a bureau drawer, and there were Rollo's socks, each one smoothed flat and folded over once at an angle across the heel, so that foot and leg pointed in the same direction. Then the socks were stacked, like the tea bags, one on top of the other.

"The man was compulsive," Caledonia muttered. "Shorts and shirts I'm used to seeing folded and stacked. But socks? That's weird!"

"Well, of course you'd think that, Cal," Angela said. "You throw things into your drawers any which way—it's a wonder to me you ever find anything. You could take a lesson from this ... although I admit Rollo went a bit overboard."

"I think you're right," Caledonia said. "He didn't have another thing in the world to do, so he folded and straightened, probably every evening of his life. Look ..." She waved an arm around the room. "No letters, no newspapers, no books on the shelves ... I guess nobody ever wrote to him, and I suppose he never just sat and read for entertainment ..."

"There's only one piece of reading matter here," Angela said, picking up an outdated *TV Guide* that lay upside down on top of the nineteen-inch color set on the rolling cart, neatly pushed back against one wall. "Mph! Of course! I might have guessed!" Angela had just looked behind the set to see that the cords were neatly rolled, the rolls held securely by "twist-em" ties; only enough cord was left to reach from the set to the outlet, when the set was pulled into viewing position—and not an inch more.

Within a half-hour, the disappointed women had searched every shelf and cupboard, the closet where a single suit hung beside three clean, starched shirts and a nylon windbreaker, under the bed where three pairs of shoes stood neatly lined up and where there was not a single dust kitten, and even around the edges of the cushions of the only overstuffed chair—the one where Rollo apparently sat to watch television. But nothing was hidden, nothing had been dropped and forgotten, and even the wastebaskets were sparkling clean.

Angela gave up. "There's just plain nothing here in the way of a clue. The man was a compulsive about being neat," she concluded.

"It's almost inspiring," Caledonia said. "I feel as though I ought to go home and scrub my own place from picture molding to mop-boards, throw out all the junk, empty the table tops . . ."

"It may be inspiring, but it's not very helpful. We haven't found a thing!" Angela complained.

Caledonia was resigned and cheerful. "Okay, so what say we go on home?"

She turned toward the exit and stopped dead in her tracks with Angela coming up short against her. Footsteps sounded—more than one person's—not loud, but audible through the closed door, coming toward the garage apartment down the concrete ribbons of the drive.

"Hush," Caledonia said, but for once, Angela was already hushed, standing absolutely still, hardly breathing, her ear cocked toward the door.

"I can't hear," she pantomimed, with hand signals and shakes of the head.

Caledonia held up a warning hand. The gesture was quite unnecessary; Angela was not about to speak. They both stood absolutely still, listening.

There was a scraping of feet on the concrete stoop outside the door, then a heavy-handed knocking. The women stared at the door, willing the people outside to go away . . . go away . . . go away . . . but it didn't work.

The door slammed violently inward, and at what seemed the same moment a hoarse voice shouted *"Police!"*—and Sergeant Benson appeared in the doorway. He seemed to the startled women to have gotten very much shorter: he was in a half-crouch and turned sideways to make a smaller target. In one hand he held a gun that seemed to them to be the size of a Colt Frontier model. Behind him, also half-crouched and partly shielded by the door frame, was Officer Jeffers, also carrying a very large, very menacing revolver that looked, as Caledonia said later, "suitable for bringing down an elephant!"

Four pairs of lungs deflated simultaneously with four audible gasps, and Benson was moved to speak first. "What the living hell . . . you two! I should have known!" He holstered the gun, and gestured to Jeffers, who followed and also put away his weapon.

"Sergeant Benson. What are you doing here?" Angela challenged. The admiral had always said that the best defense is a sudden and surprising offense, and she had protected herself often with just such strategy.

Benson was not to be diverted. "You first, ladies. Why are you here?"

"There wasn't a seal on the door," Caledonia said. "And we did knock. I didn't see any sign that said Do Not Enter, either!"

He shook his head in reproof. "Now, now . . . don't play games with me. They . . ." he gestured at the empty-looking main house "told us someone had broken in and was rummaging around out here. So we came. Fast."

"It wasn't my imagination!" Angela crowed. "There was somebody watching from the house."

"You bet," Benson said grimly. "Hernan Estevez and his wife live there with three cousins and their wives and about eight kids."

"Children?" Caledonia exploded. "I don't believe it! What are they? Deaf-mutes? You can't keep eight children that completely quiet."

"You can if they're illegal aliens," Benson said. "I have a hunch the Estevez clan have just barely got toweled off—"

"Toweled off?" Angela said blankly.

"I think he means they're wetbacks," Caledonia interpreted.

"Dripping," Benson confirmed. "It's not my job to hassle some poor shlubs who just want to make a decent living for their families, and who couldn't bear to leave the wife and kids behind in Mexico when they headed for the border. So I'm not going to speculate. Leave that to immigration. But let me tell you, people like that can keep their kids quiet! They don't want any problem with the neighbors, any complaints about a kid's ball thrown through a neighbor's window or a game of tag through the neighbor's garden. Those people work at having the best behaved youngsters in town! You bet you didn't hear 'em ... they probably sat like church mice going 'ssshhh' to each other the whole time you were sneaking past and going 'ssshhh' to each other."

"But if they're afraid of the authorities, why did they call you?"

"Well, for one thing, I've been here before—looking the Bagwell apartment over—and I hadn't turned 'em in to immigration. So maybe they trusted me a little. And the men are gone to their jobs—they work in the sewage plant. So are the older women. They work down the coast in the flower-growing fields. Mrs. Estevez is here with just the three youngest and the oldest daughter—girl about thirteen who helps care for the family. The middle kids are off in school. Learning to read, Mrs. Estevez says, and she's proud of it. But when they saw you going by, obviously heading to the Bagwell apartment, she got scared."

"Scared?" Angela sounded a little pleased. "Of us?"

Benson ignored her. "She watched you go into the apartment, and she waited and waited for you to come out—and you never did. Finally she couldn't stand it—she just had to ask for help. This is the apartment of a man who was murdered—viciously slashed to death. Who knows whether the killer is watching the place or not? And what he might do to someone nosing around? The Estevez woman thought he might have been lurking there and got both of you—or even that you might be the killers yourselves ..."

"She could have come out to find out, surely," Caledonia said.

"Not everybody's got the colossal guts you two have! Mrs. Estevez wasn't brave enough to go see for herself ... so she sent for me." He nodded with satisfaction. "Smart woman. Exactly the right thing to do ... send for the police."

"And you came charging down the driveway with guns drawn ..." Caledonia said scornfully.

Benson looked faintly embarrassed, but he defended himself with vigor. "Well, Mrs. Estevez had the oldest kid call us from a neighbor's house. The adults don't speak English very well. The daughter speaks it better—at least well enough to make us understand two strangers were in the murdered man's apartment." For a moment he looked disgusted. "She didn't say the strangers were two little old ladies—so the one thing I never expected was it would be you two! Listen—hasn't Lieutenant Martinez talked to you about all this yet? He promised he would."

"Oh, he did," Angela assured him, with a protective tone in her voice. Nobody could imply in her presence that Martinez was derelict in his duties. "He came to Camden yesterday to talk to us."

"Well, didn't you *listen*?" Benson shouted.

"Please!" Caledonia made a gesture as though to shield her ears. "No need to raise your voice to us."

"Didn't he explain that the Bagwell killing might be connected with your place up there—with the retirement center—in some way? That it might be dangerous for you to . . . to . . . Well, didn't he tell you?"

"Yes, he did," Angela said, "but you see, if there's nothing of importance to be found here," she was reviving the argument she'd used on Caledonia, "and everything that's significant is up there at our place, then it really doesn't matter if we do poke around down here. And if there maybe should be something important here—well, then you people have missed it, and two more pairs of eyes just might find it. Either way, you can't lose by having our help," she finished triumphantly.

Benson sat down on a bright yellow kitchen chair with a red-and-blue hex sign painted on it. He looked tired and exasperated. "Cute argument," he said wearily. "And dangerous. We're dealing with a cracked filbert who slashes people up . . . some character whose dipstick registers about three pints shy of a gallon . . . and you two want to play Miss Marple!"

"Oh," Angela said with pleasure. "Do you read Agatha Christie too? Don't you just *love* those stories? So clever and . . ."

"What's the matter with you two anyhow!" Benson's voice had risen again. "I'm working away at the office . . . I know you don't believe it, but we do a lot of research on our cases—get into a lot of background stuff on people and places that requires searching through piles of documents and mountains of computer printouts . . . and half our work is done right at our desks! So there I am, working as hard as I know how to find something—anything—that would have made these two guys candidates for murder—and here you are, marching in to leave your fingerprints on every-thing, move everything around, destroy and take away lord knows what kind of evidence . . ."

"I thought you looked this place over thoroughly al-ready," Caledonia said.

"Oh, we did. We did."

"But then we could burn the place down, and—so far as getting evidence goes—it wouldn't matter a bit! If you peo-ple are any good at your jobs, you already have all the ev-idence there is."

Again Benson managed to look embarrassed. "Well, that may be true. But there could be something that looked per-fectly innocent to us at the time, but in the light of facts we discover later, it might turn out to be important. That kind of thing." He groaned. "I'm starting to sound like you!"

Caledonia smiled, but Angela nodded eagerly. "I do un-derstand what you're saying. It's been that way with every single case we've worked on, hasn't it, Cal?"

Benson buried his face in his hands. "Did you hear what you just said?" he challenged through his fingers. "Did you .hear?" He took the hands away from his face, knotted his fists, and shook his hands at heaven. "They think they are working on cases. They think they're detectives!"

Angela stood up. "There's no need to be so insulting. Of course we don't think we're detectives. You're just trying to put us in the wrong over everything we say."

"No, I'm not, but I'm trying . . ."

"You're trying to embarrass us and scold us at the same time," Caledonia said. "We can see your point, but you ought to try to see ours."

He stood up. "I see yours," he said with a deep sigh.

"You want a little excitement in your lives, and this murder is a lot more fun than playing in a checkers tournament or knitting a tea cozy. Right?"

Caledonia looked at her feet and shrugged. Angela cocked her head and looked at him out of the corner of her eye. "I think she was flirting with me," Benson told Martinez later, amazed. "White hair, spectacles, wrinkles all over, looks like my grandmother, and she's flirting! My God!"

Now he shook his finger at them, scolding. "Doesn't the death of someone you knew upset you?" Benson asked. "I haven't seen one person who shed a single tear for either of those fellows, even though you knew them both. I haven't seen one person who turned a hair at all the blood and gore. You act as though murder was a crossword puzzle or a cryptogram—loads of fun to try to solve, and no harm done when it's over. But two men who were alive two weeks ago are dead this week. Dead! Don't you have any respect for human life?"

Caledonia moved forward to stand in front of him. "I suppose we do look callous, treating murder as though it were a game staged for our benefit, to keep us amused. But you have to remember we look at life and death from a little different perspective than you do. In general, to most of us who are old, it's just another fact of life—just another thing you have to do, like eating and sleeping. We do it. We don't much like it, but we do it. And we all do it. And Rollo did, too."

Benson nodded. "Okay. But remember this. Rollo Bagwell and Enrique Ortelano weren't old and they weren't ready to die. They had another thirty, forty years left and somebody stole that time from them. Now I consider that something to get excited and angry about. And I intend to find out who did that and punish that person, sane or insane."

Both women stood silent.

Benson went on. "Furthermore, I'd take it as a favor if you didn't put temptation in his way by nosing around where he could see you, get scared, and decide you needed stopping."

Angela opened her mouth and raised a hand. "Argument" was written all over her face, but Caledonia put one huge hand on Angela's little shoulder, the other into the small of Angela's back and pushed. It wasn't much of a push, considering Caledonia's size, but it was sufficient to propel Angela toward the door.

"We're going, Sergeant," Caledonia said. "You've made your point. I'm sorry you find it distasteful that we get excitement and stimulation out of the puzzle of a murder case—and we can't help that—but we can stay on our own turf, so to speak, and leave you to do your job. Come on, girl, come on ... I don't like to face the prospect of the walk back up the hill to the center, but it's time to head home for a sherry. I don't walk fast, so we should just make it. Mush!" And they left without another word.

Jeffers turned to his superior. "What are you going to do about them?" he asked. "Just let them go that way?"

Benson shook his head. "I really can't stop 'em from nosing around, I guess. But I can try to put a few roadblocks in their way. I'm going back to the office, right now, and talk to Martinez again. He seems to have some influence on them, and maybe ... just maybe, if he tries again, he could find the right words. Lord knows I don't think one thing I said will make a difference to those two."

How right he was.

Chapter 9

PERHAPS BECAUSE of unfortunate associations with the two previous Tuesday nights—or perhaps because someone had complained about the Jackson twins' winning so frequently—the bingo game was canceled for the evening. The Residents' Entertainment Committee had met in emergency session and decided on the alternative of a community sing in the lobby.

"Dear Mrs. Webster will play the piano," Trinita Stainsbury warbled into the public address system in the dining room, "and our dear Mr. Torgeson kindly had the office staff type out and mimeograph some copies of the words to a number of old favorites. Speaking of dear Mr. Torgeson, by the way, he has had this old public address system fixed so it finally works! I hope everyone noticed?" She waited, as though expecting a round of applause, but if that was her expectation, she was doomed to disappointment.

Caledonia rolled her eyes to heaven. To be more accurate, she rolled her eyes upward toward the cracked stucco ceiling of the dining room. "That woman," she said. " 'Dear Mr. Torgeson' indeed! And a community sing! I'm sorry I asked her to our tea yesterday. This is how she pays me back?"

"Well, be fair, Cal, she isn't the whole committee. She's just part of it. And she only announces what they decide."

"I can just barely tolerate the bingo. I don't think I can put up with a community sing at all!"

"That's just because you can't carry a tune," Angela smirked. Angela had sung in the choir in whatever church

116

she and her late husband, Douglas Benbow, attended at their various stations throughout his career, and she regretted that Camden's chapel boasted no choir. She had thought of organizing one at Camden, but when she consulted Mr. Palethorpe, the Episcopal priest who served Camden's chapel one Sunday in four as part of their pastoral rotation schedule, he was discouraging in the extreme.

"That old dear wants to sing in the worst way," he told his young assistant, "and that's exactly how most of them would sing—in the worst possible way." Episcopalians are nothing if not realists.

"I can just imagine what a choir would be like—cracked voices that can't reach the notes, most of 'em slightly off-key because they're too deaf to know different, half of 'em singing a beat or two behind the other half, a few who are on the wrong verse, and always one who gets onto the wrong page and sings the wrong hymn entirely. When you get your own church, remember that. The old ones love to sing, but in a choir they're á positive negative, so to speak."

So Angela still had no chapel choir as an outlet in which to raise her voice in song. And the announcement of a community sing pleased her very much. The murder had temporarily been forgotten, not only because of Trinita's announcement, but because both women were deeply embarrassed by having been discovered in the midst of investigating the Bagwell apartment. Benson had expressed his displeasure all the way back in the police car.

"He didn't have to haul us back home as though we were under arrest," Angela complained. "He isn't the least bit pleasant when he scolds!"

"He probably thought if he left us to go back on our own, we'd get into more mischief on the way," Caledonia said placidly. "Besides, I appreciated the ride. It's too far to walk both ways, no matter what you say!" And that was the end of the discussion. Neither mentioned the afternoon's adventure the rest of the day, and all the way through the evening meal.

"Everyone go back to your rooms after supper, and get on something comfy before we begin the sing. Slippers, a loose-fitting dress, a slack suit—whatever you can lounge in." Trinita simpered as though to imply some wicked double meaning. "And now, let us bow our heads in grace . . ."

Everyone in the dining room obediently bowed, so that no one could tell just by looking who was joining in the grace and who wasn't—except for Grogan, who had arrived to stand, red-eyed and unshaven, swaying in the doorway, late to dinner as he often was, and now peering left and right, waiting for the prayer to finish and looking at his fellow residents rather than to his God.

"Amen!" Trinita sang out cheerfully. "Well. Let's say seven-thirty to start, shall we? See you in the lobby, then, at seven-thirty!" She turned and put the public address microphone down on the little stand beside the amplifier panel and started to walk away toward her own table.

Almost at once, a man's voice came over the loudspeakers that circled the room, hanging high near the ceiling: "Not if I see you first, you won't, you silly old cow!"

"Grogan!" Caledonia exclaimed, with a yelp of laughter.

Grogan, staggering past the spot where Trinita had stood, had obviously intended to mutter only to himself, as he so often did. He was as startled as anyone else to hear his private thoughts echoing from above his head. He looked left and right in bewilderment, and then saw the little red lights of the amplifier still glowing.

"She left the damned mike on!" his voice rang metallically from the ceiling. "Dumb, stupid-ass thing for the woman to do! *SHUT UP!*" Grogan had picked up the microphone and was waving it aloft at the speakers. "Shut up, I say . . . where the hell is the switch on this thing!" There was an audible click, followed by welcome silence. Grogan's bleary vision had cleared enough that he found the on-off button and used it. At last.

He set the microphone down, thought a moment, weaving unsteadily about, and then picked up the microphone again. Thumbing the switch, he pronounced, "Sorry about that, everyone. I didn't know that gun was loaded! Hyuh-hyuh-hyuh . . ." His snicker cut off abruptly as he once more turned off the mike, and weaving profoundly made his way to his own table.

"Cal," Angela coaxed over a tiny helping of chocolate

mousse that tasted rich enough to buy and sell IBM, "Cal, please come ahead to the singing. It won't be nearly as much fun if you're not there with us."

Caledonia shook her head. "Thanks, but no thanks. I'll do the bingo, I'll watch the old movies, I'll tend a booth at the bazaar, I'll clap in time while somebody square-dances—even though I'd rather be dragged behind a stage-coach than square-dance myself—but I have to draw the line somewhere. Just one thing—are you sure you want to go sit in the lobby tonight? What if Mrs. Gardner is there?"

"Oh," Angela said apprehensively, "I never thought of that! I haven't seen her since the party yesterday, and it went right out of my head. I suppose she's been sleeping off all the sedatives. Of course, I'm hoping her nephew was right. He said she might just have forgotten about the whole thing." She thought a minute. "Oh, I think I'll risk coming down to the lobby. I don't want to miss the fun."

"Fun? Miss the fun? Hah!" Caledonia gathered the folds of her caftan, tonight a blue-and-brown tapa-cloth pattern, tight around her so she wouldn't trip as she rose. "All I can say is 'Happy Trails' to you, then! Enjoy—if you can!" And she swept out majestically, through the double doors to the garden, and down the path to her own apartment.

Angela, coming to the lobby just at seven-thirty, found the best seats already taken. The definition of "best seats" varied with the person. For Emma Grant, who turned off her hearing aid for loud entertainments, and Sadie Mandelbaum, whom no hearing aid would help, the front row was best. For Caledonia and other overweight residents, the end of a row would be best, or one of the big easy chairs set around the perimeter of the center section where smaller chairs had been organized into rows, theatre fashion; if these people overflowed their seats, at least there was nobody next to them to object. For Mr. and Mrs. Trimble, there was only one pair of "best seats": halfway back in the audience, on the south edge, directly behind one another rather than side-by-side, because George and Adele suffered from a common complaint of the elderly, and they didn't want to disturb others as they made their way to the public restrooms, just down the hallway off the main lobby.

For Angela, "best seats" were those in the back row when she was in the chapel, and any seat away from the Jackson twins or Trinita Stainsbury if she were at some gathering where one exchanged conversation with one's neighbors. But tonight the back row was filled, and so were most of the other available chairs. There was one obvious vacancy—in the second row directly next to the Jacksons, and directly in front of Mrs. Stainsbury, who stood up in front of the group, microphone in hand, showing her obvious delight to be acting as M.C. and songleader.

Angela sighed, braced her shoulders, and wormed her way in next to twin mountains of pink chambray. "Wouldn't you rather sit between us, so you could talk to both of us?" the nearest Jackson whispered.

"Oh, my goodness, don't put yourself out. Let's just listen and sing," Angela demurred hastily.

"Now, is everybody ready?" Trinita called out cheerfully. "Everybody got a song sheet? Oh! Oh, really! Why didn't they pass out the song sheets? Where are they? Janice . . . Oh, Janice . . ."

Summoned from her chair near the rear, Janice Felton (also an Entertainment Committee member) pointed out the stack of papers on one end of the piano bench where Mrs. Webster sat beaming, hands poised above the keys. "Frenchie" Webster (Frances at her birth) had been a piano player in a silent movie house when she was just a young girl, and though her eyesight was gradually dimming, "Frenchie" could still make the lobby's grand piano vibrate from its little brass wheels to its massive cover when she pounded out a chorus of "Tramp, Tramp, Tramp" or "The Riff Song"—or "The Battle Hymn of the Republic," which she was likely to play whenever the Jackson twins were getting too Southern for words. Frenchie's eyes were weak, but her spirit was still vibrant, and enough molasses and honeysuckle was *enough*!

"They've been there all evening," Janice hissed. "I thought you saw them."

"Well," Trinita whispered back, "I thought you were going to get someone to hand them around."

"I thought you said *you* were in charge," Janice said.

For a moment the two ladies glared at each other. Then, resignedly, Janice split the stack, taking half herself and handing half to Howard Emerson, who sat at one end of the front row. She'd have preferred asking Mr. Brighton, whom she knew better, but his hip was worse than ever tonight. He sat at the far end of the row with his leg stretched out in front of him at an angle which bent the bad hip as little as possible. No use asking him to rise and pass out the song sheets . . .

At last everyone who wanted to was holding a thin pack of the roughly typed, ink-spotted mimeographed sheets, and Trinita Stainsbury tried again, waving the hand-mike about in the manner of one of the jolly plastic clones who emcee television quiz shows, and lofting her voice so that one wondered why she bothered with the microphone at all.

"Turn over to page four, everyone. Page four. Let's try a chorus of 'My Bonnie Lies Over the Ocean.' Got it?

> My bonnie lies over the ocean.
> My bonnie lies over the sea . . .
> My bonnie etcet'ra, etcet'ra . . .
> Oh, bring back . . .
> Oh—*damn*! Oh, I beg your pardon . . .

Torgeson had intervened in the typing of the song lyrics, that afternoon, and had enjoined his staff not under any circumstances to type the same lyrics twice. "When you come to a repeat line in the chorus, just say 'Same again' or 'etcetera' or something like that. Do you see?" he instructed. Trish, his secretary, nodded patiently.

"I don't mind helping out with their little entertainment project," Torgeson said self-righteously, "but they must understand that time and paper both cost money. You'll save time if you don't retype the same words twice, and we'll save paper because it obviously doesn't take nearly as much space to print out 'etc.' as it does to print out the full line of a song, now does it? Especially where there's a whole chorus that repeats. Why bother to type *Fa-la-la-la-la, La-la, La-la* more than once? You see?" Trish nodded again.

"And be sure you run these off front and back. Let's cut the number of sheets of paper that way, too."

This time Trish protested—mildly. "They won't be easy to read—the ink bleeds through," she said. "Some of our residents don't have the very best eyesight, you know, and the lobby lighting is pretty dim . . ."

"If they can't read the words," Torgeson said, using what he thought was a perfectly reasonable argument, "they can hum! All right, get working—I've got a pile of letters to dictate, and the sooner you get done with this silly little project, the sooner you can get to the important matters for today."

The only thing was, nobody had told the Residents' Entertainment Committee about the format in which their lyrics would appear. Trinita glanced at the next song on the page and read the words to "Oh, Susannah"—complete only up to the second chorus, where Trish had dutifully typed "Oh, etc." and nothing else.

"We can't sing from these," Trinita said, outraged. "This is awful. What are we to do!"

"Everybody knows the words," Mr. Brighton suggested. "Why not just start a song and let us sing if we can?"

"But," Trinita objected, "the problem is I don't know the words!"

"That's no problem at all!" somebody halfway back muttered. Trinita looked up sharply, but nobody looked guilty or leapt to confess, and she couldn't pick out the owner of the offending voice.

"Well," she said skeptically, "what would you like to sing then?"

Frenchie Webster didn't wait for the audience to vote. She banged out a few full chords of introduction and swung into "Down in the Valley." One by one, voices took it up. What did it matter if some were singing "Down in the valley, the valley so low . . ." and others sang "On top of Old Smokie, all covered with snow . . .?" The tunes were nearly the same, and everyone seemed happy except Trinita, who was trying futilely to get them together on the lyrics.

They did "She'll Be Comin' Round the Mountain," and Mr. Brighton cheerfully injected the "Ya-hoo" at the end of each set of lines. And then they did "Sweet and Low," and Mrs. Grant wept a little because she had sung that as a lullaby to her children. "The Church in the Wildwood," "Little Brown Jug," "In the Gloaming," "Tenting Tonight," "The Spanish Cavalier," and "The Daring Young Man on the Flying Trapeze" followed each other in rapid succession. The lobby filled with sound and seemed to become brighter, as though the music—off-key, off-tempo, with faulty lyrics, and far from beautiful—gave off its own warm glow.

Mr. Emerson jumped to his feet. "How about 'Old MacDonald,' " he suggested.

"I don't know the different verses . . ." Trinita objected.

"Sit down here," he said, half helping and half pushing her into the seat he had just left. His wife glared at him. "I'll direct this one. Everybody ready? 'Old MacDonald had a farm, Ee-i, Ee-i, Oh!' "

"Old MacDonald" was done twice, for the benefit of those who had not been able to keep up the first time, and Mr. Emerson, who had just hit his stride, then led them in "It's a Long Way to Tipperary," and "Over There," and "My Buddy," and "How You Gonna Keep 'Em Down on the Farm," and "Charmaine," and "Roses of Picardy." Someone requested "After the Ball Was Over" and Mr. Emerson obliged. And finally, under this direction, people in each row linked arms and swayed back and forth as they sang together:

> After the ball was over,
> After the break of dawn . . .
> Many the hearts were aching,
> If you could read them all,
> Many the hopes that had vanished,
> After the ball.

Angela wiped her eyes and thought of Douglas and the last dance they'd gone to . . . she was too deep in her own thoughts to realize that the Jackson twins were snuffling, Mr. Emerson had turned his back and walked away from in front of the group as he mopped his eyes with his pocket handkerchief, and Mr. Brighton had hidden his head in his hands. For a long moment there was absolute silence in the lobby.

"Oh, for pity sake!" Trinita Stainsbury jumped to her feet, and for once, Angela was glad of her aggressive good humor. "Come *ON* everybody . . . this is no way for us to be at the end of a good evening. Let's do 'There Is a Tavern in the Town.' " She gestured commandingly and rapped on the lid of the piano to get the attention of Frenchie Webster, who obediently struck up the first chords, and again, one by one, people started to sing. "One more time," Trinita called out as they finished, and this time almost all of the voices joined in:

> . . . Adieu, adieu, kind friends, adieu,
> I can no longer stay with you,
> Stay with you-oo-oo . . .
> So I'll hang my harp on a weeping willow tree
> And may the world go well with thee.

The audience applauded itself with smiles and mutual good humor, and slowly began to leak away, each person to his own room and his own memories.

Angela did not have very far to go, and she felt glad of it. Crying always made her a bit tired. She didn't wait to say good night to any of the other residents—just climbed the four little steps and let herself into her own room, while the rest of the audience, one by one or in groups, departed.

"I need a hot bath with a lot of nice, blue bath salts," Angela told herself. "That will pick me up. Make me feel . . ." she interrupted herself. One of the problems with bathing in the evening at Camden was the shortage of hot water in the antiquated system—partly the fault of the system, partly the fault of the residents, since three-fourths of them elected to bathe at night just before bedtime. Angela ordinarily took a bracing shower the first thing in the morning, when she had plenty of hot water for her own use. But perhaps, she thought, if she hurried tonight, she might draw a tubful before the supply ran out.

"This plumbing may have come over on the ark,"

Angela told Caledonia one day, when they had been discussing the need for repairs to the whole, aging system,
"but one thing in its favor—the tub is deep enough so that
you can get the water right up to your chin! The tub Douglas and I had in our last apartment in Washington was a
modern beauty—and if my knees were covered, I was sitting up out of the water to my waist; if I lay down in the
tub to cover my shoulders, my knees stuck up into the air.
That's when I got into the habit of taking showers instead
of a bath."

"But there's something so soothing about a bath," Caledonia said.

"Sure. If you can fit into the tub. They don't make them
deep enough any more," Angela said. Now she poured in a
generous supply of bath crystals and let the water run full
blast, while she changed from her dress to a robe. She came
back into the bathroom from time to time, however, to
check on the water, lest it start to run cold and waste the
whole tubful by turning it tepid.

At last she had the tub filled to the overflow drain—no
use trying to fill it beyond that point, but since she was so
short, that was plenty of water to cover her completely. To
drown her, if it came to that, she thought, and shivered. She
slipped her robe off, put on a shower cap, and turned the
gush of water off . . . and that's when she heard it—a confusion of sound that, to her defective hearing, had been inaudible over the thunder of the flowing water: running feet,
voices, women sobbing, a siren in the street outside her
windows, a man standing in the hall near her front door
barking orders.

"Nobody can settle down in a bath with all that excitement going on," she told herself, slipping the robe back on
and zipping it so that she was demurely covered from neck
to toes. She stepped into a pair of fuzzy slippers and threw
aside the shower cap at the same moment, pausing for a
second to close the bathroom door (no need to waste all
that nice, steamy warmth) . . . and then she headed for the
hall.

Two men were taking the steps to the second floor in giant strides, two at a time—Sergeant Benson, followed by

Officer Jeffers. Through the lobby toward where the elevator was located came an emergency ambulance team with a rolling stretcher. Residents stood in small groups around the lobby looking stricken, whispering to each other. Torgeson was there, apparently returned from his home in town. Angela thought irrelevantly how fast he must have traveled—she hadn't been incommunicado over the tub all that long. His presence meant big trouble.

So did the identity of a man who had been hidden from Angela for a moment as she looked at the activity on the stairs and in the lobby. From a group of residents standing together in a tight knot down the hall came Lieutenant Martinez. She realized then that she had recognized something about the voice, even coming to her ears muffled, through the walls of her apartment.

"Lieutenant, what is it?" she said, reaching out a hand to stop him as he came past her toward the lobby.

"Mrs. Benbow, I'm going to tell you what I've told all the others, and I'll tell them again: get inside your apartment, lock the door, and stay there till morning. Don't let anyone in, don't stir until it's broad daylight. There's been another murder—as bad as the first two. Worse. This time it's one of your residents. Mrs. Gardner up on the second floor. Mr. Emerson found her when he was coming back from some program you had in the lobby tonight . . ."

"We had a community sing," she said faintly. "Mrs. Gardner? She's dead?"

"Oh, without a doubt," he said solemnly. "You'll hear all about it. Now, get inside and lock the door. There's nothing more to be seen out here anyway . . . and we'll be here through a lot of the night, I think. But you'll be of the most help to us if you're safe."

"And out of the way," she nodded, reading his mind. And for once, she did as she had been told.

Chapter 10

Mr. Emerson found the body. The Emersons had not waited for the elevator but went directly up the stairway off the south corridor to reach their double room on the second floor, after the community sing was over. They had watched a little television, according to Howard Emerson, who kept insisting on telling his story over and over—to the police as they came through, to the other residents standing around the lobby, to Mr. Torgeson who was walking up and down, wringing his hands, deaf to every word Mr. Emerson babbled.

Mr. Emerson was ordinarily an early-to-bedder, while his wife was one of the night owls. She was watching CNN and the last half of the 9:00 P.M. news, while he began to draw a bath.

"Get me an orange, will you, Howard?" Charlotte called from her corner of the love seat, never taking her eyes off the TV.

"I was just about to take a bath, Charlotte. My clothes are already half off. The oranges are closer to you than they are to me anyway, dear," he argued.

"I'm doing some needlework," she argued back, grabbing up some crocheting from the bag she kept on the floor beside her place. "Pretty please?"

He sighed. He ought to be used to being manipulated this way, he told Mr. Brighton, though he didn't include that comment to anybody else he told his story to.

The Emersons were a second-marriage couple. She a widow, he a widower, they had both been over sixty when they met at a singles dance club "for mature individuals," up in Los Angeles. Both had come hopefully to a club meeting, trying to find a way to relieve the tedium of solitary living. To their dismay, the club's definition of "mature individuals" included youngsters in their twenties, several divorced people in their thirties and forties, and no one else but the two of them who even had white hair! It was natural that Mr. Emerson and Mrs. Gillette, as she was then, would gravitate together.

While the younger people gyrated and gesticulated in the solo maneuvers that passed for dancing with that age group—and that Mr. Emerson told Mrs. Gillette looked more to him like the exercises his doctor made him do to loosen up his stiffening joints—the two shyly made a date for the next night to go to a small, expensive restaurant where middle-aged and older people danced to "the Big Band Sound" in comfortable closeness. "It makes me feel good to think my partner and I are communicating through the dancing. The way these kids take off on their own, they're lucky if they ever find the same partner again!" Mr. Emerson explained to Mr. Brighton, when he was telling the story of his second courtship and marriage.

"I'd give a lot to be able to dance either way . . . close or apart," Brighton said ruefully. "Oh, well—go on . . ."

"Well, anyhow, one thing led to another. We liked each other, we were both lonely, we both had money of our own, so her losing her husband's pension wouldn't hurt—it was one of the kind that they take away if the widow marries again, you know?" Brighton nodded. He knew. Everyone in the retirement center knew about those. "Besides, I thought we liked the same things, you know? We seemed to, while we were just dating. I mean, I'd suggest a picnic and she'd say that was wonderful. But I haven't been able to get her to come on a picnic since we got married!"

The activities Charlotte Gillette Emerson enjoyed did not include picnics. They consisted mainly of sitting at home watching TV, entertaining relatives—her relatives, giving parties for a small circle of wealthy and rather snobbish acquaintances, and shopping. She abhorred all outdoor and group activities: fishing, boating, square dancing, golf, and anything that Howard might do on his own, or that would put her together with people she called "strangers"—that is, anybody that wasn't immediate family or one of her particular friends.

After they married, Charlotte began to make Howard over into her image of a good husband: one who enjoyed carrying packages and watching her try on clothes and sort through embroidery yarns; one who didn't fish or golf, since those activities would take him away from her and put him with cronies she considered beneath them; one who would gladly give up a chess game with an old friend to drive her to a bridge party. Howard—being a gentle, uncomplaining soul who could almost always find the bright side—allowed himself to be remodeled from cellar to attic.

In time Charlotte had urged their moving to the center at Camden-sur-Mer. Howard had objected at first but finally agreed, and now he claimed to Mr. Brighton that was really the one good move she had recommended in all their four years of marriage. Even after they came to Camden, however, Charlotte continued work on his renovation, all of it to her advantage.

Her latest reform was getting him to stop raising the flag each morning. Camden had a flagpole, and it was traditional that one of the residents take charge of raising the flag each day before breakfast. Howard had enjoyed the duty he'd volunteered, shortly after he arrived, to take from Mr. Brighton, whose hip was getting worse daily. Howard was patriotic—he was an early riser—he was relatively strong and hale, so the weight of the flag was no bother for him—and he liked the little time alone, before Charlotte—who was a late getter-upper just as she was a late stayer-upper—arose in the morning. But after she repeatedly complained that his early rising had disturbed her enough to ruin her whole day, he agreed to pass the duties with the flag to Mr. Trimble.

Only once in a while did he struggle a little for his independence, but as he told Brighton in confidence, it almost wasn't worth while. It was easier to do what Charlotte wanted than to waste the time in argument. "She sulks, she thinks up little revenges like ordering buttermilk for me to drink when she knows it makes me sick—and it's just easier all around if I do whatever it is she wants." This evening, for instance, he made only one feeble attempt to avoid her commands. Then he sighed, slipped his bedroom slippers on (he'd actually only got so far as taking off his shoes and tie when she called to him), and shuffled out of the bathroom to the little cupboard in the hallway between the living room and their bedroom. They ordinarily kept snacks there—fruit, cheese crackers in cellophane wrappers, candy bars . . . but when he got there, the cupboard was bare.

"Not even a banana?" Charlotte complained. "Oh, dear, I did want something—I wonder, before you take your bath, if you'd go downstairs and see if they won't let you have something out of the dining room?"

"The staff have all gone home by now," he protested, mildly.

"Well, they don't lock the room, do they?" she said, in a tone of voice she would have called reasonable. "Just go in and rummage around in that fruit bowl they set out on the sideboard. They usually put fruit in it the night before, ready for breakfast the next day. Go and find me an orange. And a banana, while you're at it. And a couple of apples . . . you might want a snack, yourself."

"Yes, dear," he sighed and shuffled off, took the elevator down to the lobby, went into the dining room, and in a moment or so came out juggling his trophies. He never understood how she knew such things as the fact the fruit bowl would be refilled and ready or that the dining room door wasn't locked. But he didn't ask. He just got back into the elevator, returned himself to the second floor, and started for home.

But as he turned left toward his own rooms, the law of gravity took effect on the fruit. He didn't have hands large enough to accommodate four oranges, four bananas, and four apples—but Howard had decided, while he was at it, to insure against having to make another trip later in the week (or even this same night, if Charlotte took the notion) and he was laying in supplies. He had pressed four oranges tight against his shirtfront with one arm, four apples with the other, and he had taken two bananas in each hand. So when an orange began to slip and he shifted the pressure on his arms trying to save it, one of the apples, now insufficiently squeezed against his body, also began to slip.

It was late and he really wasn't thinking all that fast. So he just stood there, looking a little foolish, squeezing his arms tightly against his body to hold the rest of the fruit and watching the apple from one side, the orange from the other, drop to the floor. The orange made an unpleasant squishing noise and stayed put. The apple was made of firmer stuff. It took off, bumping down the hall to his right, and Mr. Emerson pursued it, using tiny steps so as not to jostle loose any more of the fruit.

There was nearly zero visibility in the hall due to one of Torgeson's perpetual attempts to save money; half of the lights in each hall were turned off by an automatic timer precisely at nine o'clock. The theory was that, by that hour, most of the residents should be safe in bed. The fact that they often were not—that, like tonight, there were often herds of people wandering the dimly lit hallways, tripping on the carpeting, clutching at the railings, muttering in anger and occasionally cursing—did not discourage Torgeson from sticking with his half-the-lights-out policy.

Thus Howard Emerson, operating on "Instrument Flight Rules" through the gloom, came upon the apple with one foot before he realized it and inadvertently kicked it, rolling it farther down the hall until it finally came to rest in a wedge of light that spilled from a door standing ajar.

"I couldn't help but look inside," Howard told anyone and everyone. "I mean, you just do. You don't have to be a nosy person. But when a door's open . . ."

Everyone assured him they understood.

"She was right inside the door. And even if I hadn't been able to see her there on the floor, I'd have seen the blood soaked into the carpet. So much blood!"

Mrs. Gardner had been stabbed to death with a silver-handled letter opener she kept in her tiny rolltop desk. The desk stood open, the papers on its top awry as though a hurried hand had rummaged among them, spilling a number of them to the floor. The body was surrounded by a shower of paper clips, rubber bands, old check stubs, and unused postcards.

"Well, I could see she was dead. I mean, there wasn't any use calling Dr. Carter. I just put the fruit down in the hall, went back to the elevator and down to the front desk, and got Jimmy to call the police. And Mr. Torgeson. I mean, the administrator should be here for emergencies like this, don't you think?"

Just at that point, one of his auditors thought to ask after Charlotte, and Emerson was stricken. "My wife! Lord, I forgot my wife!"

"Do you mean," Emma Grant asked, shocked, "that she's still sitting up there waiting for you to bring her an orange?"

He looked embarrassed. "And it's been nearly an hour now," he said.

"It's a wonder she isn't already down here hunting for you, wondering what on earth happened to you," Tootsie Armstrong put in.

He shook his head sadly. "She's probably so wrapped up in TV and in her needlework, she hasn't even noticed I'm gone. But I had better go up there and tell her about all this. She'll be furious if she's missed all the . . ." he started to say "fun" and changed at the last minute to "excitement."

Howard left hastily, stopping only long enough, when he reached the second floor, to collect his fruit, an action which caused a brief argument with the uniformed policeman by Mrs. Gardner's door, who apparently thought the little array of bananas and apples and oranges dumped next to the door might be some kind of clue. After that, things were very quiet in the lobby for some fifteen or twenty minutes, and the residents began to disperse and go back to their rooms. They knew that they would hear about everything the next day, and it really looked as though the police and the medical team would not be coming down again for quite a while.

Angela, who had paid no attention at all to Lieutenant Martinez' warnings but had stood around in the lobby watching and listening to Howard Emerson's tale, returned to her rooms to find that her bath had reached the point of being too cold for comfort. She emptied out some water and tried adding hot, so as not to waste all the lovely blue bath salts, but the hot water supply in the main tanks had been drained, as usual, by other bathers, and though the tanks had refilled they had not reheated yet. She sighed and pulled the plug to let the rest of the tub drain away. "Tomorrow morning I'll shower, as usual," she told herself. She felt her eyes getting sandy and starting to close in spite of her excitement, so she slipped on her pajamas and went to bed and immediately fell asleep.

On Wednesday nobody could talk of anything but Mrs. Gardner's death. There were more people up for breakfast than on any usual day, and plenty of wild speculation, including Cora Ransom's gently pixilated suggestion that perhaps it had been done by agents of the Kaiser! She could not elaborate her idea beyond that, and of course since everyone knew her and knew about what was referred to as "Cora's problem," nobody paid the slightest attention.

At nine o'clock Caledonia Wingate appeared in the dining room, where Angela still sat. Caledonia blinked in surprise. Her tiny friend was usually well away, shopping or watching television or in the middle of some activity like a quilting bee or a craft class by this time. Caledonia stopped at the side table where fruit juices were kept, poured herself a water tumbler full of cranberry juice ("Good for the kidneys!"), and came to seat herself in her accustomed place.

"Here?" she said. "Well. Why?" Caledonia wasted little effort on speech until revived by breakfast coffee.

Angela filled in the rest of the statement for her. "You're surprised I'm still in the dining room, right?"

"Right." Caledonia held the sleeve of her aqua crinkle-cotton caftan aside so it wouldn't drag on the plate as she reached across to the coffee thermos. "Cream. Sugar," she said. "Please."

"I just had to talk about our latest with everybody else, that's all," Angela said. "Oh, by the way, the waffles are particularly nice today. Pecan waffles. And there are little sausages."

"Good," Caledonia said and dipped into her coffee. "Ump! Hot!"

"Have some more cream, and don't be so greedy. Oh, Chita . . . Chita . . . Mrs. Wingate wants a waffle and a couple of sausages."

"Two!" Caledonia rumbled. "And four."

"Two waffles, and four sausages, please, Chita," Angela said. "Sorry, Cal, I forgot. How about a sweet roll on the side?"

Caledonia shook her head and reached silently for the thermos and a refill of the coffee.

"I swear we've had the most exciting and the most frightening week! This isn't like Rollo and that little man who did the machines, and I think that's probably because it involves someone we knew even better. Or rather, I guess when you come down to it, we didn't know her all that well. But because she's a resident, it just feels like we did . . ." Angela was rattling happily along, quite unaware that Caledonia, the fog gradually clearing from around her head, hadn't the least idea what Angela was talking about.

At last, a waffle and a half and three sausages and another cup of coffee later, Caledonia settled back in her chair with a slice of buttered toast covered with black-cherry jam. "Dessert," she said contentedly. "Now, you're talking about the brooch, right?"

"Brooch? What about the brooch?"

"I mean," Caledonia said, "this thing you say we're all upset about that's worse than Rollo's death."

"Oh, Cal! Are you going to tell me you don't know about the latest murder? Didn't you hear all the excitement last night?"

"Yes, and no! Yes, you're right that I haven't heard anything about any murder. And no, I didn't hear a sound in the night!"

"You better get your hearing checked, Cal. There were sirens, and people running around till all hours! The police were upstairs for the longest time; we finally all left the lobby and just went home. Oh, and Martinez was even here for a while."

"Martinez? Upstairs? Who was murdered then? You mean one of *us*?"

"Yes-yes-yes . . . Mrs. Gardner!"

"Lena Gardner, the new woman? The Mrs. Gardner we just gave the party for? The one with the nephew and the brooch and . . . well, for heaven's sakes, who did it?"

"They didn't say. I suppose it's whoever killed those other two."

Actually, that was exactly the thought that was being tossed back and forth by Sergeant Benson and Lieutenant Martinez. "It's probably your case, or just an extension of it," Martinez was saying. "No need for me to be involved, just because I was at Camden and available at the right time . . ."

Martinez had been doing another good deed in the name of romance, delivering his tall young aide-de-camp to Camden to pick up Chita Cassidy after work. Martinez and Swanson had been in town on an unrelated matter, and Martinez had volunteered to let Swanson, who ordinarily drove for him, stop off for a date with his girl. Martinez would drive himself home. Swanson had just disappeared into Camden's main door when Martinez' radio had come on with the word that there was a murder and Benson was being summoned. Martinez called in explaining where he was and that he'd respond till Benson could arrive . . . and simply shut off his motor and came inside, at the double.

"But that doesn't make it my case," he was saying now to Benson.

"Well, of course, they may be separate cases after all," Benson argued. "They may not be connected, see? And just happened here at this place. And what I'm saying is, if that's so, this third killing is yours. Don't think I'll care if you take it on your desk."

"Look," Martinez said reasonably. "We'll be tripping over each other if we both work down here at this place. Better talk to the captain about it and see how he wants to make the assignment. He said he'd see us about ten-thirty this morning, and I propose we let him decide. But one police team on that site should be enough, whether the killings are related to each other or not. The only question is—you or me?"

"Tell you the truth," Benson said, "being up there is kind of getting to me. I told you before. Bullwinkle the Moose and her little sidekick Rocky are really bugging me, now. I think you know how to handle that pair. But I tell you, I sure don't!"

"Actually," Martinez told Swanson privately in his own office, while he waited to see his captain, "I think we would be a logical team to assign. We do know the place well, and we would probably have had the call on the Ortelano murder to begin with, if we hadn't been tied up with something else. The Bagwell killing went to Benson, too, because it was logical to connect it with the first murder. But whether or not these are all three connected in some way that isn't obvious yet, I think we might get better results with the residents—have less background to dig up—than Benson would."

"Why don't you ask Captain Smith to put us on it, then?" Swanson said, trying not to sound too eager. He had two reasons to want to be assigned to work at Camden, the food he and Martinez were allowed to share with the residents, and Chita Cassidy's presence. Both were, to him, compelling.

"Maybe I will, Shorty," Martinez said. "But it's a matter of tact, here. Benson was there first, it's really his case, and I don't want him to get the idea I'm trying to take over just because he hasn't found the killer yet. I may need him some time, and I want a friend to work with, not an enemy."

"Oh, I understand," Swanson said, hastily. "But I still think, to tell the truth . . ."

"Tell the truth," Benson said to his captain when he and Martinez finally came into their boss's office, "I think Martinez probably should have been assigned in the first place. Oh, I know he was busy. But he knows Camden and the people and that saves a lot of background investigation. They trust him, too, and they'll tell him things . . ."

"If there's anything to tell," Martinez said. "Benson says he can't get a handle on any connection between the first two victims and the place or the residents. But we think there's bound to be one, since three people have died now—all by stabbing, and all right there at the retirement center."

"Captain, long before this third murder happened," Benson said, "I was thinking about asking you to assign me somewhere else and letting Martinez take over. Now, I really want you to consider it."

And so it was that Martinez and Swanson, just before noon, found themselves driving up the San Diego Freeway, heading toward the Camden turnoff and the retirement center—and toward lunch, as Swanson reminded Martinez almost blissfully. "Chita told me last night that tonight it's shepherd's pie for supper tonight, and Mrs. Schmitt does that up so good! Oh, and this noon it's souvlaki with rice. I sure hope we get there in time for lunch!"

Martinez was mildly surprised that even Torgeson, Camden's manager, seemed glad to see them. Of course Torgeson had been dismayed at the lack of a solution to the two previous murder cases, because that meant the continued presence of the police and endless explanations when potential residents came to look at the center and to view the only empty apartment—the one Sue Nancy Butler was using.

Even this last two weeks, before Sue Nancy had taken temporary possession of the room, the crews had been busy repainting the walls and replastering where the rain had come in one winter evening when the former resident forgot to close the window. New curtains and a new carpet had been installed only the week before, and the place was now ready for a permanent occupant.

"If," Torgeson told his secretary crossly, "anybody dares move into a retirement center where somebody is running around the halls stabbing people! I know I wouldn't want to rent a place here! They've got to get this business settled, and fast, or the tenants will start moving out. This could really finish us."

So when Martinez and Swanson showed up at the office, just at noon, to announce that the case had been passed into Martinez' hands, Torgeson actually smiled at the men and with a burst of unaccustomed warmth and generosity said, "And I trust that you both will dine with the residents as our guests—as you have done on those unhappy occasions when you have had to visit us in the line of duty in the past."

"It's a wonder he couldn't just come out and say 'Eat with us,' " Swanson complained as they left the office.

"Don't look a gift horse in the mouth," Martinez counseled. And they went gladly in to lunch.

When the men walked into the dining room, every eye in the place was turned on them. But neither paid the slightest attention. This was their third case involving Camden, and they were quite used to their presence being considered the floor show at the meals.

"Was this worth waiting for?" Swanson asked with a sigh, as he forked in a tiny cube of seasoned beef.

"I haven't had souvlaki this good since Mr. and Mrs. Georgopolis went back to Greece," Martinez said. "The couple who took over their restaurant simply didn't have the same love for their work . . . and it takes love to produce food like this!"

"It sure does," Shorty agreed, "it sure does," but he was gazing across the room as he ate, his eyes never leaving Chita Cassidy's trim form as she picked up empty plates from the first diners served and brought them tiny squares of apple custard cake for dessert.

After they finished eating, Martinez and Swanson headed out, intent on starting to work at once, chatting with no one except to say "Good day," and "How are you" as they passed. But both detectives hesitated an extra second and smiled an inch more broadly as they passed Caledonia and Angela, still nibbling at the apple custard and sipping coffee. There was no point in showing favoritism, but there was also no denying that these two were special. The men left the dining room feeling warmed in the sunny smiles of their friends.

"I hope we can do something about this mess," Martinez sighed. "They deserve a peaceful life and safety to enjoy it in . . . they don't need to be locking their doors and walking in pairs at night here in their own home!"

The second-floor sewing room was beginning to feel like a second office, as they set up their papers and notebooks, and Martinez ordered Swanson to ". . . ask that nephew to come see us. Right away!" as he swung off down the hall to Mrs. Gardner's room for a firsthand look at the scene.

Chapter 11

No GENERAL announcement was made of the change in police assignments that put Martinez in charge. The residents of Camden, as much in the dark as ever, could only speculate.

"Would they eat here if they had to pay for meals? Not on a policeman's salary!" Caledonia reasoned. "That means Torgeson is letting them freeload."

"Cal! At least say, '... letting them come as his guests.' It sounds so vulgar to say they're freeloading," Angela protested.

"Whatever you want to call it, they're here on the cuff. It's a tradition, like the apple from the fruit stand. But think about that tradition for a minute. Those old time grocers didn't give free apples to just any cop who walked by. They gave 'em to the man on the beat! The guy who protected them. It was a bit of quid pro quo."

Angela beamed. "And you always pretend you didn't have enough college to know any Latin!" She wagged a finger. "Tut-tut-tut . . . your education is showing!"

Caledonia waved her off with a good-natured hand. "What I'm trying to say is that I don't think Martinez and Swanson would be eating in our dining room if they weren't back on the case!"

"Oh, Cal, do you really think so?" Angela said, delighted. "How can we find out, do you suppose?"

"Well, we could consult a gypsy and ask her to read the tea leaves, or we could hire a private detective to plant a listening device in the sewing room, or . . ."

"Oh, be serious! What's the best thing to do to find out?"

"Why don't we ask them?" Caledonia said in a confidential tone. "I realize it's unheard of, but why don't we just walk straight up to Martinez and Swanson and ask them?"

"There's no need to be snide. It's just—I hate to seem curious . . ."

Caledonia's glance was made of pure derision as she rose from the luncheon table, flinging her napkin cheerfully into her chair, and started for the door. After a moment, Angela decided to be amused rather than to defend herself; she put down her napkin and pattered along behind her larger friend. "Should we just go on up and ask, do you suppose?"

"Do what you want, girl," Caledonia rumbled. "For myself, I'm going to do what I always do after one of Mrs. Schmitt's lunches—go and lie down and take a nice little nap."

"Now?"

"Now. And how come you don't do that, too? You'll fall asleep in your chair at supper, if you don't take at least half an hour now."

"Oh, all right," Angela pouted. She knew Caledonia was right; if they didn't take their usual naps, they ran the risk of ending up by supper time as cranky as kindergartners. With a sigh, she retreated to her apartment. "Not that I can close my eyes," she told herself, as she removed her dress, put it carefully onto a hanger, and lay down on her bed, pulling up the light-weight afghan to shield her shoulders from the breeze that stirred through the open window. "It's much too exciting to sleep and there's too much to think about. I wonder if the nice lieutenant really is back here to stay . . ." and she fell asleep.

By the time she woke, nearly ninety minutes had passed. "I would think," she said aloud, as she dressed herself, "they'd got themselves nicely settled, whoever is in charge today. I do believe I'll just stroll past the sewing room and see if it's still that Benson fellow or if by any chance Martinez really is there . . ."

As it happened, just as Angela was working her way past the sewing room door, trying her best to look absolutely innocent, the latest interviewee was leaving. It was the Jacksons' niece, Sue Nancy Butler. She had shed her fishnet stockings in favor of skintight blue jeans, and she had replaced the outsized tee shirt with an extra-large, blue-and-white shirt held in around the hips by two narrow belts in two shades of blue. Today she wore a pair of very high-heeled light blue shoes, and her frizzled, untidy-looking hair was held in place by a blue scarf, folded over and tied across the forehead like a sweatband. The jeans were so close-fitting that to Angela's eyes it appeared that the girl had wound color-coordinated elastic bandages around both legs. And Sue Nancy's walk was most peculiar, a kind of strained tiptoe, because if her stilt-heeled shoes had been one-quarter-inch higher, the balls of her feet might not have touched the ground at all, for her toes surely could not have bent to any more of an acute angle.

"I'm sure her ankles are hurting, with her feet held in that position," Angela was thinking, "and tonight, she'll need to rub those arches and take a long, hot foot bath!"

As Sue Nancy caught sight of Angela she shied nervously. "Oh, hi there," she said. "I know you, don't I? I mean, I met you around here?"

"I'm Mrs. Benbow," Angela said, stepping forward into better light.

But seeing her clearly didn't appear to help Sue Nancy's powers of recognition. Her eyes were still a bit unfocused and her brows knit in concentration. "You're a friend of my aunts', aren't you?"

Angela did not dispute the word "friend" but simply nodded.

"Yeah," Sue Nancy said. "You're the one with the stolen pin or something. The one that old lady was yelling at, aren't you? I remember because you're so short. I'm sorry not to remember right off, honestly. Truly, I am. But every one here is just faces to me. I can't keep 'em separate. Except for Auntie Donna and Auntie Dora, of course. Well, I'm off . . . I've got a date with Robbie for a concert down in San Diego tomorrow night and we're going to drive down this afternoon and get the tickets. 'Bye . . ."

She started off down the hall with a little stutter-step, catching her spike heels in the carpeting, then regained her balance and stumped toward the elevator. But as the elevator door opened, and she began to move from view, her jaunty bearing sagged, her shoulders slumped, and just as the doors swung shut, she let out a big, gusty breath.

"A sigh of relief, if I'm any judge," Angela told Martinez, when she was inside and the door safely closed. For it was indeed Martinez she found in charge in the sewing room, when she finally entered. "What were you asking that child about? She's a stranger here. She won't know anything about us."

Martinez smiled. "Possibly so, my dear lady, but she's very important to the case, all the same. She is the alibi for one of our suspects, Robert Hammond."

"Hammond . . . Hammond . . . Oh, you mean Robbie? The nephew?"

"I don't know about 'Robbie'—he didn't tell us his nickname. But 'nephew' is correct. Yes. Mrs. Gardner's nephew."

Angela was outraged. "But why on earth would you suspect him? He's such a nice young man . . . a student up at Camelot College studying computer science, and . . . and he has the most beautiful smile!"

"Mrs. Benbow, even students of computer science with beautiful smiles have been known to kill their elderly relatives. The largest number of murders are committed by a member of the victim's family. As a result, we simply never exempt relatives from suspicion . . . not till we have some reason to."

"Whatever happened to 'innocent until proven guilty'!" Angela said indignantly.

"That's for the courts. That's not for the police. To us it's the other way around. We're not supposed to take anybody's innocence for granted. We suspect everybody, though perhaps some more than others . . . and it stays that way until we can prove otherwise. In a manner of speaking, that's our job."

"Well, after you met him," Angela said, "surely you realized he's a gentle, quiet young man and that he loved his aunt."

Martinez nodded. "Uh-huh—so he told us. Several times.

But we have only his word for that. And the way he repeated himself made us take a second look at him, all right."

"What do you mean?"

"Well, surely you've noticed that somebody who's not certain you'll believe him will say 'honestly . . .' or 'I swear to you . . .' or 'really! . . .' a lot—along with whatever he's telling you? Quite possibly the reason he's not sure you'll believe him is because he knows he's lying!"

Angela beamed and nodded. "That Sue Nancy protested that way to me just now—she said more than once how sorry she was she didn't remember me. She kept saying she truly was. But I knew perfectly well she didn't care a scrap whether she remembered me or not. Of course, I really don't much care what the child thinks. Really, I—Oh! I did it too, didn't I?" Angela said, and then put her hand to her mouth. "I mean, I said it. I said 'really.' "

Martinez grinned at her. "Now, Mrs. Benbow—those aren't always signs of lying. There are other things we watch for. Like the repetition I mentioned. If a person desperately wants to be believed, he'll say the same thing over and over . . . as though repeating it could make you think it's true."

"But everybody repeats himself. Old people do—a lot."

"Well, I didn't say that was the only reason you might repeat yourself. But it's one indicator we watch for. And all I'm saying is that the nephew seemed nervous that we wouldn't believe him."

Angela was still on the defensive. "Robbie was just upset and unhappy about his aunt's death. And talking to you certainly didn't help. Don't you realize that you make people nervous? Being questioned about a murder isn't an everyday thing for most people. Just talking to the police used to make my heart flutter. Before I got to know you personally, of course," she added hastily. "Robbie's shy and quiet . . . wrapped up in his computers and his textbooks half the time, they say—and nice! Besides, you say he has an alibi?"

"He surely does. The best kind. The kind that involves

another person . . . in his case, your Miss Butler. They were together—out on a date—down at the beachfront here."

"At the beach? At night? Whatever for?" Angela was innocently bewildered. "You can't see a thing, and . . ."

"Mrs. Benbow, they claim they were just sitting building sand castles and watching the moonlight on the water . . . and that may be so. Though I doubt it. But at any rate, Miss Butler agrees that they were together the whole evening, starting from about five minutes after dinner. And Mrs. Gardner was alive at dinner time, because a nurse brought a dinner tray up to her room. The nurse came back about half an hour after dinner, and Mrs. Gardner was alive then, too." He shrugged. "So, Hammond has a very good alibi. Now to your business—do you have information for me? Is this an official call, or are you just passing the time of day?"

"It's actually a fact-finding mission," Angela said.

"Fact-finding?"

"Yes. We're dying to know if you're going to be assigned to work here permanently, or whether Sergeant Benson will be back. Not that we didn't like him, you understand . . ."

Martinez smiled. "Well, at least for the moment, I am the person in charge. Captain Smith moved Benson to another assignment and passed the files on the first two murders to me. I might add that Benson was agreeable. It seemed reasonable that, knowing you and the place here as I do, I might be able to work a little faster than Benson could. I need less background information on people than he does.

"For instance, I said we never eliminate any suspects. But the truth is, unlike Benson, I feel confident enough of you that I don't really consider you a suspect."

"Me! Surely—"

"Mrs. Benbow, you must realize that to Benson you're the second most likely suspect after the nephew."

"Me!"

"Absolutely! Granted relatives of the deceased are most often to blame. But after that quarrel you had with Mrs. Gardner, it seemed logical to Benson to suspect you. It wasn't logical to me, of course, because I know you. But

Benson would have started a background check, to find out all about you, whereas I don't intend to bother."

"I don't know whether to be pleased or annoyed. It's nice to be in the center of things, but it's not so nice to be a suspect. I can't believe Sergeant Benson really suspected *me* ..."

Martinez shook his head. "It's like the nine-ounce glass that has four-and-a-half ounces of water in it. Is the glass half-full or half-empty? Depends, they say, on whether you're an optimist or a pessimist. Either Benson suspected nobody—or he suspected everyone about equally. You choose the way to say it. Benson did have a careful eye on you. But he had a careful eye on everyone else around here as well. However"—he beamed down at her—"though I believe you capable of many things, dear lady, murder is not one of them. But I did want to see you, all the same. In fact, Shorty is downstairs right now hunting for you and Mrs. Wingate ..."

And at that highly appropriate moment, the door to the sewing room opened, and Caledonia flowed in, a white brocade caftan swirling about her like the movement of a brook foaming around a boulder that lies in midstream—a very large, very bumpy boulder, to be sure. Holding the door open and following close behind her was Swanson, who started talking before he was in the room.

"We couldn't find that little one, Lieutenant," he started ... "Oh, gosh! Hi, Mrs. Benbow."

"Hello, Swanson. I'm already here is why you couldn't find me," Angela said amiably.

"Won't you sit down, Mrs. Wingate?" Martinez said. And with the two ladies seated on the uncomfortable straight chairs—Caledonia's completely hidden by her bulk and by the folds of the shiny white caftan—Martinez pulled up a chair of his own so that he was facing them. Swanson had retired to his corner at the far end of the big table, where he had his notebooks lined up and several sharpened pencils at the ready.

"Now ..." Martinez said. And for the next few minutes, Angela and Caledonia told everything they knew about Mrs. Gardner.

"Okay," Martinez finally said. "Let me sum this up. As you see it, she was not what you'd call wealthy—"

"Right. At least, she didn't dress that way," Caledonia said. "Off-the-rack can be quite expensive these days, it's true, but her clothes weren't. They weren't cheap and shoddy, certainly. But they weren't costly, either."

"Still, she apparently owned some nice jewelry," Angela said. "After all, she seems to have had a pin like my pretty little brooch, and mine, at least, was quite expensive."

"Because it's an antique," Caledonia said. "I don't think it cost all that much originally. Pearls, for instance, shot way up in price back in the seventies. But before that they were really very reasonable. By comparison with other stones, I mean. Besides, Lena Gardner only inherited that brooch—she didn't buy it. So even if it was expensive, it doesn't tell you anything about whether she had money or not."

"She doesn't seem to have had much jewelry of any kind," Martinez said. "We've looked through her things, of course. She didn't even have an engagement ring. Of course, she wore a wide wedding band that left no room for a diamond ring. But it all seems to support your theory of her financial status. Naturally we're checking with her bank for details. But for now, I just wanted a general impression—something to start on—and you've given me that. You think she wasn't well-to-do."

Both women nodded.

He went on. "So that would make killing her for money an unlikely motive." The women nodded. "You know for a fact she was unhappy about coming here, that she wasn't making a good adjustment and she still missed her own home"—they nodded again—"and she felt her nephew had talked her into coming more or less against her will. In fact, he told you just about the same thing. Right?"

"Right," Caledonia nodded. "That's about it."

"And finally, she seems to have been slightly unstable," Martinez said. "Is that a fair assessment?"

Angela and Caledonia looked at each other a moment. Finally Caledonia said, "Lieutenant, Angela and I would both have to say 'Yes' to that, after seeing her outburst at the party. But when she first moved in here and I talked to her the first time, I didn't see a thing wrong with her."

Angela nodded vigorously. "We found out only later about things she'd been doing . . . the trouble she'd been having taking care of herself. We realized it was a good front she put up—but she was worse off than we knew. So we have to agree that she was really a very disturbed person. She just didn't look it. And that's how she got into Camden. The management won't take you if you're already so off balance that you need constant watching. You have to be able to care for yourself, to start with."

"Lieutenant," Caledonia growled. "Was she robbed when she was killed? I mean, had somebody taken things from the apartment? That occurred to me this morning."

Martinez shook his head. "My team's still looking the place over, you understand, but so far we can't see that anyone went through the dresser drawers or the closets. Her desk was a mess, but I think that was partly because the killer grabbed at the letter opener and knocked some of the papers and things to the floor. Furthermore, her purse was there on a chair, open, and she had about twenty-five dollars in bills and another couple of dollars in change . . . they weren't touched."

"Just like the soft-drink man!" Angela said. Martinez looked at her sharply. "Oh, I know that," she said apologetically, "because Sergeant Benson told everyone the man wasn't robbed. I wasn't doing any investigating on my own or anything. Honestly. Truly."

Martinez nodded. "I see. Right. Okay, so we scratch robbery as a motive. It makes our job harder, losing such an obvious motive, but we keep digging. And in the meantime, do me a favor: keep your ears open and your doors locked, especially at night."

"Lieutenant, don't you have any other suspects besides me and young Robbie?" Angela asked.

"You? Lieutenant," Caledonia rumbled. "Surely you don't think Angela . . ."

Martinez gestured soothingly. "Of course I don't. No, no . . . it's just that, before you joined us, I was telling Mrs.

Benbow that because of her quarrel, she seemed a logical suspect to Benson, and—"

"Oh! *Him!* Hah!" Caledonia's snort was a clap of thunder.

"What we're looking for now is some link among the three deaths. There are all kinds of possibilities for those two men, besides this retirement home."

"Oh?" Angela breathed eagerly. "Such as?"

"Well, for instance, the smuggling in of illegal aliens. There's still a lot of money in those activities. A 'coyote' can earn $200 to $300 a head for people he brings over the border, in spite of all the immigration law changes they've had in the past few years."

Caledonia frowned. "Those people who live in the house where our gardener Rollo had his apartment—the Estevez family—they all seem to be illegal aliens, apparently. But has anybody found a connection between Rollo and the way the family got into the country? And I don't see how our soft-drink man Ortelano figures into that."

"He was of Mexican parentage," Martinez said. He looked faintly embarrassed. "I know that sounds like prejudice, but we have to think about it."

"Well, is it a possibility? Did Ortelano know the Estevez family, too? Is that what you mean? It's a little confusing."

"Look," Martinez said. "We don't know illegal aliens are the answer. But we have to look at the possibility. Just as we have to consider drugs coming in from Mexico."

"That sounds awfully farfetched to me." Angela looked skeptical. "Even if you found some connection with both men, which I don't believe for a minute, how on earth would you ever tie Mrs. Gardner into something like that? You can't think that dear, gentle soul was a drug smuggler, or that she drove truckloads of illegal aliens over the border, or anything like that."

Martinez just shrugged. "I only gave that as an example. We're doing a lot of looking without any particular direction, hoping to turn up any motive that will account for at least two of the victims. Then perhaps we'll find some way to tie the third one in, as well. So far we haven't been successful, but that doesn't mean they weren't all tied together in some way—and if they were, we'll find that link sooner or later. But till we do—"

"Yes?" Angela leaned forward eagerly.

"Till we do, I'll be obliged if you remain very quiet and very circumspect about it all. In fact, I'd be happy if you stayed out of this entirely." The women seemed about to protest, so Martinez hastened on. "I said it before—we don't know what's behind these deaths. There have been three—that may mean there could be more. The killer may not be finished. So please . . . this time . . . try to stay—" He cast about for some way to avoid saying ". . . out of mischief" and ended lamely ". . . to stay uninvolved."

The women nodded in unison, their expressions serious, as though to match his mood, and they left meekly. But Martinez knew them well by this time, and he was not at all sure they intended to obey his injunction.

What they did when they left Martinez, in fact, was to go down into the lobby and sit in its cool gloom for a while talking over what they knew and deciding that really wasn't much. "It's so frustrating," Angela said. "If only it had been one of our friends who got killed!"

"Angela!"

"Well, you know what I mean! I didn't mean that the way it came out. I meant that if it was, we could be more helpful . . . we'd know more about them. This Mrs. Gardner was as much a stranger as that little Henry Ortelano the soft-drink man. Certainly more of a stranger than Rollo!"

"Oh, I don't know," Caledonia said. "We really didn't know a lot about Rollo, either, and that's the truth." She sighed mightily. "Well, what will we do this afternoon?"

"How about walking back to Singletary's with me and picking up my pin? I'm sure it's ready," Angela suggested.

Caledonia made a face of distaste. "My lord, girl, you're starting to be like one of those joggers we see trotting along Beach Lane every morning at dawn!"

"What do you mean 'we see'?" Angela said. "You're never up before nine."

"Well, you know what I mean. An exercise freak! I tell you what . . . I'm going back to my place and read my book. I just got to the exciting part where the wind is creaking through the old house and the shutters are banging and the heroine is upstairs in her bed, trying to decide whether there's somebody prowling around downstairs or not. And when you get back, you come and join me and we'll have tea—or sherry—depending on the hour. Okay?"

"Cal, you're not helping your heart a bit, just sitting so much. You really should make an effort to get more exercise, you know," Angela scolded. But the arrangement suited her. She really wanted to consider that blue topaz dinner ring Mr. Singletary had told her about, and Caledonia's looking over her shoulder sometimes inhibited her impulse to indulge herself with expensive trifles. "See you later," she said and swung out the side door of the lobby on her way downtown, while Caledonia groaned herself out of her chair and rolled off toward her own apartment.

Angela found it warm going, walking to the jewelry store in the heat of the July afternoon, and had to catch her breath a moment when she entered the air-conditioned shade of the shop. But Mr. Singletary had a customer at the moment anyway—a teenaged girl with a mahogany brown suntan who was wearing running shorts, slit up the side to show more leg. Mr. Singletary cast a despairing eye across her bent head, as the girl huddled over the counter, and said, "Sit down or stroll around as you like, Mrs. Benbow—I won't be long." His expression said "I hope" though his mouth did not form the words.

The girl had picked out an identification bracelet for her boyfriend's birthday. So far so good. Now she wanted "something cute engraved on the back." But she had spent most of her money already, just to buy the bracelet, and she was trying to fit a suitable message to her remaining budget, adding and subtracting words and making a difficult job harder by fussing about every suggestion Mr. Singletary made, but finding nothing useful of her own to contribute.

"How about 'L'AMOUR, TOUJOURS L'AMOUR,'" she was saying. "He's taking French in school. He doesn't like it, but he's taking it . . ."

Mr. Singletary counted. "That's twenty-three characters," he said. "That would be eleven-fifty at fifty cents a letter."

"I only count twenty letters," the girl protested.

"Count the comma and the apostrophes," he said, pointing to her sheet of paper, where she had written out the phrase.

"Oh, shoot! You're not going to charge me for a little old apostrophe, are you?" she said. "That's *mean*."

"I don't make the rules, young lady. I just send the work away to the engravers. That's what they charge me—and yes, they do charge for apostrophes."

"I only have about five dollars left though," she protested.

"Then you'll have to find a message with ten letters or less," Mr. Singletary said, reasonably.

Angela strolled across the shop to the antique counter, feeling much more like herself, after drying off her forehead and breathing a little cooler air. Mr. Singletary had arranged a new selection of pieces since Angela had come in the day before. One in particular drew Angela's attention. On a headless neck of black velvet he had hung a pendant, a rectangle of frosted crystal an inch wide and an inch-and-a-quarter long, on the flat surface of which was carved a spider-web pattern, the incised marks filled in with delicate lines of black enamel. Caught in the web was a single dewdrop . . . a tiny diamond. Singletary had hung the little "picture" by a thread-fine silver chain that hooked into the silver filigree frame. Angela was enchanted.

"I like the idea of something in another language," the teenager was saying, reaching back to scratch her hip through the garish satin of the running shorts, blissfully unaware of and unconcerned about anyone watching her. "It's kind of romantic."

"How about this," Singletary sighed. "How about having the word 'AMOUR' put on with a little 100 above it and after it . . . to the hundredth power. See what I mean? That would be only eight characters, or four dollars."

"Hey! That's a neat idea," the girl said. And so the deal was completed, the bracelet boxed to send to the engravers, and a receipt placed in the girl's hand. "So long," she called and swung out of the door and into the lavender Volkswagen bug parked directly in front of the shop in a NO

PARKING ZONE. As Angela watched, the girl revved the little engine and swung in a U-turn to pull into a space directly across the street in front of a little cafe where several other bronzed teenagers were sitting laughing and talking at sidewalk tables.

"Look at that! She drove just to go across the street," Angela marveled. "Mine must be the last generation that walks anywhere!"

"Here's the pin, Mrs. Benbow," Singletary said, at last free to lay out on a black velvet cloth her little antique pin. "Got everything secure now. If you catch these prongs on so much as a thread, they're not going to hold up. But for the moment everything's fine. Please be careful of this—it's 22 karat—much too soft, really—and therefore vulnerable. Now, can I interest you in something else?"

"Well," Angela confessed, "I came down the street thinking about that dinner ring you described, but this little crystal and diamond pendant you have here really intrigues me."

"This is another of the pieces Ruthie brought in with the other things, if it matters. Would you like to try it on?"

"No use . . . it wouldn't show up well against my flowered print silk. I think I can see well enough how it would look . . . and I love it. Tell me, what would you want for this—with the chain?"

And so the two old acquaintances spent a happy twenty minutes in the elaborate mating-ritual dance of merchant and customer . . . advancing, retreating, offering, withdrawing, accepting, rejecting, considering, and teasing . . . until at last a bargain was struck. The dancers took their bows and rested, and the music died away. Angela wrote her check, Singletary put the pendant into a box, and the adversary position was forgotten in companionable agreement.

Chapter 12

THEY SAY that Lord Byron, while taking "the Grand Tour" of Europe as a young man, found himself in the middle of the French campaign in Iberia. He was camped on a hillside overlooking the field of battle, and as it raged below, Byron nevertheless insisted, the story goes, on bathing and dressing for dinner and further insisted that although he had to dine at a foldaway table, his butler serve him on fine china and white linen just as though they were at home in England, instead of a tent in a war zone. Circumstance was not going to dictate to Lord Byron what he could and could not do; he intended to impose his customs and manners on circumstance instead. He might find himself in barbaric surroundings, but there was no need for him to become a barbarian himself!

In much the same way, the Camden residents, almost all of them adopted rather than native Californians, might lounge through their days in relaxed California clothing, and might take for granted California manners—manners they considered better suited to the beach than to the drawing room. But when the sun went down and it was time for dinner at Camden, they reverted to what had been considered well-bred dress and behavior back in Chicago, in Cincinnati, in Charlotte, in Cleveland, in Columbia ... wherever.

The gentlemen donned suit jackets and ties, albeit many of them had adapted so far as to wear the Western bolo tie; the ladies wore dress-up clothing—not formal wear, you understand, but clothing suitable for entertaining company or going to church on Sunday ... that kind of dress-up.

154

They might dwell among the barbarians (and they might enjoy every minute of it!), but they reserved the right to return from barbarism to civilization at least once a day.

Thus when Angela returned from her jaunt into town, she changed her clothes from her flowered dress to a pink linen suit and navy silk blouse. She had a reason for that particular choice: she wanted a dark background against which to show off her new acquisition, the crystal pendant. And she hurried her toilette so that she could get to Caledonia's place in plenty of time for a leisurely sherry before dinner. Besides, she had another motive—an idea that had occurred to her as she dressed.

"Angela! You've got a new pendant. Stand in the light where I can see it," Caledonia said. "Stunning! Absolutely stunning! I've never seen anything like it, and it's fantastic. No wonder you bought the thing! I wish I'd seen it first!"

One thing you had to say about Caledonia—she could be counted on to notice new things, and when she liked something, her praise was unstinting. She was a satisfying sort of person to show off to. Angela beamed and accepted her tiny glass of amontillado with grace. In fact, she was preening herself with such pleasure, it was several minutes before she remembered her good idea.

"Cal," she said, "you know, I wonder if we shouldn't get Emma to run us over to Escondido."

"To Escondido? Why!?! There's nothing over there but a lot of small manufacturers, shipping firms, a college, and six or seven motels. Or maybe you've got a yen to visit Lawrence Welk's restaurant. Have you? I know they say the food is pretty good, but we have such elegant food here that . . ."

"No-no-no . . . I thought we might go and talk to Mrs. Gardner's neighbor."

"Her neighbor?"

"Well, you remember Robbie talking to his aunt the day she moved in about how she'd left the iron on one day? And she said a neighbor had found it and turned it off . . . a Mrs. Walters. And then she said . . ."

"I do remember," Caledonia interrupted. "She said Mrs. Walters checked on her every day! You may have something—this Mrs. Walters may be the perfect person to ask for details about Mrs. Gardner. But, Angela, you don't mean to go now, do you? Why not leave it till tomorrow?"

"Oh, we can't do that. Remember Robbie also said that the reason they couldn't count on Mrs. Walters to keep watching his aunt was that the lady was going to get a job?"

"Oh yes. At K-Mart."

"Well, she'll be busy during the day, then. We have to go in the evening, after working hours—or on a weekend. And I don't want to put this off. If we do, anything we find out might not be as useful to the lieutenant."

"Uh-huh," Caledonia grinned. "You mean that if we wait, the police also might find out the same thing for themselves, without our help. And that would mean we had no excuse for poking around. Isn't that what you're thinking?"

"Sort of," Angela admitted sheepishly. "But it's also perfectly true that women sometimes talk to women. This neighbor might tell us something interesting that she wouldn't tell the police, you know."

"Tell you what," Caledonia said. "It's too late now—it's nearly supper time. But we'll talk to Emma Grant at supper, and if she's not planning anything special this evening, maybe she'll take us on over tonight."

"Wonderful," Angela beamed and extended her glass. "I think, Cal, that I'll have just another tiny drop of your sherry . . ." a sure sign that she was pleased with life.

Supper was a cozy little helping of shepherd's pie and some broccoli with a pungent cheese sauce . . . nothing to complain about, but nothing to slow down over, as Angela told Caledonia. So the women finished quickly and found Emma Grant just as she finished her dessert. Emma was at the table with Tootsie Armstrong, who was having a second cup of coffee.

"Ooooh," Tootsie said, her eyes round and her hair bristling out fuzzily into an even larger halo than ever, as though it too was excited and interested in the proposed trip. "What fun! Oh, Emma, *do* say yes! Angela and Caledonia are always thinking up such exciting things to do!

I'd be thrilled to be in on one of their schemes, just for once!"

"Oh, dear," Angela said. "We hadn't thought about . . . that is, Tootsie, are you sure you want to come? It might be—well, it might be dangerous!" The idea of a third party to their plan was bad enough, but they'd had no alternative to telling Emma Grant, since it was her car they were planning to use. But Tootsie too? Angela looked across at Caledonia, who merely shrugged and spread her big hands in a gesture that said, "Oh, well . . ."

"Surely there can't be much danger with the four of us," Tootsie bubbled. "Escondido! My, oh my . . . did you ever think of what the name means? It means 'hidden'—and that sounds exciting and adventurous enough to me, doesn't it to you? When should we start? Right now? Does anybody have to go back to the room for a minute?"

"If that's a polite way of asking if I have to go potty," Caledonia growled, "the answer is I don't."

Emma Grant held up a hand. "Wait. I'm not sure anybody is going on this trip, if you're counting on my driving. You know I don't see very well after dark . . ."

"Oh, Emma," Angela urged. "It's the middle of July . . . the days are long and with daylight savings, it doesn't get dark till late. Escondido isn't far . . . we'll be there in less than an hour, and we can ask a couple of questions and be back here before nine o'clock. If we start right now."

"Well . . ."

And that is how it was that the four women found themselves in Emma's car, entering the outskirts of the flat little inland city at 7:30 P.M., hunting for Mrs. Gardner's former address. The first step hadn't been hard—they simply stopped at a public phone booth next to a gas station on the edge of the town, though they'd had to drive to three gas stations before they found a booth that still had enough of its phone book left for them to locate Mrs. Gardner's name, the street and number. Then they located a Walters on the same street and made a note of that number as well.

For a wonder they got lost only twice, once while finding their way through a loop of one-way traffic in one end of the downtown district, the second time when they turned on Tarnhouse Way instead of Tarnhouse Lane, which was the next street over. Once on the right street, however, finding the Walters house was no problem. Tarnhouse Lane was only two blocks long, and the houses—all erected by the same developer—had foot-high ornamental numbers in brass-finished metal fixed to garage doors which were invariably a dark, intense forest green, making the brass numbers even more evident. The houses were a uniform cream stucco with terra-cotta roofs of imitation Spanish tiles. The front lawns were of dichondra, so green and smooth they looked as though they'd been spray-painted in position. This was the California equivalent of Levittown.

Emma Grant slowed the car in front of the house numbered 143—the Walters house, if their research was accurate. Lying on the front step was a large, orange-striped cat—probably answering to the name of "Morris-Two," if indeed he answered to any name at all. Most cats, of course, will not.

"Well," Caledonia said, "aren't you going to park? Just swing into the driveway."

"Oh, I can't do that!" Emma Grant protested.

"It'll be all right. She's not going to need to go out till we're gone. Just pull in behind her car there. At least, I guess that's her car—it's in her driveway."

"I can't do that!" Emma protested again.

"Well, for Pete's sake, why not!"

"I can't back very well," Emma confessed. "I'm going to park in front, by the curb. Then I can drive to the end of the street and make a U-turn when we're ready to go. I always try to park somewhere where I won't need to back. I go so crooked and I run over things . . ."

"You do that when you're driving forward, too," Caledonia growled so low that only Angela could hear her. Then, as though ashamed, she added, "Park where you want to, Emma dear . . ." and Emma pulled the car up to the curb in front of the house, where the four women got out.

"You go in front," Emma said, dropping back as they started up the walk. "I'm just the driver, after all . . . don't put me in the lead." She let the others move ahead and she stepped into the last position.

"I don't want to be in front, either," Tootsie twittered nervously, edging off the walk to let Caledonia move in front of her.

"This was Angela's idea," Caledonia said. "Don't put me in front . . ." and she edged Angela around her into the lead.

Maneuvering and whispering, the group moved toward the single step that led to a screen door through which they could see a TV broadcasting the bonus round of the evening version of "Wheel of Fortune." As they approached, the orange-striped cat rose majestically, gave its shoulder a swipe with its tongue to demonstrate its lack of fear, turned its back on the women, and making a question mark of its willowy tail, stalked gracefully in the direction of the garage.

"I'm going back and sit in the car," Tootsie Armstrong said, her voice quavering with nerves, just as Angela pressed the front doorbell and they heard chimes play the first phrase of "Bless This House."

Caledonia grabbed at Tootsie's arm. "Stay put," she hissed. "It'll look funny if you're running away when Mrs. Walters comes to . . ." A young woman appeared at the door. Caledonia tightened her grip on Tootsie's arm, forcing Tootsie to stay close by her side.

The young woman was a very pale blond dressed in the uniform of the young California housewife: faded denims rolled midway up her calf; a pair of worn tennis shoes with no socks; a shirt open in a deep vee, its tail tied up around her midriff, exposing a generous portion of flesh around her waist. She wore no makeup, and she was quite pretty, with light blue eyes and fine skin that was not at all like the tanned leather hide of the California teenager who spends every day on the beach. She carried a damp mop in her hand, and with the other she pushed the hair back from her sweaty forehead.

"Ladies?" the blonde said. "Can I help you?"

"I knew she was either a waitress or a sales clerk the way she said it," Angela remarked when they were in the car going back. "She had that deferential tone—she's used to waiting on people."

"Yes, you can," was what Angela said at the time. "We're sorry to interrupt your chores ... but we're from Camden, where your former neighbor lived up until her death? You know? And we came to find out a little about Mrs. Gardner if we could. Are you Mrs. Walters?

The blonde nodded. "Why do you want to find out about her?" she said, neither stepping aside nor inviting them in.

Caledonia moved toward the front of the group crowded onto the little stoop, Tootsie—still restrained in Caledonia's iron grasp—stumbling beside her. "We're giving the eulogies at the memorial service," she lied boldly. Tootsie Armstrong gasped "Oh, dear!" and Caledonia rocked her weight so that her foot came down firmly on the side of Tootsie's foot. "Oh, ouch!" Tootsie gasped, hopping onto her other foot ... "That hurt!" Angela glared at her.

"Perhaps," Caledonia said sweetly, "you had better sit in the car, Tootsie, since your foot is giving you pain." She let go of Tootsie's wrist.

Tootsie looked startled and scuttled gratefully off to take up a position in the back seat, from which she watched through the screen door while the ladies talked. "I couldn't tell one thing you were saying," she complained when they returned. "I wish you hadn't gone on inside; I could have heard, if you'd stayed closer by."

"Well, would you ladies like to step in for a moment," the blonde said, and opened the screen door. "I can spare a minute or two. But I work for a living, so I have to do my chores around the house whenever I can—weekends and evenings—this was my evening to scrub the kitchen floor." As the women sorted themselves out onto various Naugahyde-covered chairs, the blonde glided over, slid the mop inside the kitchen door, and on her way back to them, reached over and shut off the television. The hush that followed was almost eerie.

"I thought," Angela said later, "of Dorothy Parker's line: 'In my ears there was a silence like the sound of angel voices!' "

"What do you want to know?" the blonde said, perching on the far end of the couch which Caledonia had chosen as the only piece of furniture that would hold her without her overflowing.

"Well, Mrs. Walters," Caledonia began.

"Call me Terri," the blonde said. "I'm Teresa Walters, but everyone calls me Terri."

"If it hadn't been Terri it would have been Kim or Sherry," Angela said later. "It seems to me that women who wear their shirt tails tied around their waist are the sort to have 'cute' names."

Terri's request to call her by her first name made Caledonia so uncomfortable that she could not call her by any name at all. Instead, she looked pointedly in the blonde's direction whenever she spoke to her. "Tell me," she said, looking at Terri Walters' pale blue eyes, "why Mrs. Gardner came to us in the first place. I mean, do you know what made her finally decide to move from here?"

"I don't think she ever really wanted to move," Terri said. "But there wasn't much choice. Robbie said she needed more looking after than he could give her. I tried to help out, but she—well, she forgot things—like turning off the iron. And Robbie decided—" she paused. "Her nephew, you know?" She peered at them, and was satisfied they understood. "Robbie decided it was just too dangerous for her to be living alone. She needed to move into a sheltered environment, he called it."

"How did he find Camden?" Angela asked.

"I was the one who knew about it, actually. My girlfriend's mother applied to go in, and my girlfriend was simply raving about it. Her mother died before she could move, but I remembered and told Robbie and he applied for his aunt. He wasn't sure at first—I mean, it's so awfully expensive—but she had to go someplace, and he finally decided this was for the best. But we had to wait and wait . . ."

"He says it took quite a while," Caledonia said. "After she applied and before the room was ready."

"Well," Terri said, "from the time Robbie put in the application, it was four or five weeks. I guess that really isn't much, but it seemed like forever. He was going crazy waiting. He used to come over here and he'd go on and on about how long it was taking—but finally they phoned and said there'd been a vacancy, and after they'd cleaned and painted the room, she could move in—maybe another week. So Robbie and some of his college friends quick put on a garage sale and got rid of some of her older junk and they helped her pack the rest. The house sold pretty fast. Good price, I think. And before I knew it, she was gone."

She sighed. "I really miss them, you know? She was always a good neighbor—at least till she started acting funny. And she was still awfully sweet to me. And Robbie . . . he was a real friend—somebody near my own age to talk to—I get pretty lonesome since my divorce."

"Oh!" Angela was startled. She belonged to a generation that did not speak easily about divorce, if they acknowledged it at all. "Oh, dear, I'm so sorry!"

Terri shrugged. "No need. I don't miss that guy. I just miss somebody to talk to in the evenings. Robbie gave me that, while his aunt lived here. Of course, he's kind of a funny kid—not funny ha-ha, of course, because he has no sense of humor. At least, he doesn't get jokes till you explain them. And he doesn't always know how to take what people say. But pleasant company. And really very good-looking," she added shyly.

"I thought once—you'll laugh—but he's only five years younger than me—and I thought maybe we'd . . . but he's not really my style. I need somebody who can laugh. And somebody who cares what I think about things. I don't think he means to be cold and shut people out—it's just that he's pretty wrapped up in his classes and his ol' computers. Well, I should be fair about it—he did come by here to talk every evening for a while. It was nice, having somebody come by after work. Now all I've got is . . . him!" She gestured to the orange cat, who had come stalking silently in from the kitchen, looked around the room with great indifference, and turned his back on the guests to sail nonchalantly through the air and land on top of the television.

Terri laughed. "A little like Robbie . . . got his mind on his own things and doesn't care what everybody else thinks . . ."

"How did he get in?" Angela said.

Terri grinned. "I had a cat door put in the kitchen. He can't open the door for himself yet, but he sure has learned to get everything else he wants in this house."

Angela sighed. "That would please Mrs. Gardner. She worried about him. That is her cat?"

"Sure. Have they found out who did it yet? The papers don't say much."

"Did it?" Caledonia rumbled. "Did what?"

"You know, the murder. Gee, I felt awful about her dying that way. It didn't seem a bit fair—she was a nice lady."

"Not a clue," Angela said. "They don't even know why she was killed. All they know is, it wasn't robbery. At least, it doesn't seem like it."

"Robbery! What did she have anybody'd want to steal?" Terri said. "Robbie told me the house brought just enough to buy her a place in that retirement center of yours. It must be awfully expensive to get in. And Robbie says there's monthly rent, too . . . Well, of course there was her jewelry. She was selling off the stuff to make the monthly rent, huh? It was family things she owned, so she told me. She must have hated to sell it."

"I don't think she sold anything," Caledonia said slowly. "At least not while she was with us. News travels fast around there, and nobody heard . . . of course, her nephew said she lost a brooch . . . but I don't believe he said she sold anything."

Terri looked surprised. "Sure she did. I bought a nice little ruby bracelet of hers, and . . ." She turned to Angela. "Well, pardon me for saying this, if it's something you don't want people to know—but didn't you buy that pendant from her? The one you've got on? There can't be two like that in the world, and it's either hers or one exactly like hers!"

Angela's hand flew upward defensively to the crystal and diamond pendant, as Terri spoke. Then she stood up and walked over to the young woman and held the pendant out. "Take a good look . . . are you sure this is hers? Because I just bought it today from a dealer in Camden . . ."

Terri also rose and tucked her arm under Angela's, guiding her toward the view window. "Come over to the light a second . . . let me take a good look. Sure that's hers. I'm positive. Well, almost positive."

"Oh, dear," Angela said, unhappily. "I'm certain there's no problem about it, but there seems to be some kind of mixup . . . I'll ask my jeweler, of course. He probably bought it from her . . . but . . . well . . . the thing is, he said he got it from someone else, not from Mrs. Gardner."

"Gee." Terri shook her head. "I'm almost sure it's hers. Could somebody else have sold it for her?"

"I'll ask the jeweler."

"But there's my bracelet, too. She sold that. Cheap, too, or I couldn't have bought it. So I know she was selling stuff."

"It's all really very puzzling," Angela said with a sigh.

"We were wondering, too," Caledonia boomed out, "whether your friend Mrs. Gardner ever knew a Rollo Bagwell?"

"Oh! Oh, yes," Angela said, with a start. She had been daydreaming about her jewelry. But she realized there was more to be accomplished before they took their leave. "Or an Enrique Ortelano? That is, Henry Ortelano. His name was spelled in the Mexican way, but we called him by the English form . . . Henry. When we talked to him, I mean. I mean, not that we didn't talk to him when we saw him, of course—but we didn't see him very often, you see. I mean . . ."

"Angela!" Caledonia stopped the spate of explanations. "I'm sure Mrs. Wal—Terri—isn't interested. All we need to find out is if your neighbor knew them . . . if they called on her . . ."

Terri Walters just shook her head.

"You have heard of Bagwell and Ortelano, haven't you?" Caledonia said. "You surely read about them in the papers."

Terri still looked blank. "Are they astronauts or something?"

"Local people," Angela said. "Those are the men who were killed at Camden-sur-Mer the week before Mrs. Gardner died."

Terri shivered. "Ooooh! Well, I guess I do remember

reading about them, but of course I wouldn't remember their names. You mean they were killed right there in your apartment house, too?"

"Well, not exactly. More like on the patio," Angela said. "In the garden. In fact, Rollo was our gardener."

"No kidding," Terri said. And there the conversation sat, lumpish and unmoving.

Finally Angela got to her feet. "Is there anything else you can think of that we should know about her?" she asked, but in an offhand way, as though she were really no longer interested. In fact, she was beginning to fidget. She wanted to leave—to get home—to get to the lieutenant and to tell him about their expedition. To talk to Singletary . . .

Angela needn't have fidgeted. Terri Walters seemed anxious to get them out of her house, after that. It was as though, having told them all that she had, she now regretted it. At any rate, that was Angela's impression, as they were edged toward the door and out onto the walk. As they climbed into the car, they heard the TV go back on inside the house. Perhaps Terri wasn't anxious to have them gone, but only to get back to watching her favorite quiz show.

As she had promised, Emma did a U-turn at the dead end and headed the car back toward Camden at her habitual thirty-five miles an hour, right through Escondido's residential districts and onto the freeway, while Angela reviewed the visit for Tootsie's benefit, talking incessantly. Angela was in the front seat next to Emma, but as they drove along, she turned half-backward, so that Caledonia and Tootsie in the back seat would be sure to hear everything she had to say. Even more important, that position kept her from having to watch Emma's driving.

Emma was cheerfully oblivious to Angela's ill-controlled apprehension. She drove easily, her hands relaxed on the wheel, seemingly unaware that in turning out of Tarnhouse Lane, she had driven over the curb and flattened a hibiscus bush. She sailed through a stop sign, although she appeared to be looking straight at it, squinting slightly against the setting sun. And as they came to the section of downtown Escondido that had the one-way streets, she turned confidently onto the wrong one; fortunately, nobody else had entered that section at the same time, and she exited the one-way street, blissfully unaware of having done anything unusual.

So Angela talked and studiously watched the back seat. Tootsie, her eyes slightly glazed in bewilderment (she had not yet understood what the problem with the jewelry was), watched Angela. Emma watched something ahead of the car—presumably the road. But Caledonia watched everything—including Emma's driving—and her smile was rigid on her face, her knuckles white as she gripped her hands together and hung onto the arm of her seat.

"You were saying?" she primed Angela through clenched teeth.

"That it's so embarrassing . . ." Angela said. "So embarrassing. Because Mr. Singletary really is completely honest. I just know it. And now we're going to have to ask him all over again about some of this jewelry . . ." She lifted the pendant slightly so the women in the back could see it. Emma turned her head at the movement . . .

"No need for you to look, Emma," Caledonia said quickly. "It's the same pendant you saw before! There's— there's a truck . . ." Emma swerved back into her own lane, and the truck passed them safely, though Caledonia was able to catch sight of a startled expression on the driver's face as he wrenched the wheel to give their car a wide berth.

Tootsie waved a hand like a schoolchild asking to leave the room. "Wait, wait, wait . . . I don't understand. Why do you have to talk to the jeweler?"

"Because," Angela said rapidly, "Mrs. Walters says this pendant is something that once belonged to Lena Gardner, and that's two pieces of jewelry I own that I've been accused of stealing from her or buying from her or something, although neither one is supposed to be hers at all! They're supposed to belong to a girl who inherited them from her mother. You know, if these pieces were worth thousands of dollars each, I could understand. But they're hardly the crown jewels."

Finally Caledonia put a hand forward to rest like lead on Angela's shoulder. "There's nothing you can do about all this tonight, girl. Now, we sympathize with you—we certainly do. I know you're upset and embarrassed—but right now, don't you think it's more important that you keep relatively quiet and let Emma concentrate on her driving? Sorry, Emma, but I can't concentrate, and I don't know how you can . . ."

In the few remaining blocks till the car reached their street, they sat silent, except when Tootsie spoke up to apologize to Caledonia. "I meant to say before—I'm sorry I made a noise when you were telling that story, Cal," she said. "You know, back at the Walters house when we first arrived? I just couldn't help it. I don't remember when I've heard you tell an outright lie like you did!"

"Oh?" Caledonia managed to choke out, as Emma's right front bumper clipped the leg of a newspaper vending machine on the curb as she cornered off Camden's main street, whimsically named Maine Street. "Did I tell a lie?"

"You most certainly did," Tootsie said stoutly. It didn't seem to bother Tootsie at all that Emma again swung the car very wide at the next turn, forcing a pedestrian who had ventured off the sidewalk on the opposite corner to jump backward to safety. He was a spry young fellow and fortunately able to make the leap without straining anything but his nerves. "You told that Walters woman that we were going to give the eulogy at the memorial service. I couldn't help but make a noise. But you know, you didn't have to step on my foot quite so hard!"

"Oh!" There was a gasp and an intense sigh from Caledonia. "We're *here*!"

They were just pulling into the little Camden parking lot down the block from the main building. Emma rolled over the curbing as she turned into the lot, and as she pulled into a parking space, she let the car nudge hard against the back fence—not hard enough to dent anything—just hard enough so that you knew she was tight up against something very solid.

"Well done, Emma, well done!" Caledonia said, clambering with difficulty—but with gratitude—out of the back seat. "Okay, Tootsie, I apologize for stepping on your foot. That wasn't necessary. But the lie was. I couldn't think of any way to explain why we were asking questions. And speaking of that, I'm going to suggest that none of us says anything about the jewelry—not where we can be overheard. Let's keep this our secret until Angela has time to tell Martinez tomorrow. Is that all right with you?"

Emma put her car keys into her purse and snapped it firmly shut. "It's fine with me. I'll certainly keep quiet." She sighed and stretched her arms out. "Oh, I just feel so *good* whenever I get back from a trip!"

"I know just what you mean," Caledonia said, and Angela gave her a meaningful elbow in her ribs . . . or at least where Angela assumed Caledonia's ribs to be, under the layers of flesh.

"Naturally, I'll agree to keep our trip secret," Tootsie said, with a little frown on her face. "Because I haven't quite understood—you know—about the jeweler and all . . . maybe someone will explain . . ."

"Tomorrow, Tootsie," Caledonia assured her. "We'll explain it all tomorrow. After Angela's had a chance to talk to the lieutenant. Maybe then we'll know more than we do now ourselves. I agree that it's confusing now. Even Angela's confused."

Tootsie was appeased, and they walked together back to the building, where they separated to go to their own rooms. Caledonia took the chance to pat Angela soothingly on the arm, just as they entered the lobby, as though to say, "Nothing to worry about," but she did worry, all the same—both of them did. For both had the same nagging sense of something important that was passing them by.

Chapter 13

ANGELA WAS waiting in Camden's lobby when Swanson wheeled the official car into position under the broad canopy that shielded the main entrance, and he and Martinez swung through the double front door and turned toward the dining room to start their morning's work with a hearty breakfast.

Angela pounced before they got halfway from the entrance to the dining room and told her story excitedly, breathlessly, as she pattered along beside them. Martinez handed her gracefully ahead as they reached the dining room, so the three of them would not have to attempt an entrance while walking abreast.

"Join us for coffee and tell us the rest of the details, Mrs. Benbow," Martinez invited.

"But I thought you'd want to see Mr. Singletary *right away* about the pendant," she protested.

"Oh, definitely," Martinez said amiably. "But he won't be at work till nine-thirty, and there's really no use talking to him by phone while he's still at home, because the record books are back at the shop." Angela looked disappointed, but trotted obediently along to have a second cup of coffee while the men ate.

By eight-thirty the two policemen were finishing their bacon and eggs, and Angela excused herself to hurry down the garden to Caledonia's cottage. "I really would like Cal to come with us. I mean, she knows everything about it ... and she has such good ideas ..." she explained.

Martinez grinned. "That's fine with me. I already told

you I would be happier if you traveled in pairs, while this case is still unsolved. All three attacks have been against people who were alone."

"But this is broad daylight! All our murders happened at night! Or not at night—at twilight, really."

"Owl light," Martinez said softly.

"Beg pardon?"

"Owl light. A romantic way of referring to the time of dusk. British, I seem to remember. But that's neither here nor there. The point is, you don't want to take anything for granted. You must be careful at all times—owl light or not. So by all means do go and get Mrs. Wingate to join us. Provided she's awake and stirring." Caledonia's reputation as a late sleeper was well known.

For a wonder, Caledonia was already nearly dressed when she answered the door to Angela's excited knocking.

"Well, I was pretty het up about all this, too," Caledonia confessed, smoothing the folds of her raspberry and lime jersey caftan and putting on the rope of pearls she always wore about her neck, whatever other ornaments and jewels she might choose. "That's why I'm up so early. I thought about it some before I went to bed last night and again this morning—and all I can see is that if there's no mistake—if those things really are Mrs. Gardner's—somebody is going to have a lot of explaining to do. And maybe it's that jeweler friend of yours."

"Or this Ruthie person. Don't forget her." Angela sighed. "And either way, Robbie really would seem to be involved somehow, wouldn't he? And I simply hate that! I really like that youngster! Of course, he's terribly young! He's really more like a boy than like a man, in spite of Terri Walters' having a crush on him!"

"You registered that too, did you?"

"Oh, of course. She said he really wasn't her type, but she got all dewy-eyed when she talked about him. Anyway, that's what I thought."

"Me too. Though personally I can't see it. I like men with a little substance to them. That skinny kid . . ."

"Actually, he's fairly wiry, Cal. Remember how he worked carrying his aunt's things in?"

Caledonia humphed. "Looks like a wimp to me, girl. A bookworm. Or is it a computer worm, these days?"

Angela tossed her head in disagreement. "He's a nice young man, whether he has muscles or brains or not. I worried so about it all last night, it kept me rolling and tossing for simply hours!"

"Hah!" Caledonia was bending slightly to lock her apartment door behind her, so her explosion of disbelief was slightly muffled. "I know you, girl. You worried a whole five minutes after you finished your bath and hit the mattress ... then it was Snore City. Am I right?"

"Well, but I worried while I bathed, and before and after my bath. And while I was getting into bed. I really can't help it," Angela protested, "if I fall asleep easily when I'm in a horizontal position. It's a conditioned reflex, that's all. It doesn't mean I'm not worried about all this."

The women arrived in the dining room and Martinez rose to gesture them to the "Official Police Table," as the residents now called the table in the corner. Once they had settled themselves, while Angela continued telling Martinez the details of their visit to Terri Walters in Escondido and of all they'd surmised and guessed and reasoned, Martinez was treated to his first closeup view of Caledonia's idea of a light breakfast.

"I'm afraid I can't eat much," she said to Chita Cassidy when the girl came to take her order. "I'm not sick or anything—just upset and worried over this business with the murders." So Caledonia drank just a water tumbler full of boysenberry juice and ate a half-dozen little link sausages, two eggs over easy, four slices of whole wheat toast, a bowl of milk and cereal with a sliced banana, and finally a couple of fresh-baked sweet rolls with butter. All of this was preceded, accompanied, and followed by hot coffee.

"At least you'll keep your strength up, Mrs. Wingate," Martinez finally remarked in an awestricken voice, and then immediately hoped that he hadn't sounded too disrespectful.

But Caledonia just smiled. "Nothing makes me lose my

appetite completely, including having the flu. I remember the last time I had the flu—I was dreadfully ill all day and then ravenous by supper time. I was too weak and sick-feeling to eat without help. But I managed a light meal—a small salad, a little steak, and a couple of slices of Texas toast," she said reminiscently. "Murder doesn't blunt my appreciation of food—because nothing does! And you can't get me riled up merely by acknowledging what's true, either."

"Well," Martinez said, amused, "I really wasn't trying to get smart or start an argument with you. I found your breakfast menu intriguing. Unusual. That's all."

"I take it," Caledonia said, finishing off a final cup of coffee, "that you want the two of us to go with you to talk to Singletary, and that's why I'm breakfasting with our favorite policemen?"

Martinez nodded. "And, of course, there's always the chance you might think of something you heard or saw that Mrs. Benbow hasn't remembered to tell us. But if you're done with breakfast, perhaps we'll just drive down to the jeweler's store. Together."

And thus it was that the four of them came into Singletary's shop almost the moment he opened for business.

The jeweler's brow furrowed as he saw them. "More trouble?" he said.

"More information," Martinez corrected him. "We need to ask more questions. First of all, are you sure the pieces you sold Mrs. Benbow—the gold brooch with the black enamel, and the crystal-and-diamond pendant—are you sure they came from the group of pieces your little lady Ruthie brought in?"

Singletary spread his hands. "I'd have sworn . . . but let me get the records out and check again to be sure." He pulled out the large, black, leather-bound book. "Here. You come around the counter with me, lieutenant, and we'll look together." He opened the register on the flat surface of the glass case. "Here it is," he said, moving his finger to a series of entries. "I was right."

"Okay, I see it," Martinez said. " 'Virginia Ruth Robertson.' And the list of pieces . . . yes, you've listed the ones we're interested in. What do you know about the girl, John?"

"Known her since she was little! Of course, she's just a kid, and kids these days ... I really knew her folks better than I know her." Singletary sighed and put the ledger back with the others. "You ladies ought to be able to tell the lieutenant about Ruthie. You must know her fairly well yourselves."

Caledonia and Angela looked at each other. "No, I don't remember any 'Ruthie.' Up at Camden, do you mean?" Caledonia asked, waving a hand in a westerly direction, more or less toward the retirement center.

"She works on the kitchen staff," Singletary went on. "You might not see her every day, but once in a while she waits table in the dining room. I tried to tell you about her when you were down here before."

"Oh, dear," Angela said, guiltily. She vaguely remembered his starting to tell her all about the girl he called Ruthie, and she also remembered that she had interrupted him because the story had sounded as though it would be dull. "Of course. And I never did let you finish explaining about her. Oh, I'm so sorry!"

"Well, I probably told you that she's a hard-working girl. She has two part-time jobs I know about besides working in the kitchen up at your retirement center."

"Three jobs! Good glory!" Caledonia sounded impressed, and probably was, since three jobs would mean rising early as well as working late.

"One is as receptionist to a chiropractor who splits his time between here and an office in Oceanside. Ruthie announces his patients and gets their records out and sends his bills and answers his phone all morning long, as soon as she leaves your place after breakfast. Then she comes back to Camden to work your lunch-time shift. And when the kitchen's slicked up after lunch, she goes off to the movie house in the mall and she's the matinee ticket seller. I expect that when they've started the last matinee, she just has time to run back to Camden and work the dinner shift."

"Very commendable ambition," Martinez said. "But that

doesn't tell us much about her except that she hasn't much free time."

"And that she needs money," Angela put in sharply.

"Well, that's why I wasn't really very surprised when she wanted to sell her mother's jewelry," Singletary said. "At least—well, she told me those were her mother's things. Her parent's didn't leave her much. Long illnesses eat up all the savings, you know. First it was her father's heart attack—then her mother got cancer—it took nearly everything they had. Ruthie never did get the chance to go even to business school—and she wasn't prepared for any career. So she picks up these odd jobs. With the three of them, she makes enough to keep going, I suppose. At any rate, that's why it seemed logical to me she'd want to sell her mother's old jewelry. I mean— well, I believed her, you see." He sighed and fell into a mournful silence.

Caledonia was still shaking her head. "Ruthie . . . Ruthie . . ." she mused. "I thought I knew all the girls. There's Suzi . . . and Laura . . . and Mary Jean . . . and Ginnie . . ."

"Well," Singletary said, "maybe that's her. Ginnie. Her first name is Virginia. But we always called her—"

"Is your Ruthie a pretty girl with light auburn hair and kind of amber eyes?" Angela asked excitedly. When he nodded, she didn't wait for him to speak. "Then that is her. It is Ginnie. You see, we don't get to know the last names of these youngsters who help out now and then or who work entirely in the kitchen. We hardly even get to know their first names!"

"Names aside," said Caledonia impatiently, "I still can't imagine what the connection in all this could be . . ."

"But we'll surely find out," Martinez promised, looking at his wristwatch. "It's ten-thirty—she'll be reporting to work soon. I think we'll all be getting back up to Camden and see what we can find out. Thanks, John—we appreciate your help."

"Listen," Singletary said, worriedly. "She's just a kid . . . and her folks were decent people. So if she needs help—if there's anything I can do . . ."

"Trust me to call you," Martinez said. "Shorty?"

Swanson swung out the door, holding it for the two ladies and loping ahead of them to the official car by the curb, and then again opening the door and ushering them into the back seat. As Martinez joined him in the front, Shorty said hopefully, "Siren?"

Martinez shook his head. "Not even for the amusement of our two passengers, Shorty. You know how I hate it. Let's just drive quietly back up the hill. There's plenty of time."

And so there was. Ginnie-Ruthie didn't report to Mrs. Schmitt till 11:00 A.M. Perhaps more people had come to her chiropractor for an adjustment that day, or perhaps there were more bills and overdue notices to send out than usual. Whatever the reason, Ginnie swung into the kitchen breathless from running the ten blocks between her two jobs.

"They want to see you in the sewing room," Mrs. Schmitt said, without preface or elaboration. "Now."

"But the tables ... lunch ..." The girl gestured to the trays of silverware waiting to be set out at the tables in the dining room.

"The waitresses will help if they have to. You just get upstairs. Take these back stairs here—they're closer." And Mrs. Schmitt watched while Ginnie climbed the narrow service staircase that ran to the second floor and brought its users out nearly opposite the door to the big room the police were using for their interviews.

Angela—having heard the lieutenant send for Ginnie—had lingered purposely in the sewing room, chatting pleasantly with "her" policemen, hoping to be able to hear the interview. But when time passed and Ginnie did not appear, Angela gave up and started to leave. At that very moment the girl appeared, hesitant, in the doorway. Angela turned hopefully back into the room, curiosity shining from her face. But to her disappointment, Martinez seated Ginnie by the table, then showed Angela politely out.

"But it's my mystery—my jewelry—" she whispered to him at the door.

He nodded, amused. "Don't worry, Mrs. Benbow. You'll be the first to know, if we find out you're really handling stolen property. And I know you'd burst if your curiosity wasn't satisfied. But I must be the judge of how much to tell you, how much to hold back."

"Hold back!"

He nodded. "I will not tell you something I think it's dangerous for you to know. You must trust my judgment. Have a good lunch—we'll probably see you in the dining room." And he swung the door shut, leaving her in the shadowed hallway, her lower lip stuck out, at least metaphorically speaking, in a pout that was anything but metaphoric.

If Angela had been a child walking along outdoors, she'd have scuffed her shoes and kicked at pebbles and tin cans in her sulk. But as it was, she could mutter to herself (after looking carefully to see that no one was listening—she tried so hard not to let anyone notice, if she talked to herself), but that was small release for frustration.

"I need a tin can or a little rock to kick," she said as she got off the elevator.

"Why?" Tootsie Armstrong said, walking across Angela's line of vision from her right.

"Oh, I'm just feeling frustrated," Angela said hastily, "because we don't know anything more than we do about our murders. That's all." She had no intention of being more specific.

"Come along to the library," Tootsie said. "Work a jigsaw puzzle. Or look at the newspaper before lunch. Reading about other people's troubles might make your own seem less important!"

"Why, Tootsie," Angela said, surprised. "That's a very good suggestion. Taking the mind off does help—you've made a really profound observation."

"I have?" Tootsie smiled rather vaguely. "Well, reading's what I always do, anyhow. Right now I'm reading the most wonderful book—all about place names here in California. I do about a chapter a day ... before meals. It's big and heavy so I just leave it in the library. But those Spaniards named their cities for the strangest things ... did you know that 'Vista' means 'view'? But the town called 'Vista' doesn't have a view ... at least, I always think of the ocean as *the* view in California, and they can't see it from six miles inland." Tootsie was chattering away and Angela had no trouble ignoring her and letting her talk, while her own mind moved around pieces of a puzzle far different from the jigsaw that awaited her on the big library table.

All four walls in the room designated as Camden's library were fitted with bookshelves, wherever doors and windows did not intrude, and most of the shelves were full. Almost all the books were donations from the private libraries of new residents who found their apartments too small for them to keep any but a very few old favorites. The largest number of the books were novels, and the largest number of the novels were Westerns, mysteries, and lurid romances with embarrassing pictures on the paper covers— the kind of romantic novel one can take up just before bedtime, read for a few minutes, and put down again. If you take it up and read a bit more tomorrow night, well and good; if you forget and reread the same chapter twice, you probably won't even notice. And if you never pick the novel up again, no harm done either, for you can predict the plot long before you read the author's version. These were not classics.

At one end of the room there was an oak pedestal stand that held a gigantic unabridged dictionary, and in one remote corner of the bottom shelves there stood an encyclopedia and a few reference works of the popular type. That was the corner that drew Tootsie Armstrong, who pulled a copy of *California Place Names and Their Meanings* from its shelf and sat down to read.

Almost reluctantly, Angela followed Tootsie's suggestion and went to work on the jigsaw laid out on the central table that ran the length of the room and held, besides the inevitable puzzle, the latest newspapers. Camden-sur-Mer subscribed to all local papers, but most of the jigsaws were, like the books, contributed by the residents and were available for anyone's use. Those really addicted to jigsaws—or monumentally bored with television—could take puzzles back to their own apartments to work.

But someone always started one jigsaw on the central table, and people coming into the library would stop and add a piece or two, then go on to read the daily paper or find a book. Little by little the puzzle grew—first the outer borders, then the identifiable figures—an animal or a human being—a bowl of roses on a table, the door of a barn, a boat at a dock. The last parts to be worked were those amorphous stretches of forest, sky, and water with their confusing lines and blended colors. At last someone would sit down and fit in the last ten or twenty pieces. The completed puzzle would stay on the table for everyone to admire for a day or two, and then someone would break it apart, put the pieces into the box, file the box on a shelf (beneath the small collection of science fiction—not a popular item for Camden's readers), and take out a new puzzle.

Angela was not really fascinated with jigsaws, but as she fiddled idly with a few pieces, she found herself putting together the shape of a sundial ... then a rosebush grew under her fingers. Neither had a place in the puzzle that was obvious yet, so she set the finished mini-puzzles aside till more of the framework would be complete. She picked up the box from which the pieces came and saw that she was working on a formal rose garden with white statuary, backed by Lombardy poplars. Italian horticulture, she thought. European, at any rate. American gardens were much more given to free-form and random plantings, fewer formal, sculptured outlines. Less planning, more a riot of color. She yawned. Something was nagging at her subconscious again as she worked and fitted pieces, chose and discarded. Something about the roses and the sundial and ... she yawned again.

"Oh, dear," Angela said aloud. "I don't want to go to sleep before lunch! And after lunch is quite enough."

Mr. Brighton appeared in the doorway, leaning heavily on his cane. "Ah, dear ladies," he greeted them. "Charming to find such lovely company while I read my daily paper." He moved forward and gasped with pain at each step.

"Can I help you?" Angela said with concern.

"No, no, dear lady. It's just a bad day, that's all."

"Can't they do anything about that, Mr. Brighton?"

"They're talking," he said sadly, easing himself into a chair at the central table, "about a hip-joint replacement.

Frankly, I'm a little apprehensive about losing my own bones and having to go through life with a stainless-steel ball-joint in a plastic, teflon-lined socket. Some days—like today—I'm tempted. Other times, I just think—well, I'm getting on, and it's only a few more years ... 'Time is the great physician!' as Disraeli said. Or was that Sir Walter Raleigh? No, I think he was the one who touched the headsman's ax and proclaimed it '. . . a sharp remedy, but a sure cure for all ills.' Same principle, of course. The point is, I'll be gone soon enough, and what's the use then of that elaborate operation and all the expense?" He sighed and pulled the daily paper over towards himself.

"Oh, dear Mr. Brighton, I wish you wouldn't talk like that," Tootsie said. "It's so gloomy of you!"

"Not me, dear lady," he said, smiling over at her. "Disraeli. He's the gloomy one, not I—I was merely quoting. Of course it might have been Raleigh. I must look that up one day."

Angela moved one seat over, closer to him. "Mr. Brighton, I hate to have you feeling so blue," she said sympathetically. "I wish there were some way to cheer you up ... Have you talked to Hazel Hanson? I mean, she had the same operation two years ago, and she walks a half-mile before breakfast and a half-mile after supper every day."

"She does that much, eh?" Brighton sounded interested.

"She surely does. I wish you'd talk to her. She might change your mind about the operation. She can give you the name of her doctor."

"It was Disraeli," Tootsie said.

"I beg your pardon?"

"Here ..." Tootsie held out a heavy reference book—*The Oxford Dictionary of Quotations*—which she held open, her finger pointing to the left-hand page.

"Ah, yes, dear Mrs. Armstrong," Brighton said, peering at the printing. "So it is. Disraeli for sure. Do you see, Mrs. Benbow? The relevant quotation ... 'time the physician' seems to be from a book called *Henrietta Temple*. Ever read it? I never even heard of it! But then I never had pretensions ..."

Angela was peering into the collection of quotations, but

looking at the right-hand page, which was closest to her.
"Well, can you believe ... listen to this." She read aloud,
"Let me die eating ortolans to the sound of soft music."

"What does that mean?" Tootsie said. "What is that
you're reading to us?"

"I haven't any idea what it means—it's just another quotation from the same author, Disraeli. But the word *ortolans*
caught my eye. Because it was like the name of our soft-
drink man. You know ... Enrique Ortelano?"

"Henry. Certainly. But what on earth is an ortolan anyway?" Brighton said. "It sounds like a fancy cookie!"

"Maybe that is where they got *Oreo* from!" Tootsie
cried.

Angela ignored her and went across the room to the unabridged dictionary, ponderous on its oak stand. She
couldn't recall ever having used it before in all her years in
Camden, though it had stood there as long as she could remember coming into the library. "Let me see—*orthograph,
orthopteran, orthorhombic, Ortler Mountains* ... here it
is—*ortolan—a small brownish bird eaten as a delicacy.*"

"Oh," Tootsie said. "How disappointing. It's only roast
chicken he was talking about. I thought it was going to be
something romantic and exotic and ... foreign!"

"Do you mean to tell me our soft-drink man, Mr.
Ortelano, was named for a bird?" Mr. Brighton said curiously.

"It says here that *ortolan* is *applied to any one of a
number of birds like the bobolink,*" Angela read.

"Mr. Henry Bobolink?" Tootsie laughed. "Oh, I know I
shouldn't. He's dead. But that's so funny ..."

"Surely he wasn't the Spanish equivalent of 'Mr. Bobolink,' " Mr. Brighton smiled.

Angela went on reading. *"French, from Provençal, from
Latin hortolanus—horticulturalist."*

Brighton closed his eyes. "Hortelano ... Ortelano ...
yes, that's it. I think you've got the translation. I seem
to remember from my Spanish in school—a man who
works in horticulture, a gardener. But they don't pronounce the *H* in Spanish, so they dropped it in the spell-
ing. The same way he was called 'Henry' without the

H—'Enrique.' Do you see? 'Enrique Ortelano' is 'Henry Horticulturalist' or something like that. He wasn't Mr. Bobolink—he was Mr. Gardener. Dear lady, is something the matter?"

Angela had stood up and she was quivering like a newly tuned violin string. Her eyes were snapping with excitement. "Oh, oh, my, oh, dear—oh, don't you see it?" she bubbled. "Oh ... I have to go and tell our Lieutenant Martinez ... because that is the connection between the three murder victims! Mrs. Gardner, Mr. Ortelano-Hortelano-Horticulturalist-Gardener, and Rollo our gardener! In one way or another, they were all three gardeners!"

Tootsie looked a trifle doubtful. "But, that doesn't make sense," she said nervously. "Why would anybody want to kill three gardeners?"

"Well, I don't know! That's what the police are here to find out, surely," Angela said impatiently. "All I know is, that's a connection nobody's seen before. And I should tell the lieutenant! Right *away*!"

Brighton heaved himself up to his feet. "I agree. It doesn't make much sense to us, but then nothing about these murders does. But it may to them. And if it doesn't, they still should know about it. My dear lady—"

They were interrupted by the sound of the Westminster chimes ringing their little tune that signaled the opening of the dining room.

"Oh!" Angela said, excitedly. "They'll be coming down to lunch. Will you both excuse me if I run ahead?"

"Please do," Brighton said. "I'll be slower than anybody else today. And that suits me—I don't want to be walking in a crowd and risk being jostled."

"Oh, go ahead, Angela, don't wait for me," Tootsie said. "I'll be putting books away and tidying a bit before I go in to lunch ..." Tootsie, for all she was disorganized about her own life, had taken over the library chores and managed things very well.

So Angela skipped on ahead to find the policemen with her latest idea. Sherlock Holmes might have disapproved—it was more intuition than solid deductive reasoning, perhaps.

But Angela knew that her intuition was often more reliable than her logic, and she'd have told Sherlock that to his face, if she had been able!

Chapter 14

IT WAS an intense disappointment to Angela that neither Swanson nor Martinez emerged for lunch. It would appear the men were spending their lunch hour working in the second-floor sewing room, or at least that was a logical deduction. Just as Caledonia and Angela had reached approximately the halfway point in their main dish, a succulent stuffed pepper redolent with Greek seasonings, Chita came bustling through the dining room with a tray of covered dishes.

"Oh, dear! That must be for our policemen!" Angela said. "I hate that!"

"What on earth are you talking about?" Caledonia said, forking in another helping of the stuffed pepper. "This is great stuff! Hooooo, this spice ... You know, of course, that people will smell us coming a mile off, as soon as we exhale, all afternoon long! But who cares! I don't understand how you can hate something so good!"

"Not the food," Angela said impatiently. "The lieutenant not being here. And Officer Swanson. I *so* want to tell them about my find!"

"Oh, that. I was thinking about the stuffed peppers. Another triumph."

"Of course it was mostly luck," Angela said modestly.

"What?"

"How I found out about the gardeners being the murder victims. It's really too obvious, once you see it, to be an accident. The lieutenant kept saying there was nothing that tied the victims together except this place. But now, you see, we *know* there's something else . . . a profession. Two were named 'gardener,' and one *was* a gardener!"

Caledonia shivered hugely. "It's frightening, is what I think. More frightening than before we knew that about the gardeners. Because what on earth can it mean except that somebody's flipped out completely? It's like that Sergeant Benson said . . . remember all those funny words he had for 'going crazy'? But he was right. Someone has one foot out of the stirrups! Otherwise why make a dead set—no pun intended—on gardeners?"

As they left the dining room later, Angela insisted that she was going to her apartment for her usual nap. But Caledonia guessed—correctly—that first Angela would wander by the second-floor sewing room to see if Martinez was available. Her discovery was not going to let her merely go off to take a postlunch nap. It was exactly the same when she was a child and her mother gave her a dime. She could not rest until the money was gone—and now she knew she couldn't rest until she had told Martinez her discovery. Of course, half her motivation, if the truth were known, was to bask in his praise, for she felt that she had been unusually clever.

As she approached the east end of the second floor, the door to the sewing room swung wide and Robbie Hammond came out. He was mopping his brow. "Wow!" he said. "Mrs. Benbow, they're in a mean mood. If they've sent for you, watch out! They really took me apart in there." He grinned. "Not that you can't hold your own, the way I hear it . . . people around here say you can defend yourself pretty well . . ."

"Are you all right, Robbie?" Angela said, concerned. "You're awfully pale."

"You would be too. Those fellows think I killed my aunt! I can't believe it but they made it perfectly obvious that's what they think!"

Angela patted his arm. "There, there . . . you may be mistaken. After all, your aunt wasn't even a resident here at Camden when the other two were killed, so they couldn't think you murdered those two, could they? And the deaths are definitely connected with each other! There's a pattern, you see—Oh, it's so exciting. Promise not to tell anyone, but they were all gardeners!"

"Excuse me? This—this is a theory of some kind?"

"Yes! I just worked it out! It has to do with the names and what Rollo did for a living—oh, dear—it's so hard to explain. But believe me, the clue is that they were all gardeners."

Robbie raised his eyebrows. "Well, I don't think I quite understand. But if you're right, I suppose things would look a little brighter for me, wouldn't they? I mean, I don't have any grudge against gardeners. So I'd be out of it as a suspect. I guess," he grinned at her crookedly, "I should wish you luck in convincing the lieutenant. You're on your way right now to tell him about all this 'gardener' thing?"

"Certainly. He's got to know that all three murders are part of a pattern. It's very important! And I share everything I know with the lieutenant," she boasted. "He relies on my opinion," she beamed, obviously very pleased with herself.

Robbie only looked gloomy. "Mrs. Benbow, the police may just be too dumb to see what you're pointing out to them! After the way they went after me, I don't have too much respect for their intelligence, believe me." He sighed. "I mean, you can always figure out what a computer's going to do, because you know that in a given set of circumstances, it will always do the same thing. Computers are so logical." He sounded genuinely admiring. "I really can't figure human beings. These police . . . they seem to jump in their thinking. First they're going in one direction, and then all of a sudden . . . I mean, out of a clear blue sky, why am I the favorite suspect? It doesn't make any sense!"

Angela patted his arm again, reassuringly. "Well, not to you, Robbie. But I assure you that the lieutenant—"

The door behind Robbie opened abruptly and Martinez peered out. "Oh, it's you, Mrs. Benbow," he said. "I thought I heard voices . . . please come in." He hesitated, glaring at Robbie. "That will be all for now, Hammond, but don't forget we'll want to talk to you again."

Angela eased in past his outstretched arm holding the

door, and Robbie started off down the hall toward the elevator, his shoulders bent under the weight of his cares.

"Well, now, Mrs. Benbow, I was about to get in touch with you. Then Swanson reminded me you take a nap after lunch each day. So we didn't call. But here you are anyway."

Swanson looked up from a double-decker sandwich and grinned over a frill of lettuce. "We figured there was time to let you sleep, ma'am, while we finished our meal. We couldn't get to the dining room today, what with two people to talk to, but they sent something up."

"I know," Angela smiled at him. "I saw Chita staggering under that tray-full of food! Enough for four of you. But you seem to have done all right with it. And besides . . ." She broke off sheepishly. "Oh, dear . . . Caledonia says I wander around the point, sometimes, and I do believe she's right. Because I act like I'm only here to pass the time of day, and I have such news . . ."

Martinez gestured her to a chair. "Do sit down. Do you mind terribly if I eat as well? We've been working hard this morning, and we'll go flat out this afternoon."

"Oh, please," she beamed at him. "Do go right ahead. I don't mind."

"A cup of coffee for you?" He gestured at the pot and the cups on the tray. She nodded and he poured for her, then turned to his own sandwich while she added cream and sugar.

"Now," she said, "may I talk while you eat?"

He smiled. "You're obviously controlling yourself with the greatest of difficulty. So please go right ahead. I promise I can listen over the sounds of lunch."

"Well," she said, hitching slightly forward in her chair, her eyes bright with excitement. "I think I've found the common factor."

"Common factor?"

"Among the murder victims! The thing that ties them together."

"I told you I already figured that out, Mrs. Benbow," Martinez said regretfully. "It's this place. And of course all three were stabbed, which may be significant."

"Oh, but it's more than that! It's the garden . . . and gardeners."

"Say what?" Shorty said, looking up from a slice of raw onion that he was adding to his second sandwich. "Gardeners?"

"Well, they were all killed in the garden . . . except for Mrs. Gardner, of course. But she *is* a gardener, you see. And so is Rollo Bagwell. I mean, that's her name and it's his job. But today I found out something else. The third element."

"Uh-oh," Martinez said. "And I think I see the rest of this coming. After all, I speak Spanish," he said to Shorty, "and *Hortelano* is Spanish for gardener."

"Of course," Angela explained, turning directly to Swanson, "our Henry Ortelano spelled it without the *H*, because the *H* was silent anyway. As in *Enrique*, which was his real name. But that's only *Henry* without the *H*, if you see what I mean. He was Henry *Hortelano*"—she deliberately pronounced the *H* in both words—"or *Enrique Ortelano*. Or actually," she finished triumphantly, "Henry Gardener! So you see, all three victims were gardeners!"

Swanson looked stunned, but Martinez nodded. "Believe it or not, I really do see. Furthermore, they were all killed at dusk while they were alone, they were all killed here at Camden, they were all stabbed to death. Oh, and they were all killed on a Tuesday night. The three deaths do have quite a lot in common, as you say."

Shorty, about to bite into his sandwich again, hesitated. "But what does that mean? It doesn't make much sense to me."

"That," said Angela loftily, "is because you're a sane person. The lieutenant said before that madmen have patterns the rest of us don't understand. I hope," she said, turning back to Martinez, "this means you won't be pestering that nice Hammond boy any more. I mean, just to begin with, he isn't crazy, and only a lunatic would run around killing gardeners! Of course Robbie only comes around here because his aunt is here—was here, I mean—and she moved here *after* the two men were killed!"

Shorty dived back into his sandwich and Martinez swallowed a bite of his own before he spoke. "I'll concede all that. Robbie Gardener looks less and less like our man, Mrs. Benbow. By the way, he has a perfectly simple explanation for the jewelry that's been worrying you."

"Oh, I was hoping you'd find something out. Well, is it mine or is it Mrs. Gardner's? Who owns it?"

"It's Mrs. Gardner's. Rather, it was. Robbie sold it, and Mrs. Gardner never knew about it. Apparently he used that girl Ruthie as his agent. I wanted you to know that, to help put your mind at ease. Well, perhaps not completely at ease. The matter is legally complicated, but eventually I think you can get the jewelry back. In the meantime, I'll need to hold it, till all the questions are resolved."

"I'll get it for you later," Angela said. But her little brow was furrowed. "I really don't understand. If Robbie sold the jewelry, what was all that Mrs. Gardner was talking about then? About *losing* the brooch?" she asked.

"Well, as he tells it, the family had limited resources, and when he decided his aunt had to come into the retirement center, he was able to meet the down payment by selling his aunt's house. But there was still the monthly rent here to worry about. It's not enough just to be admitted here; you need some income to maintain yourself. So he took the old jewelry Mrs. Gardner never wore and asked a longtime friend, this Virginia Ruth, to sell it for him."

"Oh! I see. Well, that makes sense. It doesn't sound very open and aboveboard, but it certainly makes sense." Angela thought a moment. "But why didn't he sell the jewelry himself? Why did he need someone to do it for him?"

"Good point, Mrs. Benbow. He says he didn't have time, what with helping pack the old lady up and giving that garage sale to get rid of furniture and things, and studying for his own exams at school . . . Virginia Ruth is a friend. One day he was talking about having to sell his aunt's jewelry, and Virginia Ruth offered to help because she knew this jeweler who bought old things. So he says."

"What does she say?"

"Oh, pretty nearly the same thing. Except she says *he* asked *her* to do it. I'm not sure it matters whose idea it was. They do agree on one thing—that he offered her five percent as a commission for the work involved."

"I see." Angela sipped her coffee a moment. "But why did she lie to Mr. Singletary and say the stuff was her mother's?"

"I'm not quite certain of that, either. She kept sobbing and it was hard to get her to talk sensibly. But she did say she didn't want Singletary to think badly of her. I took it that she meant it might have sounded mercenary if she told him she was doing it for a commission. Or maybe she thought Singletary would suspect that she stole it. At any rate, I fully intend to go over it all with her again. Perhaps later today."

Shorty looked up from his sandwich with a grin. "The lieutenant can handle almost any situation but a woman who cries," he said. "That girl started snuffling as soon as she got in here, and the lieutenant was embarrassed from that minute on."

Martinez glared Swanson to silence, but his voice was light as he spoke. "I don't like to admit it, but he's right. One thing about you, my dear Mrs. Benbow—no matter how you've felt about things, you've never wept in my presence. I suppose it's my early training," he sighed. "My mother and my two sisters were weepers. And it was a sure and certain way to get whatever they wanted from me and from my father!" He smiled mischievously. "My father was a wise man and taught me everything I know about women. But that is the one thing about which he told me nothing— what to do when a woman bursts into tears!"

Angela laughed in spite of herself. "I come from a generation that was taught not to display what we call 'negative' emotions in public—fear, anger, sorrow—My mother always said, *Laugh and the world laughs with you; Weep, and you weep alone* . . . and taught me to hold my tears till I was alone, in private. The younger generation is more demonstrative, of course—but possibly it's for the best. They won't have ulcers."

Martinez frowned. "I really don't like it. It's manipulative. Why, even young Hammond wept! In my book, men don't cry, Mrs. Benbow. But he did. When we questioned him closely about the jewelry, he just plain broke down and sobbed."

Angela shook her head. "He was upset at being suspected, no doubt. And it's all very bewildering to him. Besides, I'm sure he's still feeling perfectly awful about his aunt's death—his only living relative, after all. And she only died less than a week ago . . . at the hands of some lunatic who kills gardeners . . ."

Martinez added, "Always on Tuesday evenings, of course, and only here in your establishment, and only with a sharp-pointed instrument."

"You don't seem to be taking my suggestion very seriously, Lieutenant. You disappoint me. And I think the boy had a valid reason to be upset."

"So do I. But I'm less charitable about him than you are. I think part of why he wept is that his conscience is hurting him. It certainly should be. He deceived his aunt shamelessly. He signed her into this place over her strenuous objections, he supported her here by selling her treasured family mementos without even telling her, and he generally acted as though she were feeble-minded. When she missed her brooch, he told her she'd lost it, and that made her feel even more unhappy and insecure about her failing memory. In my opinion, that was cruel and arrogant."

"Well, she was failing," Angela reminded him unhappily.

"Ah, but not all that fast," he retorted. "You said yourself she acted fairly normal most of the time. And the thing that galls me is that he nearly got away with all of it. Your buying that brooch was terrible luck for him, and he's still incredulous over the unfairness of it all! But I can't forget how hard it was on his aunt. She couldn't understand your having her pin. And imagine her frustration when nobody would believe it was hers. Well, it was hers, as she saw it, for she didn't have any idea it had been sold. All in all, young Hammond had a lot of explaining to do to us, and he'd have been better off doing the explaining earlier on, to his aunt! It would have saved a lot of trouble and suspicion."

"Not a nice kid at all," Shorty mumbled through a mouth full of ham-on-rye.

"As for your Ginnie Ruth," Martinez continued, "she was even more deceitful than just fibbing to John Singletary. She told us her commission was supposed to be five percent of $600, and that would be a nice little thirty dollars for running one errand and telling one lie. Well, apparently she skimmed $100 off the top before she gave Robbie his money. She only gave him $500 . . . claimed that's all she got from Singletary. Robbie told us the figures because he was explaining how annoyed he was it wasn't more. He was even annoyed that he had to give her the commission he promised! Incidentally, he rationalizes taking his aunt's jewelry because it really wasn't worth very much."

Angela was shocked. "Are you saying that Virginia Ruth is a thief?"

"Essentially, that's so. She made a cool profit of $125—the $100 she took off the top, and the twenty-five dollars Robbie paid her as a commission on the $500."

"Oh, dear! I never!" Angela took a deep breath. "And she looks like such a nice, honest girl, too!"

"Well, she's only reasonably nice, and only reasonably honest."

In the late afternoon when Ginnie came back to the detectives' room, she was no longer weepy and distraught, but haughty and defiant. Her pretty auburn hair shone very red in the slanting rays of the late afternoon sun, and she flounced across to take her place in a chair—not the one Martinez had gestured toward, but one a little farther off. "Pure stubbornness," he said later to Swanson. "Just showing me she was in control."

"We do have a few more questions," he began.

"I told you everything I know this morning," she said indifferently. "Robbie is a friend. I've met him a lot of times with other kids we know—at the club we all hang out at . . . The Vein of Silver."

He looked a question.

"It's downtown here. In Camden. You know—they serve beer and wine, they have a band on Saturday night and a jukebox the rest of the time—and, oh, I dunno—it's popular—absolutely everybody goes there . . ." and that obviously seemed to her to answer all possible queries.

"Well, that isn't really what I want to hear about. I want to hear about your transaction with Mr. Singletary."

"Again?"

"Again. Start with why you told him it was your mother's jewelry?"

"He wanted to know where I got it. I had to tell him something!"

"Why not the truth? Why didn't you say you were simply handling it for a friend?"

She looked sullenly at her shoes. "He wouldn't have given me so much for it. It was a pile of junk. He didn't have to say so—I could tell. But I knew he was crazy about my mom. After Dad died, I thought for a while that maybe he and Mom would get married. So I knew he'd give me more if he thought it was Mom's."

"I see. And he gave you altogether . . ."

"Six hundred dollars," she said promptly. "You've seen the books, you said so yourself, so you know."

Martinez nodded. "Just confirming. And you were to get a commission . . ."

"Five percent. Thirty dollars off the top," she said quickly.

"Well, that's interesting. Because you should have given Robbie Hammond $570, then. But he says you only gave him $500, and he paid you twenty-five dollars commission out of that amount."

Her jaw dropped. "Do you mean you went and told him about the $600? What did you want to go and do that for?" Her pretty brow furrowed into a dark scowl and the corners of her mouth turned down. "You had no business to talk about that to him. What I paid him and what I made off that deal was *my* business—mine and his!"

"Why did you cheat him, Miss Uh—Miss Uh—"

"Robertson," Shorty spoke up from his corner for the first time since the girl entered.

"I needed that money," she said defiantly. "I barely make it holding down three jobs. Besides, Robbie's got plenty of money."

"He says not. He says he had to sell that jewelry to pay his aunt's rent here."

She tossed her auburn hair in a gesture she must have picked up from the old movies on TV, probably watching the late Susan Hayward in her early films. "They had a big house he sold," she insisted stubbornly. "He got plenty of money from that. And he paid a *huge* amount to get her in here. And there's a big rent to stay here, too. She must have had plenty of money herself. You know that all these folks here are rich. They have to be or they can't get in. They never miss a little bit of money like $100 . . ."

"But if he had to sell that jewelry, surely that means he and his aunt had very little to spare," Martinez argued, reasonably.

She thought a moment, then shook her head. "Well, he *says* he had to sell the stuff. But personally I think she had plenty without that extra—he was just getting a little bit of cash for himself, because he was short. That'd be just like him. All these rich kids that pay their way through college without taking a job! I earn every penny I make, not like him . . . living off his aunt . . . going to school free . . . she got him a terrific car, and his own computer for his dorm room. Listen, I could never even afford to go to college! Don't you think I wanted to? I wanted to make something of myself, too!" Her voice was rising in agitation.

"Miss Robertson, sit down. Lower your voice." Martinez was scolding like an irate parent. She sat. "Now, Miss Robertson, am I to understand you took the $100 because (a) you thought he could spare it, and (b) you were jealous because he could go to college and you couldn't afford to? Is that what it boils down to?"

She nodded. "I suppose you want me to give it back? You want me to hunt him up and apologize and give him the eighty-five-dollar difference between what I took and what he thought he was paying?"

"Ninety-five-dollar difference," Martinez corrected. "And I think that would be a very wise idea, Miss Robertson. You might also hunt up your friend Mr. Singletary and apologize for lying to him."

"Awww, you're not going to tell him *tooo-oo-oo!*" she wailed.

"He'll find out sooner or later, whether I tell him or not,"

Martinez said. "Trust me, young woman, it will be better if you confess first than if you let it go till afterward. He'll forgive you if you go to him now. He won't forgive you if you wait until he has to ask you for an explanation. Take my advice and go tomorrow—as soon as you can."

She sighed. "All right. But I don't think I have ninety-five dollars to give Robbie . . . I bought some clothes . . ."

"Well, make whatever arrangements you can with him," Martinez suggested. "Why not offer to pay off a week at a time, every paycheck, for a while? He'd probably accept that."

"You're right. He'd accept it," she said sulkily. "But it'd be hard on *me*. Well, what does he care? He doesn't care about me! I don't suppose he ever did, really. He's got that new girlfriend . . . that Miss Round-Heels of Alabama! She's older than she looks, even if she's dressing like a teenager," she said angrily. "What he sees in all that eye liner beats me! Sure he wants money—so he can buy a little grass for their dates, so he can impress her. Listen, isn't smoking marijuana a crime or something? Why don't you go arrest them instead of picking on me!"

Swanson cleared his throat and looked earnestly at his notes. Martinez looked out the window at the sunset.

"Well," the girl went on. "If you're done making me feel bad, I guess I have to go to work and smile at all those wrinkled old mummies in the dining room and make nice for Mrs. Frankenstein in the kitchen . . . you two have no idea how bad it is, working around here. Especially if you're young . . ."

When neither man said anything, but both simply looked at her, she started for the door.

"That's another thing," she said as she turned to go. "You'd take money, too, so you could go out and have fun, if you had to work with all these old people all day long. Bo-*ring*! You wouldn't believe . . . half of 'em don't know what day it is. And they yell at you if you forget the slightest thing, like if you don't put a knife at their place. I'm glad when I can stay out in the kitchen. Which I do most of the time. If I'd had money, things would be different!" And on that note, she left.

"Wow," Swanson said. "I thought this morning she was a nice girl!"

"I did too," Martinez said. "But only up to a point. No 'nice girl' skims an extra ninety-five dollars of her friend's money, after offering to help. No 'nice girl' hates her employers and mocks them behind their back. She wasn't crying this time, you notice—that was just a pose to impress us, this morning! That kid carries a load of resentment and rage so big it's a wonder it isn't visible!"

"She sure was mad ... about everything! Or maybe about nothing!"

"If our three murder victims had been rich, I'd be looking at her as suspect Number One. I'd think she hacked them up in a tantrum over other people's having money when she didn't! But at least two of the victims were worse off than Virginia Ruth Robertson ... and maybe all three. Shorty, have those bank statements come through on them?"

Swanson grinned. "You know how it is doing business with banks," he said. "They act like they were doctors and you asked them private stuff about their patients' health! But I have statements on the two men." He reached into his briefcase and brought out two sheets on a bank's letterhead. "Same bank for both. Right here in town. Mrs. Gardner still had her money in a bank in Escondido where she was living. They dragged their feet a little, but they'll have a statement for us tomorrow."

Martinez looked at the statements and sighed. "$11.80 left in checking, $123 in savings ... some fortune our Enrique Ortelano had!"

"He had child support payments to make," Swanson reminded him. "Maybe he sent some to the ex-wife, too."

"Well-well!" Martinez was surprised. "Listen to this. Our gardener, Rollo Bagwell, had a tiny $17,500 in savings and over $1,000 in checking! There was a man who hung onto his money. Of course he didn't drive a car, he wasn't married, he didn't seem to have any hobbies at all, and the rent on his place wasn't awfully high. He saved what he made, I guess. It's no fortune, but people have been killed over less. Listen," he thought a moment. "Are you done with lunch? I've got an idea we should go talk to the police department's psychiatrist about this business with the gardens and gardeners. Maybe an expert can see something in that pattern. I confess it beats me, but there must be something . . . come on," and he headed for the door.

Shorty wiped the crumbs from his second sandwich off his shirtfront. "I kind of had a notion you didn't think too much of that gardener business, while Mrs. Benbow was telling you about it."

Martinez shrugged. "Tell the truth, I just don't know what to think about it. But it worries me. It's—oh, I don't know, it's too cute, somehow. All the same, I don't dare turn down any lead, because I really don't have too many."

Shorty unfolded his considerable length and brushed at more crumbs lodged in the folds of his slacks and his sports coat. "We got a little bit . . ."

"What? A nephew who isn't as thoughtful and loving as he seems? A young fellow whose idea of 'mine' and 'thine' is a bit too elastic to be really ethical? Sounds good till you stop and think about motive. The nephew doesn't stand to inherit much with the old lady gone. But she was a source of good things for him, while she was alive. She kept him in college, for instance. Then she apparently ran out of money. Because he had to sell her house and her possessions—never mind that he chose to cut corners by not discussing it with her."

"The Robertson girl says they had money."

Martinez gestured impatiently. "I wouldn't believe her if she said Tuesday followed Monday. I'll wait for more objective evidence than that. No, the nephew doesn't look quite as good to me anymore. They don't send you to Death Row for being inconsiderate."

"Well, we have Singletary . . ."

"Not John. I've known him too well for too many years. Of course, the Robertson girl looks better as a suspect. I think she'd kill if everything was right. Then there's that neighbor of Mrs. Gardner's . . ."

"The neighbor?"

"The Walters woman. The one we interviewed early on.

The one who identified the pendant, when our helpful ladies called on her in Escondido."

"She's a suspect?"

"As much as anybody else, I suppose. She knew the Gardner woman, and that means I have to look twice at her. Mrs. Benbow swears the girl had a real soft spot for the nephew—and Mrs. Benbow's got a shrewd eye. So maybe there's something there."

"What?"

"Darned if I know, Swanson. Darned if I know. Oh, and then there are the illegal aliens. I don't know if they have anything to do with this at all. But we can't overlook the possibility."

"And then there's this stuff Mrs. Benbow was talking about . . ."

"Mmmmph! Gardeners. Well, I guess having a grudge against gardeners is as good a reason for the murders as any we've come up with so far."

Swanson wrapped an uneaten sandwich in a napkin. "Might come in handy later," he said sheepishly. "How about maybe you got three different murderers, then, since you can't find a real connection? How about the killings aren't really related at all?"

"I hate coincidence," Martinez frowned. "I like things to make sense. Coincidence doesn't make sense—it just is. It violates my need for order. I want pattern. And I want it badly. So I say, come on—stuff that sandwich into your pocket, and let's go talk to our police psychiatrist. Maybe there's something in that pattern . . ."

"Gardeners?"

"Right. Crazy, isn't it? Gardeners." Martinez headed for the door and Shorty followed. Fast.

That evening, the two policemen were back at Camden—no wiser than before—with as many loose ends and unresolved ideas as ever. They officially closed up shop but before they headed home for the night, Shorty went to the kitchen and perched on a stool as nearly out of the way as his long legs would allow him to be, watching Chita and another younger girl work around Mrs. Schmitt, preparing the meal and setting the tables and making the coffee and

cutting the pound-cake servings that would be dessert after
the addition of a rich mocha-cream sauce. Virginia Ruth was
nowhere in evidence, and Mrs. Schmitt was muttering
crossly under her breath about the irresponsibility of the
younger generation, banging the pans around as she worked.

Shorty was hoping for two things: a bite of dinner (he
loved Mrs. Schmitt's *coq au vin* with a passion he reserved
for few things in his laid-back life) and a chance to talk
with Chita. She had refused a date after work ("I got to
wash my hair tonight, Swans-sohn. Honest. Don't look like
that . . . it's really true!") and he was feeling sorry for himself in a way that only she—or food—could cure.

He got a plate of dinner—Mrs. Schmitt's anger did not
extend to a satisfactorily hearty eater like himself, and her
temper eased as he forked in *coq au vin* and made appre-
ciative noises. He did not get the chance to talk much with
Chita, since Virginia Ruth's absence made her do double
duty helping to set up the residents' tables for the evening
meal. But, he thought happily, there were worse things than
eating Mrs. Schmitt's food and getting a glimpse of Chita's
shapely legs, as she raced in and out of the swinging doors
leading into the dining room.

Martinez took the time to walk down the garden path and
call on his ladies. When Caledonia admitted him, he was
pleased to see that Angela was there as well. "Yes, I'm off
duty officially," he said in answer to Caledonia's invitation,
"and yes, I'd love a little sherry. My neck aches all the way
down to my ankles! And sherry is next best to a professional masseur working me over. Your company, of
course," he bowed slightly toward them and smiled that
brilliant smile of his, "your company goes far to make the
day less burdensome."

Over the little thimbleful of amontillado, he told them
about the interview with Virginia Ruth.

"Oh, dear!" Angela exclaimed. "What a loathsome child!
And I thought she was so nice!"

"Well, be reasonable," Caledonia said. "You don't know
her . . . you have only seen her."

"Yes," Angela conceded, "but she looks so nice!"

"You mean," Caledonia snorted, "she looks so pretty.

I've said it before and I say it again—ugly people are easy to suspect of any atrocity. We have a tendency to think the good-looking ones are innocent. It's a kind of a trap we fall into."

Martinez sipped and nodded. "I think we all have a feeling that the insides and the outsides should match. But in my line of work, you learn that the handsomest men can be the meanest liars, and the prettiest women the most cold-blooded, self-centered, inhuman . . ."

"Isn't that going pretty far to describe Ginnie?" Angela asked.

"I didn't mean her, especially. I only meant—well, sometimes motherly looking women are pickpockets, and meek-looking little wimps are muggers, and happy, smiling faces can hide murderous rage. That's all I meant. She fooled us—"

"Well, me, anyway," Angela conceded. "You saw through her pretty fast."

"To be fair, she helped by coming right out in the open. And that was one thing that both led to her embezzling the ninety-five dollars and to her confessing to it—the arrogance. She felt somehow she had a right to the money, that her reasons for taking it were perfectly valid—that life owed it to her. When she told us about it, she was simply explaining to us—not apologizing. She's protected herself against the world by wrapping herself in a cloak of arrogance."

But by the next day, it began to seem that Virginia Ruth had apparently cloaked herself in something else, as well: invisibility.

Chapter 15

"IF I knew where she was I'd tell you! (*Clang!*) If I knew where she was, I'd go and haul her up here by the scruff of her neck myself! (*Clash!*) I have two waitresses out with flu, one on maternity leave. I need that girl!" (*Bang-Bang-Clatter!*)

The ring of metal on metal as pan met stove and pan met pot and pot met sink punctuated Mrs. Schmitt's irritated responses to Martinez' inquiries about Virginia Ruth's whereabouts. "If she's not in her own home, I have no idea in the world where she'd be. Out on the beach with some boyfriend, probably. These kids . . . now, if you two will kindly step aside—I need to get muffins out of the oven . . ." (*CRASH!*)

Breakfast, Martinez decided, was really not the time to locate a missing person. But missing was what Virginia Ruth Robertson seemed to be. She had failed to show up for work, as the detectives discovered when they arrived at Camden early and went to the kitchen to summon the girl for yet another official interview. Martinez had intended a businesslike breakfast of bacon and eggs, followed by more questions to the Robertson girl, but instead he and Swanson found themselves on the telephone, starting a chain of inquiry to locate her, wherever she'd got to.

"Not that we'll find her, if she's run away," Martinez sighed. "I always think Southern California is the perfect place for someone who wants to disappear and take a new identity. Almost nobody is a longtime resident in the same location. Neighbors don't know their neighbors—renters appear and disappear every six months—even people who own their own homes sell out and move more often than anywhere else in the United States. A whole population of fly-by-nights and newcomers . . . one more will just get lost in the crowd."

"Well," Swanson said, "there's always a possibility she hasn't just run away, isn't there?"

Martinez nodded. "She put herself in a dangerous position—right in the middle of not-too-honest activity. And someone may have had a reason to remove her from that position."

"Do you want me to get a couple of the men to hunt around the grounds and down on the beach?"

"Yes. I don't like to think about it. But we better do that. But quietly, and especially be quiet and behave yourselves where the residents here can see you. No need to get people upset—particularly if it might be a false alarm. She could show up yet, I suppose. But it's the kind of coincidence that makes me very uneasy. We find out she's been embezzling one day, the next day she's nowhere to be found."

"I'll call for a couple of men, okay? We'll start with the grounds here—and the basement, the attic . . ."

"Start at her house. Just because she doesn't answer the phone doesn't mean she isn't there. She could be there— and not able to answer Mrs. Schmitt's phone calls. More people die at home than anywhere else."

"I already tried that, Lieutenant. She didn't answer my calls, either. I guess I should have told you . . ."

"You're learning, Swanson, you're learning. Mrs. Schmitt says Virginia Ruth is not at home, but you check up on that. Good. Don't take anybody's word—even the good Mrs. Schmitt. Unless she's discussing chocolate cream pie or Veal Oscar." Martinez got to his feet. "Okay, then. I'll ask around here among the residents—you do the hard work—get sand in your shoes, get cobwebs on your hair, and look everywhere."

Swanson departed at a lope and Martinez began asking his questions of the early morning diners already at breakfast. Nobody had seen the red-haired kitchen helper. Two of the residents even claimed they had *never* seen her and that no such person worked at Camden. And Cora Ransom insisted the girl had been driven away in a "touring car, seated beside a young man who was quite probably Edward—you know, Edward, the Prince of Wales? I always said he would never stay with that Simpson woman. And this girl who works here is such a pretty thing, I'm not surprised she caught his eye. I said to Sadie Mandelbaum . . ." Martinez bowed slightly and eased away from Cora.

Help came from an unexpected source. Grogan allowed a loose smile to smear across his face when Martinez stopped dutifully by his table. "Oh, I saw her, all right. Yesterday, though. Late afternoon. About the time she was supposed to be setting tables. I think."

"What time would that be exactly?"

Grogan shrugged apologetically. "Time is sometimes not very clear to me, and I was having a little predinner cocktail at my place, just standing looking idly through the window. Besides, I had no reason to check the clock. Anyway, she was in the garden. Reason I say it was table-setting time—she had her hands full of napkins and silverware. She came out of the dining room with a basket of silverware in one hand and a pile of napkins in the other to talk to somebody on the patio . . ."

"Who? Who was she meeting?"

Grogan shook his head, and quickly grabbed it with both hands. "Shouldn't have done that. Mornings, these days, my brains seem to be kind of loose in my skull—seem to hang against the sides, if I move too fast." He paused and then, apparently satisfied that nothing had spilled from his head, went on. "I don't know, sir. I do not know the identity of her companion. She had walked to the end of the patio where the lounge furniture is, and he was half-hidden from me—behind that big flowering vine . . ."

"But it was a man?"

Grogan started to shake his head again, and stopped in time. "I don't know that for sure. I thought so, sir. I thought so. But I couldn't really see. I suppose it was just an impression. Because she was such a pretty little thing. It seemed logical to me."

"Could it have been a woman?"

Grogan shrugged and spread his hands. "Maybe. Maybe.

Damn eyes aren't as good as they used to be . . . I've been thinking about getting glasses. There was a vine in the way that kept me from seeing clearly, too—and the light kind of dances there, with the shadows of the leaves making lace-patterns on the patio walls . . ."

"And you were too drunk to have seen a hippopotamus clearly!" Martinez thought, but didn't say so. At least Grogan had been reasonably coherent, this morning, and relatively cooperative, instead of showing his irascible hungover personality. Martinez filed the possible sighting of the quarry in his mind under "Questionable" and kept on with his rounds through the dining room.

"Won't you join me for a bit of breakfast, lieutenant?" Angela asked, when he finally reached her table.

"I'm sorry I can't, Mrs. Benbow. Truly sorry, and that's not just manners talking. I'm starved. But Virginia Ruth Robertson seems to be missing, and we're trying to find out if anyone's seen her."

"Heavens! Well, of course I did—yesterday just after noontime—"

"No, we mean later. The first time she was really missing—that is, that she didn't show up where she was expected—was to work the dinnertime shift in the kitchen. Mrs. Schmitt thought she was just taking a holiday. But the young lady didn't show up this morning, either, and now Mrs. Schmitt is sure she's skipping work for a date."

"What do you think?"

"I don't like it, Mrs. Benbow. Not even a little bit. We've started a systematic hunt for her. In fact, you'll see Shorty and some of the uniformed men poking around the grounds and down at the beach. Please don't let it distress you."

"Looking for her body, then?" Angela asked shrewdly.

"I hope not. But—" Martinez excused himself, and Angela hastened through the last bites of her bacon and eggs so she could hurry down the garden to Caledonia's cottage and break the latest news to her.

As Caledonia, yawning, answered Angela's knock, Grogan was tacking past them toward his own cottage, his smile replaced by a scowl, his hand held to his temple—the morning sun was obviously giving him great pain.

"I'd hoped, after he stayed sober for three weeks and really tried to dry out, that these drinking bouts would be better," Angela complained to Caledonia, once safely inside with the door closed behind her. She peered out Caledonia's view window, standing to one side so she could not be seen staring, but so that she could follow the progress of the unsteady Grogan, swaying down the path in the general direction of his own apartment, though he overshot and had to come back to make it directly to his front door.

"He's not aiming for the door," Caledonia surmised. "He's flying a landfall!" She sighed. "Oh, the man will kill himself with drink—but somehow, I think that, having reached eighty, the man has a right to kill himself by whatever means seem attractive!"

"But . . ."

"And we're not going to interfere. Not again!" They had been responsible for trying, on that one previous occasion, to coax Grogan into sobriety—with poor results.

"But it doesn't get better . . ."

"Oh, yes, it does! He gets drunker and he enjoys it more."

"Hah!" Angela scorned her huge friend's little attempt at humor. "He's not drunk now, he's just hung over. And in pain. He felt so much better during the time he was sober . . ."

"Spare me. Grogan would never agree with that analysis, I'm sure. Now—do you want coffee? I'd just made myself a pot—didn't feel like trudging up to the dining room this morning, but I woke up, and once I was awake, I couldn't get back to sleep. So I figured, early as it is, I might as well stay up."

"Cal! It's not early. It's after eight. Cream and sugar, please . . ."

Caledonia glared as she poured Angela's coffee, doctored it, served it, and then relaxed onto the sofa with her own cup, still hot enough to be sipped rather than gulped. "Okay, now what brings you here at this terrible hour?"

"The Robertson girl is missing!"

"Good heavens above. Missing? Not killed, is she?"

"I really don't know—but I doubt it. Of course the police

are looking for her body—all around. They were just going into our basement when I came down the path from breakfast ... I suppose they have to do that, but it just wouldn't make sense. I mean, she's not a gardener, is she? She wasn't even the one they sent to cut the flowers for the guest table when there were special visitors—one of the regular waitresses did that. So our murderer isn't going to kill Virginia Ruth, is he?"

"Trying to save your precious theory? Well, maybe she hasn't been killed ... maybe she's just—oh, must have gone on a date or something."

"Not only is she not a gardener," Angela went on as though Caledonia hadn't spoken, "but yesterday was a Thursday, not a Tuesday. The murderer has only struck on Tuesdays!"

"So far," Caledonia cautioned and kept sipping her coffee. "You know, I've been thinking. You and I really ought to talk to young Hammond. Just to—oh! Oh, yoo-hoo ... yoo-hoo ..."

"What is it, Cal?"

"Yoo-hoo ... oh, yoo-hoo ..." Caledonia had put down her cup and walked toward her screen door, yodeling in what she thought was a friendly little voice, but which actually shook the windowpane like a sonic boom. "Oh, Sue Nancy ... yoo-hoo ..."

Angela stood so she too could peer out the screen. Into her line of vision came a vision ... Sue Nancy Butler, dressed in a flowered frock that reached nearly to her ankles. A princess bodice that Angela would have expected to hug the girl's form hung loose from shoulder to hips. "... easily three sizes too wide, and two sizes too long!" Angela said, later. A dirndl skirt started at the hipline— three-quarter sleeves had been pushed to Sue Nancy's elbows, and a white lace collar ("... like little Lord Fauntleroy wore," was Angela's judgment) topped the whole. Sue Nancy's shoes were spike-heeled patent leather with toes "... sharp enough to use picking up wastepaper out of the gutters!" as Angela put it, and with straps that crisscrossed up her lower legs like the thongs of a classical Greek shepherd's sandals. She carried a long chiffon handkerchief in one hand, a half-dozen strings of brightly colored plastic beads circled her throat, and her hair—frizzy in some places, straight in others—had been styled with that careless abandon that says ". . . sorry, I didn't have time to use a comb!"

"Cyndi Lauper strikes again!" Angela muttered.

"Yes'm?" Sue Nancy queried with her vague smile. "You called me, Miz Wingate?" Her eyes were slightly unfocused and she wobbled on the stilt heels as she walked, holding her arms a little out and to the sides for balance, as though she were walking on a high wire.

"Yes, I did. I wondered if you knew where Robbie Hammond is today?"

Sue Nancy shook her head. "At school, I suppose. He's taking these summer session classes and he has to study most of the time. It's such a bore." She leaned her weight on one hip, and propped one arm against the edge of the door.

Angela came forward to stand just behind Caledonia at the screen, peering around her shoulder because there was no room to stand beside her. "You two are going together now, I hear," she said pleasantly.

"Sort of, yes'm," Sue Nancy said. "Not going steady or anything, you know. Just dating. We've been together near about every night this week," she added with a lilt that Angela took to be pride.

"Were you out with Robbie last night, too? Wherever is there to go in a little place like Camden?"

"We were down on the beach. That's where we mostly go." Sue Nancy looked just faintly uncomfortable.

"Oh, heavens! The beach?" Angela said. "But why ever go to the beach at night? You can't swim—it's too dangerous. You can't even see the water! I can't imagine . . ."

"Angela, you really are a caution," Caledonia crowed. "You can't be that old . . . you can't have forgotten why young people want to be alone at night, far away from their elders . . ."

Angela was embarrassed and showed it. "I only meant . . . that is, I thought . . . it's so uncomfortable in the sand!

I thought, if they wanted to—you know—be alone—to . . . to . . . neck . . ."

"Neck?" Sue Nancy said blankly.

Angela threw up her hands. "What I'm trying to say is, who wants to sit on sand? You get it in your clothes, in your shoes . . . it's damp and at night it's cold. If I was their age I'd want to be sitting on a park bench somewhere, under a tree . . . on the back porch . . . on the steps somewhere . . . in a car . . . I wouldn't want to be on the beach! So I just thought they went there for some other . . . *Oh!* You get me so *rattled!*"

Caledonia was laughing and Sue Nancy was smiling languidly. Only Angela was cross.

"I asked the lieutenant the same thing . . . why they were on the beach . . . and he said they were building sand castles. I suppose he was making fun of me, like you are, wasn't he? I'll have to explain to him when I see him . . ."

"Oh, leave it alone, Angela," Caledonia advised. And then she did a small version of a classic double take. "Wait . . . when did you talk to the lieutenant about this?"

"The last time they were down on the beach. Sue Nancy, you and Robbie were down there when his aunt was killed, too."

"Oh, I know," the girl said solemnly. "I know. And Robbie felt just awful about that. He felt like if we'd only stayed around for the evening and played rummy with her or something, she wouldn't have been killed! But we never thought . . . of course he doesn't know about this yet, but I know he'll feel just awful about this, too!"

"He knew Virginia, didn't he?"

"I guess so," she shrugged. "I mean, I know he did. But I don't think he cared much for her one way or the other. She liked him, though—a lot. She was even a little jealous of him . . . she would come up to talk to him while I was along and kind of turn her back to me, like she wished I wasn't there. That's one reason we stopped going to the Vein of Silver downtown. She wouldn't leave us alone."

"You've only been here a little more than a week," Angela marveled. "That is what we used to call fast work!"

"We still do call it that," Sue Nancy said smugly. She

patted the tangled mat of her coiffure as though to make sure no tangle had let go. "I've always been able to get the boys ..." She pronounced it like a three-syllable word: *BAH-OH-YEEZ*. "I'm sure I don't know what they see in me, but they do."

Caledonia turned her back hastily and walked a circuit of the room, getting control of her broad smile before she let Sue Nancy see her face again.

"Are you and Robbie serious about each other?" Angela asked curiously.

"Oh, I don't think so," Sue Nancy said thoughtfully. "I mean, I'm not. He might be. But then, I'm not sure what you mean 'serious,' and I'm not sure what serious would feel like. But I don't *think* I'm serious about him. I mean, I'm going home to Birmingham next week, aren't I? And he'll stay here ... It would be nice," she said with a dreamy smile, "if he was to write love letters to me while we were apart, of course. I like all those sweet things boys say ..."

She moved away from the door. She had leaned against it, while she was talking, but now she seemed satisfied the building would stand without her help. "I really have to go meet Auntie Dora and Auntie Donna now. They said we were going shopping this morning so they could buy me a nice skirt and blouse before I go home ... something that really looks like California, you know?" She waved a hand along the length of her own shape to indicate, presumably, that she looked un-California. In making the gesture, she relaxed her hand on her handkerchief and it came free. But its floating length of chiffon did not drift to the ground. Rather the knotted end, which she'd held in her hand the whole time she talked, weighed the kerchief down and it fell with a plop. There was something wrapped and tied in the kerchief ... something she'd been concealing as she stood there in conversation.

Sue Nancy made a swoop toward the kerchief and fumbled the grab. It was as though Sue Nancy's vision was blurred and her depth perception off, for her fingers missed the kerchief by almost two inches. Angela, coming out of the screen door, was a little quicker, and there was nothing wrong with *her* depth perception. She stooped, retrieved the kerchief, and got a good look at the little bundle in the corner as well. "Here," she said, handing it back to Sue Nancy, who rolled the entire kerchief up into a ball and backed hastily off the little cottage porch.

"Thank you. Got to run now, like I said ... 'bye, y'all," she called, never stopping her retreat and turning as she reached the main sidewalk to move off double-time, stumbling and wobbling in her clumsy, fashionable shoes.

"Okay," Caledonia said. "What was that all in aid of? I bet you wanted to see what she'd had clutched in her hot little fist, wrapped in that handkerchief. And I take it you did see it. So? What was it?"

Angela smiled. "It reminds me of my own teens. She's trying to keep her aunts from finding out she smokes. She had cigarette butts in there!"

"Why would she carry them around with her?" Caledonia said. "Here, let's have some more coffee. I'll get a fresh pot. It really doesn't take Mister Coffee any time at all ..." She moved over to her kitchenette, working while she talked, and Angela followed. "I could understand why she'd want to sneak off to have a smoke in a bathroom or on the beach ... we all did that at her age, I suppose. But she could just have left the butts there! Her aunts would never find them in the sand. Why carry them with her so secretly?"

"To smoke later on," a man's voice said from the doorway. "Marijuana is expensive, and you don't just put the cigarette out ... you save what's left."

"Oh, Lieutenant," Angela said. "How wonderful to see you!"

"Coffee?" Caledonia boomed. "Join us ... we were about to have a little 'elevenses' here and you're welcome ..."

"No, thank you," he said. "I'm afraid I'm on duty. I came by for a very specific purpose. Mrs. Benbow, I shall have to ask for those items of jewelry you have that were Mrs. Gardner's. I'd like to photograph them, and of course they may still be evidence ..."

Angela nodded. "I thought you might want my brooch

and my pendant. I'll be glad to get them for you. But wait
. . . this has all sailed past my head a little fast here. Let me
go back to when you came in. Did you say marijuana? That
child Sue Nancy is smoking marijuana?"

"Well, that's what hidden, half-smoked cigarettes sound
like to me," Martinez said. "I could be wrong, of course.
But in fact, marijuana was mentioned once before to me . . .
Virginia Ruth tried to tell me Robbie needed money to buy
marijuana so he could impress his new Southern girlfriend.
I paid no attention at the time. I put the remark down to
jealousy. And besides, she was hardly a reliable witness.
But now—"

"Oh, dear," Caledonia said. "Sure about the coffee?" He
nodded. "Oh, dear! Do you mean Robbie gave Sue Nancy
those cigarettes?"

"Maybe," Martinez said. "Or maybe the ones you saw
were hers. At least, I took it from the conversation she was
carrying some butts and you caught sight of them."

Angela nodded. "She had them knotted in the corner of
a handkerchief. She was just coming up from the beach . . .
you don't suppose they were smoking marijuana there on
the beach last night and she was just cleaning up the evidence?"

"Ah, but I do suppose they were! And I also suppose she
was collecting the leftovers for use, not cleaning up the evidence . . . it would be typical of someone who smokes pot
frequently. She can take the leftovers of several butts, break
them out into a new paper, and roll a whole new cigarette.
Those leftovers are important . . . and I think she went
down to get them."

"*There!* I'm not so naive as you thought," Angela said
suddenly to Caledonia. "You thought they were going down
there to make love. I *told* you the sand was too uncomfortable. They were going down there for privacy to smoke
pot."

The words sounded uncomfortable in her mouth. Angela
was not accustomed to talking about drugs, and the nickname *pot* sounded awkward . . . like prudes who, reading
aloud, come across the word *naked*. They can't pronounce
it clearly, and it comes out in a half-whisper as *nekkid* be-

cause the word feels uncomfortable in their mouths. So Angela half whispered as she said the word *pot*.

Martinez grinned. "Well, I got more than I bargained for by coming down here. I got a whole new idea. A new direction to investigate."

"Why?" Caledonia said curiously. "Are you thinking this is somehow connected to drug trafficking? The soft-drink man could have been a dealer, of course."

"Oh!" Angela exclaimed. "Of course! How perfect. He could have been delivering sodas and drugs at the same time!"

Caledonia glared and Martinez went on. "It's not unheard of. A while back one of the ice cream delivery men—in South Carolina, as I recall—was dealing drugs along with the chocolate chip! It's an easy way to contact customers ... when you're already contacting customers for another product! But we looked into the background of Mr. Ortelano pretty thoroughly and he came up absolutely clean in regard to drugs. Besides, how would you explain the deaths of Rollo and Mrs. Gardner, then? Neither of them would have been involved in drugs themselves ... not as dealers and not as users. And no dealer in his right mind would have trusted either of them as a runner. We keep getting common factors that fit one and maybe two—but no more."

"Or three ... as with the gardeners," Angela said.

"Yes, like that. You know, I really thought you might have something with that notion, and I went out to talk to one of the psychologists at the college who does a little consulting for us, now and then. She said it's possible ... all things are possible ... that the occupation of gardening and the time of the attacks—on Tuesday nights—might have significance. But she was darned if she could tell me what it might be, because none of it fit any patterns she could think of. She felt uncomfortable about the whole thing ... said something didn't sit right with her. Still, I wasn't ready to give up on the theory of a crazy person. Now I don't know."

"But why do you say that drugs give you a new direction

to look in, if there's no real chance all three were involved with drugs?" Caledonia asked. "I don't get it."

"Ah," Martinez said. "Now there's the question. You see, one of the alibis in this case rests on testimony that might be made unreliable if pot were involved. I have young Hammond coming in soon, and I'll have an extra tough question or two for him, this time."

And he left.

Caledonia took a deep breath. "I'm not sure I still understand it, quite. But he'll sort it out."

"I wish—I wish I could be of help!" Angela said. If she'd had a mummified monkey's paw in her pocket, she couldn't have wished more effectively . . . or more dangerously.

Chapter 16

BEFORE SUPPER that night, the usual crowd gathered in the lobby. Mr. Brighton sat in a chair bolstered by two extra cushions friends had brought to help hold him in a more comfortable position, but his expression said he hurt badly tonight. Around him were Emma Grant, Caledonia, Angela, little Mary Moffet, and Mr. and Mrs. Emerson. As usual, Charlotte Emerson's face was set in deep frown lines, while Howard Emerson looked alert and interested in everything around him, a man to whom life was still intensely enjoyable.

"All this is beyond me," he was saying. "The two men—well, that could have been a tramp wandering through. You know, that's what I thought of first. Someone coming up to see what they could steal from the place, then being frightened when they were interrupted and just lashing out with the nearest weapon. The two men just got in the way. That's what I thought."

"I don't know about 'nearest weapon,' " Caledonia said, pulling at the sleeve on her silver-threaded, slate blue georgette caftan, unusual because the material was crystal-pleated in tiny, tiny creases from the silver-beaded collar to the floor. "Our gardener was killed with his own shears, it's true, but I don't recall that they ever found out where that knife came from that killed the soft-drink man. Drat!" She yanked at the sleeve again.

Tonight Caledonia had adorned herself with a huge cuff-bracelet of white gold on either arm, bracelets that each featured one large, perfect sapphire in a claw setting. The bracelets had been a mistake, of course; the claw settings reached out to drag at the loose sleeves on either arm, and Caledonia found herself untangling blue-gray georgette from a sapphire on one arm or the other after every gesture. She was growing steadily more impatient and pulling at the material more roughly each time a sleeve caught, so that by the time she went in to dinner, both of her sleeves had a frill of loose threads around their circumference. "I'm going to see the dressmaker on Monday," she growled, "and the jeweler as well. This is not going to happen again. Pass the cornbread!"

But now, before the meal even began, Caledonia fussed irritably with her sleeves, yanking and jerking and untangling all the while she talked and listened. And her job was made all the more difficult because she tried not to let anyone see that she was fussing with her clothing.

"But it was obvious after Mrs. Gardner died," Howard Emerson was saying, "that there was more connection with this place than we thought at first. I mean, not just anybody could get in and be wandering our hallways—especially at night—without being noticed by somebody."

"I don't know," Angela said. "If you knew this place well, there's always a way. For instance, since most of us were in the lobby at the sing-along, someone could have come in through the library without our seeing. There's a service stairway that takes off behind the library, from the hallway . . ."

". . . and comes out about halfway down the north hall. Right by Trinita Stainsbury's room," Mary Moffet squeaked excitedly. "I've gone up that way myself, when I've been in the library and wanted to see somebody on the second floor."

"You're not supposed to do that, Mary," Tootsie Armstrong said, joining the group just in time to hear the last remark. "Your supposed to use one of the main stairways in the front . . . the ones that go up from the lobby here." She gestured vaguely toward the wrought-iron railing that edged the main staircase to the second floor. "Or take the elevator."

"I don't like our elevator," Mary said nervously. "It's making more and more noise every day—it gets stuck about once a week—I think it's just going to *die* one of these days, and I don't want to be on it when it does!"

"We were on it," Charlotte Emerson said, "when it got stuck a couple of weeks ago. Weren't we, Howard?"

"Indeed we were, my dear," he agreed. "It's not a terribly pleasant experience. The lights went off and the fan didn't turn, so it got quite warm in there, as well. But we could hear them working away up above our heads on the second floor where the machinery is . . . and pretty soon the lights came on and it started again . . ."

"I don't call half an hour 'soon.' You'd think they could do better. Some of us have weak hearts and a fright like that—being locked in an elevator—might well kill some resident someday!" Charlotte Emerson said and fell silent again, her frown even deeper.

"We take the stairs more often now," Howard added rather lamely, watching his wife out of the corner of his eye. "Anyway, what I was going to say, I was going to point out that this girl from the kitchen, Virginia something, who seems to have disappeared . . . well, that just doesn't make any sense to us at all. Does it, dear?"

Charlotte looked pointedly away, perhaps watching the Jackson twins make their spectacular entrance at the other end of the lobby. Tonight the Jacksons, like Caledonia, had chosen frocks of georgette. Unlike Caledonia's, their frocks were pink, of course—and formed of dozens of triangular pieces of material, overlaid one on the other at neck and waist, so that the Jackson sisters look like dying chrysanthemums.

The skirts of the Jacksons' dresses were meant to lie flat against slim figures, so that the uneven hemline would drape like the points of a handkerchief held up by its midpoint, the four corners dangling. But the plump waists and chubby thighs of the Jacksons, which had demanded major alterations in their dresses, also made the skirts balloon outward, giving the impression that each had stepped into and decided to wear a very damp and much overused swansdown powder puff.

Their niece followed immediately behind them into the lobby wearing, by way of contrast, a white satin body stocking that covered her from neck to wrists and neck to ankles, hiding and revealing at the same time every feature of her body. Over this, she had on an ankle-length black linen skirt, fastened at her waist but unbuttoned down its length so that at every step her white satin legs were visible. She had on black boots with high heels that covered her to the knee in crush-leather splendor, and her hair was held in a black leather sweatband decorated in stars made of silver-colored studs.

"Shades of Cher!" Angela whispered.

Conversation throughout the lobby ceased completely as the three hove into view from the south residence hall, then quickly picked up in intensity, as each person determined not to stare. It was obvious that Donna Dee, Dora Lee, and Sue Nancy each regarded her own outfit as a fashion statement.

"Although I think you might say the statement was 'I have no taste at all!' " Angela whispered to Caledonia.

"Ooooh," Mary Moffet said despairingly. "When will they open the dining room door! I'm starving."

"And she doesn't want to have to say anything to the Jacksons and their niece, either," Angela whispered. "Even Mary might just have to laugh out loud!"

At that moment the chimes signaled that dinner was served, the double doors of the dining room were opened, and the crowd surged forward. But Angela lagged behind. Jimmy Taylor was already on duty for the evening shift, and after he managed to unwrap Mr. Grogan from the desk, pointed the happy man in the general direction of the dining room, and gave him a gentle shove to start him moving off on his unsteady way to dinner, Jimmy had settled down with a copy of *The Complete Plays of William Shakespeare*.

"Before you get too deep into that play, Jimmy—" Angela said with a half question in her voice.

"Oh, yes, Mrs. Benbow. What can I do for you?" Jimmy cheerfully laid the book down and came back up to the desk.

"I was wondering if you knew Robbie Hammond well? He's over at the college, I know."

"Well, he's in a different department, so I really don't

know a lot about him. He's a computer sci. major . . . I'm
going into high-school counseling. Of course I'm only a
sophomore, and he's a senior—I think. Anyhow, I know
him when I see him, and that's about all."

"Can't you tell me anything at all about him? The reason
I ask," she said hastily, "is he's obviously in a little trouble
with all that's happened. And I was thinking, if I could possibly find out something more about him, I could help. I
mean, Lieutenant Martinez certainly isn't convinced that
Robbie's innocent . . . but maybe if I could just find
out . . ."

The switchboard buzzed raucously.

" 'Scuse me a minute, Mrs. Benbow," Jimmy said, darting
over to pull a rubber cord from its brass socket and put the
plug into the hole beneath the winking red light. "Yes, sir,
can I help you? . . . Oh, sorry to hear that, Mr. Tuttle . . . I'll
call the nurses' station and get you a tray sent up right away
. . . No trouble, glad to do it." He flipped that cord free and
pulled another into position.

"Miss Washington, this is Jimmy at the desk. If you got
a minute, Mr. Tuttle on the second floor south is feeling the
pain in his leg something awful. He'd like you to stop by.
And of course he doesn't want to go to supper, so if you
could bring a tray . . . Gee, thanks, Miss Washington, I
know he'll be grateful." He freed the cord, which retracted
automatically into the orderly forest of metal plugs lined up
on the board.

"Okay, now, Mrs. Benbow," Jimmy said, returning to the
desk. "Where were we?"

"Mr. Tuttle's not well?"

"Oh, didn't you hear he fell in his room and broke his
leg yesterday? Gosh, they said they had the paramedics
come and take him to the hospital and get the thing
X-rayed and plastered up and everything . . . they wanted to
keep him overnight, but he fussed so bad, they decided it
was better if he came on home. It must still hurt like crazy,
of course."

"I didn't hear anything about any of this, Jimmy,"
Angela said. "I'm surprised. Usually news like this travels
so fast . . ."

"Well, everybody's talking about the murders instead, I guess."

"And I was out some yesterday—it could have happened while I was downtown, I suppose."

"Sure. Let's see . . . we were talking about that guy Hammond . . . and I honestly don't know what to say. I see him driving around campus in that fancy car, once in a while, is all. Wow, would I like to have one like that! But we just don't go to the same places, him and me."

"What fancy car is that?" Angela said.

"Oh, it's a Vet," Jimmy said. "Real sporty . . . one of the best." He sighed. "I'm sorry I really don't know the guy personally. I'd love to help." The switchboard buzzer went again. " 'Scuse me," he said and darted back to the board. "Camden-sur-Mer, good evening. Can I help you? . . . Yes, ma'am, but she's at supper right now. She'll be . . ."

"I'm going in to supper myself," Angela called. "Thank you, Jimmy . . ." He waved acknowledgment and went on talking into the mouthpiece of the antiquated headset, as Angela turned and hurried to the dining room.

"Where were you? I thought you were right behind me," Caledonia complained over a mouthful of cranberry mousse, the appetizer du jour. "I decided not to wait . . . you'll have to excuse me."

"I was talking to Jimmy," Angela said, grabbing up her spoon. Cranberry mousse was one of her favorites. "Mmmmm . . . this is super, Cal. Well, what it was, you see, I thought maybe he'd know something significant about Robbie. They go to the same school, after all. But they're two classes apart and in different majors . . . Jimmy didn't know much about him except that he admired his car."

"His car?"

"He said it was an older model. Jimmy really liked it, though," Angela said. "A strange taste for a young man."

"Did he say what kind it was? A rebuilt Model T? Or maybe an Edsel?"

"He didn't say. He just said it was a veteran," Angela said indifferently.

"Oh. Well, that tells me something. Veteran cars are a

class of old car," Caledonia explained. "Pass the cornbread. Any car made before a certain year is a 'vintage' car—after that but before another year is a 'veteran.' They have separate races for them over in England, separate shows ... everything. I just can't remember exactly the year that divides the two classes, is all."

Angela took a piece of cornbread for herself as Dolores, the head waitress, came by delivering plates that featured a handsome helping of pilaf that included jumbo shrimp. "I wouldn't know about that," she said. "I never got interested. Douglas tried to get me to go to some of the shows and the rallies—he loved that stuff."

Caledonia tasted the pilaf. "So did Herman. But unlike you, I went. And I enjoyed it. Oooooh, my ... another of Mrs. Schmitt's triumphs. Try it ..." And for a few minutes, neither one spoke as each enjoyed the buttery, spicy flavors of their dinner.

"Herman actually wanted to buy a Lancia Lambda once," Caledonia continued at last. "Made around 1926, if I have my dates right. Oh, it was a glorious thing—huge brass headlamps the size of a bushelbasket—in fact, the whole dashboard was trimmed in brass instead of in chrome. And inside—the owner had polished that engine and kept every part spotless and clean. His wife said that each time he used it, he'd clean it with a chamois. That man kept even the drip pan under the crankcase polished like a mirror! You could see your face reflected in that pan! And the old car would really go, too. We took a trial spin and we hit seventy-five on the straightaway. The whine of that monstrous engine when it geared down to take a corner, and the roar as it accelerated out of the turns ..." She signaled with delight at the memory. "They just don't make 'em like that any more."

"Why didn't Herman buy it if it was so wonderful?" Angela asked.

"Too much money. I mean, you could buy a half-dozen new Cadillacs for what that old car was worth!"

"Well, one thing we know for certain then," Angela said, "and that is, whatever the 'vet' Robbie's driving, it isn't a Lancia."

They ate in silence for a moment. And then Caledonia's face took on a puzzled frown. "Say that again, would you? Something . . ."

"What? You mean that Robbie can't afford a Lancia?"

"No, just before you said 'Lancia' you said 'vet' . . . I don't remember precisely, but—Angela, what exactly did Jimmy say to you about Robbie's car?"

"Nothing much. I told you. Except that the car Robbie owned is a vet."

"Ah-*hah*!" The explosion of noise stopped diners in mid-munch for three tables around. Caledonia lowered her tone and leaned forward so that no one could overhear. "Angela, I bet you anything you like the car that Jimmy was admiring wasn't a *vet*—it was a *Vette*."

"I don't see . . ."

"Of course you don't. Because you never paid attention when Douglas was trying to teach you about cars. It's the very thing a young fellow like Jimmy would admire . . . *Vette* is the kids' name for a Corvette. The American sports car with the sleek, low lines. A real classic, if you go for that sort of thing, and very hard to find. They aren't made any more. But real collectors have them and keep them up . . . they had Fiberglas bodies and the speed was unreal . . ."

"Well, but that explains it, then. Robbie could never afford one of those European cars, of course. But a small modern car . . ."

"Robbie couldn't afford to buy a Corvette, either, Angela. If he really is driving one, he either inherited it from Mrs. Gardner, or . . ."

"She would never have driven a sports car! She wasn't the type!"

"I was about to say, either he inherited it, or somebody in that family *did* have money! Or else it's a beat-up wreck of a car he salvaged from . . ."

"No. Because why would Jimmy admire it so much then?"

"Right. Where are you going?"

Angela had thrown down her napkin and jumped to her feet. "I'm going to ask Jimmy," she said.

"But you haven't had dessert yet," Caledonia objected. "It's Boston cream pie tonight, with . . ."

"I can't help it. You order one for me and eat it yourself. I want to find out about this," Angela said, heading for the door. Fast.

Caledonia beamed. "Very thoughtful," she said approvingly. "I can always eat another dessert." But Angela was already out the door, which was easing closed on its pneumatic stopper behind her disappearing back.

Jimmy was only too glad to talk about the car. "Oh, wow, yes, Mrs. Benbow . . . a Corvette. Like new, too. I could never afford one like that."

"What do you suppose it cost him?" Angela asked.

"I don't know, but I bet it was about $30,000 . . . maybe more!" Jimmy said, shrugging his shoulders. "I never priced one. He's crazy about that car—shows if off all the time . . . everybody on campus knows about it."

"How long has he had it, Jimmy?"

"Oh, not long. A month maybe? Three weeks? He'll get tired showing it off after a while, but you know . . . when it's new . . . I'd feel the same way."

"Thanks, Jimmy," Angela said. "Listen, Lieutenant Martinez and Shorty Swanson have gone home for the evening, haven't they?"

"I don't think so," he said. "I haven't seen them go through the lobby, anyhow. I thought they were still up on the second floor."

Angela nodded. "Thanks. I'll try, anyhow." She headed for the broad main staircase, which was a few steps closer than the elevator. When you were in a hurry at Camden, your feet served you best, for the old machinery creaked and sighed and groaned, and the elevator moved more slowly than Mr. Brighton walked.

At the head of the stairs, Angela hesitated. The lights of the upper residential hallway, not yet cut in half by Torgeson's computer-managed 9:00 P.M. curfew, were dim even at full strength, and Angela suddenly felt she was walking out of daylight into the gloom of a gathering storm. Colors simply disappeared in the electric twilight, and shadows lurked in every doorway up and down the silent, carpeted length of the hall.

"Owl light indeed," she whispered nervously to herself and shivered.

Taking a deep breath, she turned left, heading for the sewing room where the detectives might still be viewing, interviewing, or reviewing. But she had gone no more than a few steps, when around the far corner came Robbie Hammond, his head down, his face darker than the shadows of the hallway. They met halfway between the head of the stairs and the turning that led to the sewing room.

"Hi, Mrs. Benbow," Robbie said dejectedly. "You can guess, I suppose, they were after me again."

"About smoking pot on the beach?" Angela said self-consciously. "I thought they might be."

"Well, I spent last evening with Sue Nancy again, but I guess she must have told them we were sharing a few joints, because they kept asking me how she acted? Did she get sleepy? Did she pass out? I don't honestly remember myself, Mrs. Benbow. After all, I smoked as much as she did."

"Does it make you lose track of time? Do you get sleepy?" Angela asked curiously. "I've never understood the attraction."

"Gosh," he said, grinning ruefully, "it embarrasses me to admit I do take an occasional smoke. Yeah, I guess some people do get kind of dopey and don't know what day it is, let alone what time it is. But it feels good—like there's an awful lot of fun in the world and everything's going to be all right, forever. You don't focus on your troubles—you forget them. And with my aunt dying, believe me, I wanted to forget about things."

"You sound like people do when they're trying to justify heavy drinking," Angela said. "People say it can't hurt them, and it numbs the pain. They say they drink to forget . . ."

"Yes, yes, that's it," he said, missing her point and hurrying eagerly on. "It's sort of like that, except you don't get a hangover from pot, you see. And it's not addictive!" She must have looked skeptical because he insisted. "No, honest, it's not. I don't have to smoke it . . . neither does Sue Nancy. We just do it when we want to—not because we have to, either. See? And no hangover . . ."

"Oh, I don't know about that," Angela said. "Sue Nancy's been a little dazed and dreamy the last couple of days. I thought she was just sleepy after a late date. Now I wonder if some of the drug wasn't still acting on her system."

He shrugged. "Like I say, it hits different people differently." Then he reached out and to her surprise, he took her hand. "Mrs. Benbow, please don't think badly of me," he said earnestly, looking into her eyes. "It's just—with everything that's happened—you can understand why I wanted a few minutes away from thinking about it all, can't you?"

"I suppose so," Angela said, faintly embarrassed and withdrawing her hand. "I suppose so. But you know, I'm glad I got to talk to you. I really need to ask you where you got your car."

He had started a step or two around her, as though heading for the stairs or the elevator—or his late aunt's apartment—but he stopped. "Where I got it? You mean, the name of the dealer?" he asked, without turning around.

"No, I meant—well, I understand it's awfully expensive. I was wondering how you could afford it, that's all."

"How did you find out about my car? Nobody knows about it but the kids on campus. People my age."

"Jimmy at the front desk told me. He admires it very much—says everyone at school does."

Hammond nodded. "Well, they ought to. I tell you, it's really great." He turned fully back to her and retraced his steps so that he stood close beside her. Then he smiled that sunny, innocent grin of his. "It was Aunt Lena's graduation gift to me in advance. I had a chance to buy this terrific car at a real bargain price, you see, but only if I acted right away. It wouldn't have been available anymore if I'd waited till I graduated next year. So I asked her, and she said yes, and I got it. That's really all there was to it! Nothing strange or mysterious."

"But Robbie," Angela protested, "your aunt didn't have enough money to move in here unless she sold her house.

And she couldn't pay the rent without your selling the jewelry," she said skeptically. "How could she buy you a car like that?"

To Angela's surprise, Robbie took her hand again and tucked it firmly under his arm. She tried to pull free. She never had liked people holding onto her and making her move where they wanted her to go—even if they were going where she was headed anyway. Slightly claustrophobic, she had always hated being confined in any way. Forced body contact—like being squashed against other people on a crowded bus—made her slightly panicky. She tugged insistently at her hand, but he was surprisingly strong, and kept towing her along, all the while smiling down at her with that sweet, youthful grin.

"It's really so much simpler than it sounds! She only spent part of the money from the house to buy her way in here. She used the rest for my car. See? There just isn't anything odd about it at all!"

Angela was feeling seriously annoyed as well as a little puzzled. He was really hustling her along. "Can he be trying to get rid of me?" she wondered silently. "I bet he's got a date with Sue Nancy again!"

When they got opposite the elevator, to her intense relief, he released her hand and pushed the elevator button. He was still crowding her, though, and she decided quickly to take the elevator when it came. She could make her escape from his stifling closeness in the lobby more easily than in the narrow hall.

While Angela eyed the elevator door hopefully, Robbie went on talking. "I guess I can understand if the police think I'm a suspect in my aunt's murder," he said, raising his soft voiced slightly over the creaking and groaning of the elevator's mechanism, muttering its protest behind its stout oak door, as it raised itself painfully to their level. "I suppose they've just been doing their job when they ask me questions. It kind of hurt my feelings at first, but I really do understand. Of course, I should feel hurt that you would be so suspicious of me."

"Well," Angela soothed, "actually I think 'suspicious' is too strong. I just wondered about the car, you know."

"Sure." Robbie nodded. "Perfectly understandable. But everything is okay. Honestly. Truly it is. Besides, you must know I'm not really involved in anything bad—the murders, I mean. What reason would I have to kill two strange men?"

She nodded emphatically. "I've tried to make the lieutenant see that. The three murders are definitely linked together, you know. I felt so all along," and she patted his arm comfortingly. "They'll find the real murderer soon, I have every confidence."

He didn't move to take her hand again, and she felt faintly relieved. He beamed down at her. "You know, Mrs. Benbow, I thought you were really awfully clever to work all that out about the gardeners. That was really ingenious."

"Well, maybe it won't come to anything. But I'll bet you—and I told the lieutenant this—that they're going to find somebody whose wife once left him for a gardener. Or who got sick from using strong insecticides. Or maybe somebody who lost a fortune trying to develop the first truly black tulip or the first really white marigold . . . they're bound to find *something*!"

The mechanical groaning ceased suddenly. The elevator had arrived, and its oak door began its stately, inch-by-inch slide to admit her.

"I don't suppose they're trying very hard," Robbie sighed. "They really ought to look around here. There are bound to be several of the residents who aren't—you know—who aren't quite right in the head. I mean, you know how people get . . ."

"Oh, Robbie! For shame. You're sounding just like Sergeant Benson!"

With its usual perverse pleasure in making things difficult, the elevator floor had come to rest an inch above the hallway's level. Angela stumbled slightly as she stepped inside, and Robbie moved into the car beside her, putting a firm hand under her elbow. "Here," he said, reaching around her to push the first-floor button. "I'll see you to your room. The light's so dim around here at night that you can't really see your way properly. I don't understand why they don't put brighter lights in these hallways. You old people—"

"There you go again," Angela snapped. There was a shudder and a sigh, and the elevator door trembled in its slot, preparatory to sliding shut. The car swayed and the cable groaned. "Having known all of us here—having lived with your aunt, I'd expect you to have a better understanding of older people, not to be like most youngsters . . ."

The door settled closed and the elevator's mechanism began to groan unhappily again as it lowered its cab toward the first floor, ever so slowly.

"Well, now, understanding should work both ways," he said. "You don't understand me and people my age, either! Aunt Lena didn't understand me, close as we were. She was just like most of you—you old folks—all turned inside. Worried about herself, about what she wanted, about what was best for her—really selfish. She didn't even try to understand the things I want out of life. She was always after me to be patient, to wait, to consider other people's point of view . . . as though she did herself. She never thought about *my* point of view, did she?"

"What a thing to say! You got along so well!"

He shrugged and smiled again, that easy, boyish smile. As he lifted his head, the elevator ceiling lights reflected on the surface of his glasses, and Angela found herself vaguely disturbed that she could no longer see his eyes, as he talked, just the shiny surfaces of his glasses—great, bright, blank Orphan Annie eyes with her face reflected on their curved surface.

"You know," he was continuing, "it really took me quite a while to learn how to get along. Not just with her—with all of you. But I learned. Talk nicely, be a 'good little boy,' and say what the old people want to hear. I could get anything I wanted from her, after I figured that out. Well, almost anything . . ."

"I see!" Angela's lips were pressed tight together. "Well, you certainly had me fooled. I believed your 'loving nephew' act."

He beamed at her with obvious pleasure. "Why, thank you! But you know it wasn't just an act. I really did love her—most of the time. It was just when we fought about things I wanted to do that she didn't want me to—she could get awfully stubborn. And then it was up to me to—you know—make her change her mind, or find a way to get around her."

"Like when you sold her jewelry for her without her permission?"

"Yes. Like that. I tried and tried to talk her into it—it made no sense for her to hang onto that stuff. I mean, she never wore it. It just sat in a drawer . . . and it was all going to be mine one day anyhow, you know. She'd told me that a hundred times. So I didn't see what was wrong with getting my money out of it a little early, that's all. Besides, she needed to throw away a lot of junk when she moved in here."

The elevator stopped with a jolt. "Boy, this thing is slow," he marveled.

"It's old," Angela said tartly. "Like me. But like me, it usually manages to get where it's going!" The heavy oak door quivered in its groove—groaned—trembled—and stayed shut.

Robbie grinned at her. "And sometimes, just like my aunt Lena, it needs to be helped to make up its mind to do what's right. See?" He reached around her to thumb the DOOR OPEN button. But the door remained shut.

"Oh, dear! It's going to stay shut, isn't it?" Angela gasped. "I *hate* tiny, closed spaces! I always have. Ask anybody around here . . . I really feel as though I can't breathe . . . oh, dear . . ."

"Here." Robbie pushed with both hands against the door, trying to force it to slide open. "Maybe I can do something . . ." The door didn't budge. "Hey!" He raised his voice to a shout. "Hey! Is anybody out there? Can you hear me? I think we're stuck in here!" He banged with both fists against the oak panel.

"Oh my!" Angela took a deep breath. "It did this with the Emersons last week . . . but I've never been caught in it before."

"Well, at least it seems to have got all the way to the ground floor."

"Yes, but stuck is stuck, even if we're not caught between floors!" she said unhappily. "Oh, dear . . . does it seem warm to you in here?"

Robbie moved back to the control panel. "Let's see—there's a button marked EMERGENCY here. Let's see what it does." He gave it a jab with his thumb.

What happened was that a raucous alarm bell sounded, somewhere just over their heads. It was harsh as well as very loud. Angela jumped and clapped her hands over both ears. "Oh, dear! Turn that awful thing off!"

"Let it ring a second or two, Mrs. Benbow. Till we're sure someone's heard us!"

"Please . . . my ears . . ." she was in genuine distress.

"Oh, okay . . . I expect they've heard it by now anyhow." He thumbed the button again and the ringing stopped.

Over their heads there was the sound of distant pounding. Faintly they heard a man's voice calling, "Hello! Hello! Is somebody in there?"

"Yeah, we sure are," Robbie bellowed upward, his head thrown back. "Two of us . . ."

"We're stuck in here," Angela called hopefully. "Yoo-hoo—yoo-hoo . . . I really have to get out of here! Please? I don't like small places . . . can you do anything?" Tension was making her voice very tight and high and small, a squeak she felt certain was not going to be heard. Her breath was coming in short gasps, as she felt the car growing smaller around her. "Oh, dear . . . this is *awful*!"

Over their heads they heard another man saying "Well, can we do anything about getting the thing moving again?" and Emerson saying clearly, "Well, I can tell you it's damned uncomfortable in there. I ought to know. We should do something. Listen, whoever you are . . . we'll get this working in a few minutes. Sit down on the bench and be patient."

There was a bench built into the back wall of the cab, especially for the tenants who could not stand up for as long as the old elevator took to move between floors. Angela, who ordinarily would have scorned such weakness, sank onto it gratefully as the sounds of work continued overhead. "The fan doesn't seem to be working. It's really awfully close, don't you think?" she panted.

"Look, you need to stay very calm and very quiet," Robbie cautioned. "Breathe slowly. Deeper. And don't get in a panic. If you get upset, it might bring on some kind of attack . . ."

"I'm perfectly sound of wind and limb, thank you! Attack, indeed!" but her face was chalky white and she was perspiring.

"Well, I'm sorry," Robbie apologized. "Honestly, you're as bad as Aunt Lena. She'd get so mad when I told her to be careful with stairs, or not to get excited . . ."

Angela's frustration flared up as anger, and she directed it toward the only person within range of her temper. "You really disappoint me, Robbie. You're exactly like all those other young people . . . you really think older people are good for nothing at all!"

"Oh, on the contrary. Aunt Lena was good for a few dollars any time I needed it! She was very useful—at least, she was to me."

Angela stood up, quite forgetting to relax and breathe deeply. "The way you talk, you *ought* to be suspected of her murder," she flared. "Of all the unfeeling . . ."

"Now, Mrs. Benbow . . ."

"Lieutenant Martinez always says it's usually a family member who's the murderer anyway! And to think I have been defending you all along! I really did! I mean, I know from reading mysteries that it's never the most likely suspect. And you're certainly the most likely suspect!"

"Oh, come on, Mrs. Benbow," he placated. "We both know the police are wrong. I mean, they might suspect me of Aunt Lena's murder, but they certainly know I didn't kill those two men. Those other two murders are my protection, aren't they? Why would I do them? I had no reason . . . no motive . . ."

"I tell you," Angela snapped angrily, determined to get a bit of her own back against him. "I tell you—I always thought that if I wanted to murder anybody—not that I would, you know, but suppose I did—I always thought it'd be smart if I killed a lot of people who had no relation to my victim at all. But I'd try to make it seem somehow that the deaths were all related to each other!"

She looked at Robbie, and he was no longer smiling. "If I wanted to kill someone," she went on a little less stoutly, "I'd pick people to kill both before and after the one I really cared about . . . maybe people who all had the same hair color or the same name, you see, so the police would think there was a real connection. Because . . ." she faltered then. He was staring at her unblinking. "Because . . ."

"Because," he said, "then the police would get bogged down trying to find a connection among the three murders—a connection that didn't exist. And they'd throw out the suspect for any one murder if he couldn't be tied in with the others. Very clever. Don't you agree? And it really should have worked. If only the police weren't so stupid . . ."

"It was you then. It was you all along!" Her voice was a thread, a whisper.

"Oh, yes." He looked down at her almost with affection. "Oh, yes. And you're perfectly right about the first two murders, of course. They were just to set the stage for a manhunt for a deranged killer—some kind of serial murderer. But the police didn't seem to see the connection. It took you to do it for them. I've really been grateful to you for that. I told you so, didn't I?"

"But—you weren't here. Your aunt wasn't even living here when the first two men were killed!"

"No, and that's the beauty of it! I waited to start it all going till I was certain she had the room here. The same night they called and said there was finally space for her, I came over to start my plan working. That was easy—you don't have to have a relative living here to stroll into the garden at night. And that's all it took—just walking in. And the whole pattern was begun."

"But—but Ginnie doesn't fit the pattern. She's not a gardener!"

"Ginnie?"

"Well, I assumed . . . she's missing, you know, and I . . ."

He looked genuinely amused. "You thought I killed her? Well, maybe she deserved to be punished for cheating me—and for telling about the jewelry—but no, I didn't kill her. It's like you said. That would have spoiled the pattern. No, she's perfectly all right—unless something has happened to her in the last twenty-four hours."

"Then where is she?"

"Where she really wanted to be—in Hollywood—going to try to be a movie star. I bought her a bus ticket and gave her the rest of the $500 from the jewelry to help her get started. I just wanted her out of here. So she couldn't talk about me any more to the police!"

"She just packed up and left?"

He nodded. "I couldn't do anything to her. It would have spoiled the whole effect I created."

"You know, R-Robbie, I don't think the police are any too happy with the theory of the serial murderer—the gardener-hating lunatic. It just isn't working anymore."

"Wrong! I know it *will* work! I ran it through a computer simulation—a program of probabilities—and the computer said the police would go for the crazed-killer idea! The only mistake it made—no, that *I* made in setting up the program was that the police didn't operate very logically. I was sure they'd get the picture right away. But they didn't. Not till you pointed the pattern out to them. It was really very clever of you."

He sighed and went on earnestly. "People often disappoint me, you know ... they're not as bright as I expect them to be. A psychologist told me once it's because I don't see things the way other people do—because I'm so much smarter than they are. Did you know I have an I.Q. of over 200?"

"No," Angela whispered. "No. H-how unusual!"

"Oh, yes. I've always been way smarter than anybody else. In school—everywhere. Sometimes it's been a big disadvantage, because other people couldn't follow what I was trying to tell them. Sometimes other people think I'm making fun of them, when I'm not trying to."

"Yes, well ... well, what happens now?"

"I think that you'd better have a heart attack here in the stalled elevator, don't you agree? Before you can be rescued? You're the only one who's been smart enough to follow my plan, and now you're the only person in a position to get me in any trouble. Because you've worked it all out. So I think you're going to have a violent panic attack, while you wait for them to come and get us out."

"But that won't fit the pattern," Angela argued in her tiny whisper. Fear was making her feel weak, and her hands were trembling. "I'm not a gardener!"

"True. But you're not going to be murdered, either. Like I said, you're going to die of a heart attack! You're already pale and your skin is clammy, you know . . ." He smiled gently. "It's a shame. A delicate little woman like Mrs. Benbow was—I suppose her fear was just too much for her . . ."

"Please . . ." Angela turned desperate eyes to the ceiling of the elevator. This just can't be happening, she thought. Surely they're going to get to us and rescue us—but the banging overhead seemed to be exactly the same as it had been a moment ago and the muffled voices no nearer.

Robbie was shaking his head. "I really never dreamed I'd ever run into people as stupid as the police have been. Not finding that gardener connection. Of course, I never thought I'd run into anybody as quick as you, either . . . someone who could put the whole scheme together the way you did. The trouble is, you know, you just won't act the way an old lady is supposed to act!"

"Th-thank you!" Angela said, backing away from him till her back was against the elevator wall. "Up there . . . yoo-hoo . . ." She tried to call out loudly, but her voice had tightened to a tiny squeak. "Yoo-hoo . . ."

Terrified as she was, one portion of her brain was thinking busily, "It's like the Smothers Brothers used to sing . . . something like, *I yelled FIRE when I fell into the vat of chocolate . . . because nobody would come if I yelled CHOCOLATE!* I'm yelling 'Yoo-hoo' because nobody's going to understand what I'm talking about if I yell 'murder!' "

"Help!" she tried again. "Help" certainly seemed more appropriate to her circumstances than "Yoo-hoo," however vague and trite. "Help," she squeaked.

But Robbie was directly in front of her and his hands had found her throat.

"Please," he whispered, almost in her ear. "Please don't struggle. That'll make it painful. If you just stand still, this won't hurt much and it will all be over in a second. I really don't want to hurt you . . ." and he smiled gently at her and squeezed. "Just don't fight me . . . let's make this look like a natural death . . ."

"Help!" Angela tried again, but it was almost a token effort. She knew she could not be heard. She knew her breath was being cut off and even the tiny squeak was inaudible. She put her hands up and tried to pry his fingers loose, but it was futile. He held firmly—the pressure increased—

The last thing Angela saw as she slumped into unconsciousness was the reflection of her face, distorted in those big glasses . . . two great headlights coming through a tunnel . . .

She gave one more pull at his fingers, and managed to draw one more half-breath. *"Chocolate!"* she croaked out despairingly—and then she entered the tunnel herself.

Chapter 17

Wʜᴇɴ Aɴɢᴇʟᴀ was four years old, she'd had her tonsils out and they gave her ether. At seventy-plus she could still remember how pungently sick-sweet it smelled. She could remember that the anesthetic never really kept her completely out—that she swam along just under the surface of consciousness most of the time, faintly aware, but not awake. From time to time she would break the surface and register the bright lights of the operating room, the masked and gowned men and women, and the choking, burning in her throat. She would try to protest—to cry out. Each time, she was given more ether, and the lights would retreat, sounds would become muffled. And she would sleep again, but not deeply.

Now she lay on a bed and remembered vaguely that time long ago. Once more she was half-unconscious, half-awake, swimming just below the surface, registering sensory impressions without being able to speak or move. Once more her throat hurt, and there was light in the room, and people were talking. She could barely realize they were there. Occasionally she recognized a voice—Caledonia, and Lieutenant Martinez, and Mary Washington the nurse—and once she thought she heard Robbie.

"Help me," she knew she wanted to say. She knew she wanted to call, "Don't leave me. Robbie will come for me, if you leave me. Stay with me."

"Look, she's stirring in her sleep," Caledonia said once. "I thought she made a noise."

Dr. Carter came and gave her another shot. Another? Yes, she told herself in her unconscious dream state, he's been before; you've had a shot and that's why you can't wake up. Carter said, "I can see she's restless, tossing and murmuring. But she'll rest a little better now."

Behind closed lids, Angela shouted silently, "But I want to tell you what happened. I don't want to sleep anymore. I want to wake up! I have to wake up. I have to tell you so you don't leave me alone with Robbie . . ."

"See," Carter said, "she's making noises in her throat now. But that will pass when the drug takes effect."

And then at last she woke up, rather quickly and without much trace of drowsiness. She sat up in bed and realized the sky outside was dark. It was still night. She got to her feet, found a robe in the closet and a pair of fuzzy slippers, and scuffed into the living room.

Caledonia was the first to see her, and Caledonia's response was gratifying. "Thank the Lord!" she blared like a clarion before the walls of Jericho. She jumped from her chair and embraced her tiny friend. "Thank the Good Lord—and I don't say that very often!" She held Angela by the shoulders and held her out where she could look at her, embraced her again, and held her out at arm's length once more. "You don't look half-bad for an old lady who's been through hell and back again!"

As Caledonia released her, Angela felt herself swept up again, this time in a man's arms. "Mrs. Benbow, you gave us a terrible fright. I am so very glad you—you look so wonderful!" And Lieutenant Martinez gave her a second hug.

While he was embracing her, her hand was wrung by another pair of hands and she heard the voice of Shorty Swanson. "Oh, ma'am . . . oh, boy! Mrs. Benbow, ma'am . . . oh-boy-oh-boy, Mrs. Benbow! I'm glad you're okay . . ." Shorty's greeting made up in warmth and sincerity what it lacked in inventive diction.

It was useless for Angela to pretend she wasn't pleased at the attention and the obvious affection. Under other circumstances she might have "hmphed" and "grmphed" her way free of their attentions and made some deprecatory comment. Now she was pink in the face and beaming back at them. Truth to tell, she was feeling mighty glad herself

to be alive and in one piece ... and glad that Robbie
seemed to be nowhere around.

"I heard you talking while I was asleep." She sat down
on her little couch and curled up with her feet under her,
like a child on a cold winter evening, and Caledonia tucked
an afghan around her shoulders. "I had things I had to tell
you, but I just couldn't seem to talk. And of course I
couldn't remember what I heard you saying from one minute to the next. I could hear you talk, but the words disappeared," she told them. "But I remember I heard Robbie's
voice at least once, and I have to tell you about him! He's
the murderer." She began to grow agitated. "And he was
trying to kill me! I was so afraid you were going to leave
me alone with him ... you must do something ..."

"That was only your imagination, Mrs. Benbow. Robbie
hasn't been in here." Martinez stopped and looked across at
Caledonia. "Can we ... Mrs. Wingate, do you suppose
she's strong enough to ...?"

Caledonia nodded. "Strong as a Chincoteague pony, our
Angela ... and she'll feel better when she hears it all. Besides, her curiosity is so overpowering, it'll lay her flat if
you don't tell her."

Martinez hitched his chair over toward Angela's corner
of the couch. "Do you want to hear all about the mystery
of Camden's murders?"

"Wait." Angela held up her hand. "First ... you better
tell me what time it is."

"Ten-thirty, Mrs. Benbow," Shorty said, turning her little
enameled table clock to face toward her.

"Saturday," Caledonia added, leaning forward. "Lieutenant. I don't think she's realized she's been asleep for more
than twenty-four hours altogether!"

"Twenty-four hours! Saturday!" Angela was horrified. "I
missed a whole day!"

Martinez smiled. "Dr. Carter gave you a shot as soon as
he arrived. He said after what you'd been through you
could use the rest. Then he gave you another shot this
morning. So I'm starting my story back at the point in time
where you left us ... yesterday evening. Okay?"

Angela nodded and he started his story. "I'd called

Robbie in last evening to talk to him about the marijuana he and Sue Nancy smoked together on the beach. She was his alibi for the night of his aunt's murder, but if Sue Nancy was full of that stuff, there's no telling how reliable her testimony was! She said she remembered everything, but I had my doubts, after I found out about the pot.

"But before he could get in to see us, late in the same afternoon we finally got Mrs. Gardner's bank to give us an accounting of her financial status—and we were stunned. She had an enormous amount of money. She wasn't as well-to-do as either of you ladies, I suppose, but she was better than comfortably off."

"But her clothes and her furniture weren't expensive," Caledonia said.

"Maybe not," Martinez said, "but she didn't really need to sell her house or the jewelry, either. Shorty's more of an accountant than I am, so he looked at the figures . . ."

"It didn't take an accountant to see that she never got the money for the sale of her house at all. No deposit of any considerable size had been put into her account," Shorty said. "And no money from the sale of the jewelry either. In fact, there hadn't been any deposit recently, except for her social security checks and her interest, which came direct from her financial manager and which was considerable."

"But plenty was going out," Martinez said. "We looked over the canceled checks."

"That practically took an act of Congress," Shorty muttered resentfully.

"We found checks written to Robbie's college, checks written to Robbie's landlord, checks written to Robbie's tailor, and checks written to Robbie. She was supporting him in grand style, paying tuition and fees, rent, books, clothing, and incidentals . . . and giving him a regular allowance. A generous one."

"Was there a check for a car?" Angela asked curiously.

"No," Martinez said, "but when we were at Robbie's place today, we found a bill of sale for the Corvette—paid for, so it said on the bill, in cash! Some $30,000, as I recall. What we think happened is that Robbie took the money from the sale of the house for himself, without his aunt's permission, and used part of it to buy the car."

"He told me," Angela said indignantly, "that it was an early graduation present!"

"Maybe that's how he saw it. But as best we can tell, we don't think his aunt Lena knew she was giving him the present."

"Same with the jewelry," Shorty said. "From what he told us, he just took the stuff."

"He tried a couple of days ago," Martinez said, "to convince us that he sold the stuff to help pay his aunt's rent. But we knew when we saw that bank statement that just wasn't true. Of course he tried to put everything in a good light. He had a dozen rationalizations. And I think he halfway believed them himself. But we had already figured out that the timetable he was presenting to us didn't square."

"What didn't fit about it?" Caledonia asked.

"Well, for one thing, he would have liked us to see the sale of all that jewelry as a sort of natural outgrowth of the other sale of Mrs. Gardner's possessions. But Singletary's records show he took the jewelry into the shop a full two months before Mrs. Gardner's move to Camden was arranged.

"Knowing that he had sold the jewelry some time ago, we pushed him on the subject, and that's when he started his rationalizations. He said all right, he'd sold the jewelry well before she moved, but why not? She was going to sell everything else anyway—she never wore the jewelry anyhow—it was all going to be his soon—and besides she'd never miss it.

"Then we asked him to account for the money from the sale of the house—and he said he had merely 'borrowed' it against his future inheritance, because his aunt wouldn't lend him the money for his car when he needed it—when he found that good buy on the Corvette."

Caledonia rumbled ominously, "He had all the answers, didn't he? That little—"

"The way we think it really happened was that Robbie stole the jewelry to get some extra cash, and to his delight, he got away with it. We think that succeeding in robbing his aunt gave him big ideas. After all, if he could get away with it once—"

"Maybe more!" Caledonia growled. "How do we know that's all he took from her? Who knows what else he stole and sold, and she never knew about it because she didn't miss it right away?"

Martinez acknowledged her point by raising his eyebrows. "Good idea. That may be the way it was. But whether that was the first theft or just one in a long string, it apparently gave him what he thought was a marvelous idea for a real coup—a way to get everything else she had as well—all of it, and right away without waiting. But he had to have one element to make the plan work. She had to move in here. If he'd killed her before she did, we'd have made a beeline right for him!"

"Did the lieutenant tell you," Shorty chimed in, "that most murders are committed by some close friend or family member? Well, if she'd been killed while she was living in her own house, and her nephew was her only family member still alive, we'd surely have made a connection between the two right away."

"As it was," Martinez said, "we got a confused picture of things. His scheme to divert suspicion by making things complicated worked. For a while."

"Lieutenant," Angela put in, "how much of this is what you know and how much is what you just guessed?"

"Everything was guesswork right up to that minute that elevator door opened. Shorty here lunged in and picked you up, and people started fussing over you—protecting you with a wall of concerned friends. We had taken you away from him, at that point, you see. He wasn't going to be able to silence you, after all. And he turned right around to us and started talking—well, just about. It was nearly that easy from that moment on. Are you sure you want to hear all this? It isn't very pleasant."

Caledonia glared at him. "Don't stop now! We can take it!"

"All right. First the plan. Robbie decided to make his aunt's death just one of a series of murders by a mad serial killer. Or so it would seem. And to create that illusion, he planned to kill somebody here at Camden—just anybody—he didn't care who. Immediately after they'd received the letter saying there was finally a room his aunt could move into, he came over here one night, deliberately looking for a victim. He had decided stabbing looked crazier than shooting or strangling . . . so he brought a big knife with him. He just walked into the garden from Beach Lane, and waited in the shadows for somebody—anybody—to show up alone. It was chance—really bad luck for Ortelano as that night was the same night he came to refill the soft-drink machine."

"Are you saying Robbie confessed all this, lieutenant?" Angela said, appalled. "Or are you still telling us what you guessed?"

"A little of each," Martinez said. "But mostly, he told us. I think I mentioned some time ago that people simply love to confess. They want to be understood. They want to justify themselves. Robbie Hammond was no different. He really enjoyed letting us in on his clever scheme. He was aching for us to tell him how brilliant he'd been. Did you know that originally, the plan called for him to kill one of the residents of Camden because, as he put it, they wouldn't matter as much?"

"What!" Caledonia's explosion shook the windowpanes.

"Well, that's what he said. He said you'd lived your lives, and it was time for the older generation to step aside anyway and let the young ones have a chance."

"He sounds," Caledonia bellowed, "like John McEnroe! Do you remember him talking about Jimmy Connors and Bjorn Borg after Wimbledon a few years back?"

Martinez grinned. "I surely do! I don't supposed anyone over thirty at that time ever forgot it—or forgave it! Well, at any rate, fate stepped in to alter Robbie's original plans a little. He stabbed poor Ortelano, instead of one of the residents, and then he just went back to his dorm room and studied for an exam. Can you beat it?"

"How did he choose Rollo?" Angela asked. "Was that random, too? I thought I was so clever with that 'gardener' business, too . . ."

"You were. His plan demanded he establish a pattern,

like most serial killers have—some kind of correspondence among the victims. The day after the killing, from newspaper accounts, he learned the name of his victim. And this is one thing we can blame on higher education, I guess ... he knew the translation of Ortelano's name because he'd studied Spanish in school, and he realized it corresponded to his aunt's name. And the rest of the scheme was born.

"He hunted through the residents' roster for a name like 'Farmer' or 'Rose' or even 'Bush'—anything that would have been associated with the term 'garden.' But he couldn't find one. So he went looking especially for Rollo, because of Rollo's profession. That would set up his phony pattern, and he was satisfied he would be in the clear when his aunt was killed by stabbing, as the two men before her had been."

"My Lord," Caledonia breathed. "The incredible gall of that boy! The impudence! The conceit!"

"But there he hit a snag," Martinez went on. "Nobody seemed to see the connection he had taken such pains to work out. He says he actually felt grateful to you, when you told him you had discovered the 'gardener' connection among the first three victims. He raged at us for being so dense and ignoring his pretty pattern! I hated to have to tell him he had been just too fancy for us poor ordinary policemen!"

"Well, anyhow, Angela," Caledonia said, "you weren't wrong about your theory then. Except the murderer meant for the pattern to be discovered, and meant it to lead to the conclusion that he was a nut case."

"But Lieutenant," Angela said, "you always hung onto the idea that Robbie might have been involved, somehow. Because of the theory that relatives kill relatives, I suppose. Even my finding the pattern didn't mislead you ..."

"I'd like to pretend I was awfully smart about that," Martinez said. "But stubborn is more like it. The idea of killing gardeners was too contrived somehow. It rang false to me. And yet we couldn't find a reason for any one of the victims to have been killed in his or her own right. At least not until we found out Lena Gardner really did have money after all—enough to make inheriting from her worthwhile!

Of course, we still hadn't worked out any way her death was connected with the other two.

"But I like to think policemen are successful partly because they're such a dull group that they don't mind doing their homework! We just went ahead and worked on the one killing we had something to go on—Mrs. Gardner's. And, of course, in the end, it worked out."

"Did Robbie have an alibi for the first two murders?" Caledonia asked curiously.

"He didn't need an alibi for those two nights," Martinez said, "because he and his aunt were still unconnected with this place during the first one, and she had just arrived before the second. He judged police thinking absolutely right, in that regard. Sergeant Benson realized there was some kind of Camden connection in the two men's deaths—but it would never have occurred to him to look closely at someone who wasn't even here yet.

"Lena Gardner got her notice that she could move in, and Robbie killed Ortelano within a couple of days. Then he sat down with his reference books and worked out the phony 'pattern.' He timed his killing of Rollo exactly a week later, not only so the day of the week would be the same as the first, but so the second death would be out of the way before his aunt and he were really part of the Camden scene."

"But Robbie had an alibi for the night of his aunt's death," Caledonia said. "He was down on the beach with Miss Butler—you know, our Southern belle."

Martinez nodded. "And she was zonked out on marijuana. He claims that was clever planning. I think he was lucky again. She might not have passed out or lost touch with reality. But she did. Actually, he tells us she gets very high, giggles a lot, and falls asleep. Now, she thinks she's wide-awake the whole time, and she's perfectly prepared to say so in court. But Robbie more or less confirmed my suspicions about the way pot affects little Miss Alabama.

"He gave her a couple of joints, waited till she was snoring in the sand, and then he came on up to his aunt's place and killed her with her own letter opener. He was actually sneaking out the back door of the lower hall when Mr.

Emerson found the body, as nearly as we can figure. But it didn't matter how close the timing was, so long as it worked—and it did work. He was back on the beach before Sue Nancy opened her bonny blue Confederate eyes!"

Caledonia nodded. "I see. And she never missed him at all, right?"

Martinez nodded. "Do you know the only reason he didn't kill Virginia Ruth Robertson is . . ."

"Oh, dear," Angela interrupted. "I'm sorry—I meant to tell you that she isn't dead. She's alive and well! He sent her to Hollywood to seek fame and fortune—and be out of the way, so she wouldn't talk anymore about the jewelry he took."

"Well," Martinez went on, "we know that now, too, of course. We've located her—still doing kitchen work, but in a Taco Bell on Sepulveda Boulevard now instead of here in Camden. She spent the time we talked to her on the phone today complaining because she hasn't been able to break into pictures in just two days. But I think she's a lucky girl—lucky to be alive at all! Robbie wouldn't have hesitated to kill her, except he couldn't think quickly of any way to make her fit his beautiful pattern."

"Strangling me wouldn't have fit the pattern either, so he was going to make my death seem like an accident," Angela explained. "He was going to say I'd had a heart attack because of claustrophobia. He thought Dr. Carter would believe I'd gone into a panic because I'm so afraid of being locked in small places. I am, you know . . ."

"But, instead, when the elevator door opened," Shorty said proudly, "there we were, waiting for him. Just as you collapsed. We'd decided we had enough evidenced to make an arrest, and we'd gone to find him. When we heard the banging around at the elevator and all the shouting, and Mr. Emerson told us it was the two of you caught in the stalled cab, well, we just walked down the stairs and waited by the door till they got it open."

"I was being choked to death and you were standing by the door waiting?" Angela yelped with indignation.

"Now, now—if we'd realized he was going to try to kill you, Mrs. Benbow, we wouldn't have waited. We'd have shinnied down that elevator cable to rescue you, or forced the door or something, I promise you. Of course, when I saw you drop to the floor, I thought maybe you *were* dead. It was a relief to find out you were just unconscious."

"He choked me, all right, but I also fainted, I think— probably from sheer terror," Angela said.

"Killing you was a pretty good plan all right, for another improvisation," Martinez said. "Although I'm sure Dr. Carter could tell the difference between strangulation and a heart attack."

"Some comfort you are, Lieutenant," Caledonia said. "I'm not sure Angela would care, after she was dead!"

"Well, anyhow, considering Robbie made the plan up on the spur of the moment, it really wasn't bad. Natural death—especially under stressful circumstances—would be more or less taken for granted here. What I'm really curious about, though, is why he felt he had to kill you!"

"Well," Angela said with a touch of smugness, "I worked it all out, too, you know. In a way. Just as I got on the elevator, I said to him that if I ever decided to murder anybody, I'd kill people before and after in some way that would make everyone think my real murder— the one I really cared about—was just one of a string. And about that time I caught his eye, and all of a sudden, I *KNEW*! I knew that was the right answer! And he knew that I knew. And that's when he decided he had to kill me. You're certainly right—he did love to talk about it. He did crave applause."

"And that's what really saved your life. He stood there chatting casually—and in the meantime, they got the elevator door to working again, and we could come in and get you."

Caledonia got to her feet. "Gentlemen," she said, "it's been a long, long two days. And I suggest we postpone everything else till tomorrow. Angela must be worn out, just out of her bed and talking so late. Look, it's after eleven. Why don't we . . ."

"Of course." Martinez leaped to his feet. He took Angela's hand and kissed it in a most satisfactory gesture of gallantry. "The best thing about all that has happened is that you are well, in spite of the danger and the difficulty. The second best thing is that you have proved once more what I say of you—you would make a marvelous murderer yourself, for you hit quite naturally on what was Robbie's 'perfect murder' scheme. If you ever turn to crime, I'm done for!"

Shorty came over and put both hands on Angela's shoulders and bent nearly double so he could look into her eyes. "Gee, I'm glad you're okay, too, Mrs. Benbow. You've got grit. We're proud of you."

"We'll see you tomorrow," Martinez said from the door, "and take official statements and settle everything. But you can relax. Robbie is in prison and likely to stay there. He may not have stopped bragging and confessing yet, for all I know. Thank goodness! That universal urge to be understood and admired makes our job much easier! Until tomorrow, then." And Martinez and Swanson left.

Angela got up and stretched herself. "I don't know what everyone's going away so early for," she said rather peevishly. "I've slept for twenty-four hours and I couldn't close my eyes now if I wanted to, I'm so excited. I've got to go over everything the lieutenant has said . . . I have to come to terms with the fact I'm still alive . . ."

Caledonia sighed. "I am a wreck myself, worrying about you, and dead tired. I didn't sleep at all last night . . just sat right here watching you. Now I feel like I could sleep a week! But I did want to say how glad I am it's worked out this way. I'd miss you, girl. So—welcome back!"

"Thank you, but do you have to go? I'm wide-awake, and I want to think about everything. Isn't it amazing how being young can distort your thinking?"

"What do you mean?" Caledonia said, and immediately yawned.

"I mean, Robbie got generous gifts from his aunt, but it wasn't enough. In time he'd have had all her money legitimately, but he couldn't wait. He worked out that whole plan to get everything—and he couldn't even wait for that!

I mean, why steal the money from the house, when it was coming to him with the rest of the estate? All he had to do was hold on till after he killed her. But that wasn't good enough for him. You know, he took an incredible number of chances—and yet he really believed nobody would ever see through the scheme."

"Listen, if you want to go over all this, do it in bed. Your feet are covered in those slippers, but your ankles aren't and there's a little breeze tonight . . ." Caledonia gestured to the open window of the apartment. Then she slipped her arm under Angela's and walked her gently toward her little bedroom. "You can lie down and think about things as easily as you can sit up and think about them."

"Oh, all right . . . I'll go on to bed," Angela conceded. "But leave the window open. The fresh air is nice. Of course," she said, laying her robe aside and kicking off her slippers as she pulled up the sheet and blanket and smoothed the undersheet, "of course, the fresh air will just help to perk me up. I don't feel right now as though I'll ever sleep again." She lay down and pulled the sheet and blanket over her.

"Well, just close your eyes and try," Caledonia said. "I know there's a lot to think of, but tomorrow will do as well as today, and at our age we can use the extra sleep. Boy, every time I think I'd like to be young again, I remember something else I've outgrown . . . besides the feeling of being untouchable . . . the conceit . . . it's the embarrassment! I mean, I spent half my teens embarrassed about something! I wouldn't want to go through that again, would you?" She yawned. "Boy, I wish somebody'd give me a twelve-hour injection. Oh, could I stretch out and—Angela . . . Angela?"

From the bed there came the sound of deep, rhythmic breathing. Angela was once more sleeping. And her dreams appeared to be pleasant, for her brow was unfurrowed and her face relaxed.

Caledonia switched off the light and tiptoed to her own night's rest.

Outside the buildings, a light, mist-laden breeze off the Pacific tiptoed through the garden, shaking the bougainvillea, now past its prime, bringing down a flurry of the last blossoms. They fell silently, and tonight, there was no one about to see them as they fell.